D0192425

continued . . .

BARELY BEWITCHED

"*Barely Bewitched* is filled with humor, sass, and sizzle! Every page is a new adventure in a world of hilarious antics and smoking chemistry. I love this series and I am really looking forward to the next Tammy Jo fiasco . . . I mean, story!" —*The Romance Readers Connection*

"The amusing story line is fast-paced . . . Fans will enjoy the escapades of Tammy Jo in this jocular urban fantasy." —*Genre Go Round Reviews*

"Kimberly Frost can tell a tale like no other . . . A can't-miss read." —*Fang-tastic Books*

WOULD-BE WITCH

"A wildly entertaining read. *Would-Be Witch* has its dark and dangerous moments that should satisfy the reader's appetite for action, and the heroine's unresolved love life adds seduction and love to the mix. I'm looking forward to Tammy Jo's next adventure in magic." —*Darque Reviews*

"Hilarious start to the new Southern Witch series that will keep you laughing long into the night!" —*Fresh Fiction*

"A wickedly funny romp . . . The story trips along at a perfect pace, keeping the reader guessing at the outcome, dropping clues here and there that might or might not pan out in the end. I highly recommend this debut and look forward with relish to the next installment in the Southern Witch series." —*Romance Junkies*

"What a debut! This quirky Southern Witch tale of a magically uncoordinated witch with an appreciation for chocolate is likely to win over readers by the first page." —*A Romance Review*

BARELY BEWITCHED

KIMBERLY FROST

BERKLEY SENSATION, NEW YORK

THE BERKLEY PUBLISHING GROUP
Published by the Penguin Group
Penguin Group (USA) LLC
375 Hudson Street, New York, New York 10014

USA • Canada • UK • Ireland • Australia • New Zealand • India • South Africa • China

penguin.com

A Penguin Random House Company

BARELY BEWITCHED

A Berkley Sensation Book / published by arrangement with the author

Berkley Sensation Books are published by The Berkley Publishing Group.
BERKLEY SENSATION® is a registered trademark of Penguin Group (USA) LLC.
The "B" design is a trademark of Penguin Group (USA) LLC.

For information, address: The Berkley Publishing Group,
a division of Penguin Group (USA) LLC,
375 Hudson Street, New York, New York 10014.

ISBN: 978-0-425-26756-1

PUBLISHING HISTORY
Berkley trade paperback edition / September 2009
Berkley Sensation mass-market edition / December 2013

PRINTED IN THE UNITED STATES OF AMERICA

10 9 8 7 6 5 4 3 2 1

Cover art by Tony Mauro.
Cover design by Rita Frangie.
Interior text design by Kelly Lipovich.

ACKNOWLEDGMENTS

I would like to thank . . .

My incredible family and friends who turned out en masse for my book signings. I think it's pretty rare that a debut novelist gets to feel like a rock star at her very first author appearances. (Special thanks to Elizabeth and my parents for hosting *Would-Be Witch* launch parties.)

The bookselling dream team at Murder By The Book (especially Anne for reading *Would-Be Witch* in advance, and David and McKenna for all that you do). My friends at Katy Budget Books who were excited about the book when no one else really knew about it. Roxanne, the terrific event marketing manager from Borders, and the members of Lyceum who made my "hometown" signing in Michigan such a pleasure. Laura and Miles from separate Barnes & Noble stores, who loved the book and hand-sold scores of copies. You guys are wonderful!

My WRW family for all your support and enthusiasm (and occasional story advice on legal matters)! The reviewers and blog communities who let me visit as a guest and helped me spread the word about my books. The Houston RWA chapters and my amazing friends on MySpace.

The Berkley Publishing Group with special thanks to Leis, my editor; to the incredibly talented cover artist; and to everyone who worked on the production, promotion, and sales of the Southern Witch series.

My agent, Elizabeth, for your faith and the things you do

on my behalf. My critique partners, David and Bonnie, for seeing what I can't.

And most of all, thank you to my readers. I have been waiting all my life to meet you, and you are everything I hoped you would be and more.

1

IN THE PAST, the closest connection I'd had to criminals was rooting for Butch Cassidy and the Sundance Kid during Duvall's classic movie month. But now thieving was on my mind, and, unlike last week, I wasn't going to be the victim. Normally, I'm honest and law-abiding, but you wouldn't believe how much can change in just a few days.

"I know it sounds like stealing, but the truth is that those jewels weren't mine to sell . . . so retrieving them is really just putting things right," I explained to Mercutio as I set the bowl of key-lime batter in the fridge.

A fall breeze blew in from the open window, and I smelled freshly mowed grass. I opened the window a little wider before I walked around the counter to the couch. I sat down so we could have an eye-to-eye conversation.

"I'll make sure Jenna gets her money back. I'll even find a way to lift that hiccups hex." I leaned over Mercutio where he lay on the couch. He purred and his fur rippled, making his ocelot spots dance. He probably didn't think much of my trying to rob anyone, even if it was one of our nemeses. Before a week ago, Jenna Reitgarten had been just a snooty blond nuisance, but she'd been promoted. And Merc, who I didn't even know before last week, had become my trusted friend and sometime action-adventure sidekick. Yeah, you wouldn't believe how much stuff can change in just a few days.

Merc batted a loose strand of my red hair, catching his claws on it and tugging my head forward.

"Hey," I complained, pulling the hair loose. "Watch those paws. Remember you're not a tabby. With jungle-cat strength comes jungle-cat responsibilities. Now, when do you think would be the best time to burgle a house?"

Merc licked his paw thoughtfully, and I reached for a washrag on the counter to wipe a drop of cream cheese frosting off my Longhorns T-shirt. It wasn't that I wanted to start in on a life of crime. Far from it. But the honest approach to jewelry recovery hadn't worked.

"If I wait until they're out of town, I'd have to break in and maybe trip the alarm. Or I could sneak in when they're having their festival party and swipe the stuff and sneak out."

"Either way should be exciting," a soft voice said.

Startled, I jumped, and jerked my head to find Edie, the family ghost.

I smiled at her white trousers, navy boatneck sweater, and double strand of jawbreaker-sized pearls. Mostly, Edie sashayed around town in her 1920s flapper dresses, but sometimes she wore trousers, and she could make pants look every bit as elegant. If she were chocolate, she'd be a holiday box of Godiva truffles. Me, I'm more of an M&M's girl. As you might guess, there's a lot about her that I envy, except for the part about being dead and all.

"I thought you were out of the country," I said.

"I was traveling, but I got bored. There was no one interesting in Notre Dame, and the Scottish ghosts were off on some mass haunting. Extremely tiresome. I'll come along on the robbery, shall I? To play lookout?" Edie asked, fingering her sleek black bob.

"That would be great," I said with a smile. These days Edie was usually too busy with her own life—well, afterlife—to get overly involved in mine. "You'd be the perfect accomplice, since it's not like you could get arrested and put in jail, right?" I said.

The oven timer dinged, signaling that my first batch of cupcakes was done. I hopped up to take out the muffin pans.

"Speaking of good-looking men with handcuffs, how is your favorite member of law enforcement?" Edie asked.

Zach, I thought with a slight pang. "Right as rain," I said, hoping that he was. Truthfully, my normally ever-present ex had dropped out of my life, not returning my calls, even when I left supersweet messages on his machine. Zach's avoidance maybe had to do with the way a certain gorgeous guy—and forbidden wizard—was trying to become a fixture in my life. Or maybe it had to do with having to fight a whole mess of werewolves last Thursday night because of me. Generally, when Zach's off duty from being a sheriff's deputy, he likes to have a few beers and watch a game. And battling the supernatural creatures he never knew existed hadn't exactly gone smoothly. I wanted to make things up to him, but first I had to track him down.

"Why are you making so many cupcakes? I rather doubt you needed to go to the trouble for our cat. A bowl of cream would have sufficed, or a small rodent."

I wrinkled my nose at the thought of Mercutio eating fuzzy little mice. "I'm taking these to Miss Cookie's place to see if they convince her to rehire me. Du-Fall Fest is kicking off, so she'll need the help. With the right confectionary bribes, I think she'll realize it's a good time to forget about my act of defiance. After all, whoever said 'the customer is always right' was probably just a customer trying to use an expired coupon. I mean, if a man buys a pack of gum and then says, 'I think you should tap dance,' is he right? Ever see a cashier in tap shoes?" I paused. "I didn't guess so."

"I don't know what you're talking about, and why on earth would you want that job? You should be concentrating on learning your craft. You're a witch now."

"Oh, no. Those were special—especially bad—circumstances. I'm back to being a baker," I said, waving my arm to indicate all the batter-covered pots and pans on the flour-dusted counter. "It's my one talent. You don't know because you've never tasted anything I've made. I'm telling you, if Hershey's had a college, I'd have a PhD in cocoa."

She rolled her eyes. "Wonderful. Gives a whole new meaning to flour power. You'll undoubtedly change the world, one fruitcake at a time."

She disappeared into a small green orb and was gone. I was two steps from the kitchen counter when someone knocked on the door.

Mercutio yowled and sprang off the couch to dart down the hall.

The knocking got louder. "I'm coming!" I called, hurrying to the front door, hoping to find Zach.

I pulled the door open and did find a man leaning against the brick door frame, but he wasn't anybody I'd ever met or been married to. I looked over his preppy turtleneck, dark trousers, and gleaming smile. He wasn't very tall, only about five-six, but he was clean-cut and pretty enough to be in a boy band. I'd bet some women wouldn't find it hard to fall for him right off.

"Hey there. Can I help you?" I asked.

"You have that backward," he said in a yummy English accent.

Don't even think about getting another crush!

"I'm here to help you. Jordan Perth," he said with another flash of his wide smile. He pulled a folded envelope from his pocket and handed it to me.

There was an impressive-looking black wax seal on it that had partially cracked off. The seal seemed to be some kind of a crest.

My eyes darted to his face and then back to the envelope.

"A hand delivery, huh?" I mumbled. "I hope my mailman, George, doesn't hear about this. He's mad enough about e-mail taking all his business." I ripped open the envelope and pulled out the letter.

Dear Ms. Trask:

Having been found guilty at your hearing, you are expected to immediately comply with all Conclave directives. Details of the remuneration you must pay will follow in a separate letter. The matter of your training and placement within the hierarchy of magic must begin forthwith. Mr. Jordan Perth, the bearer of this letter, will assist you in your preparation for the Initial Challenge, which shall occur on November 1. Should you fail to comply with completion of the Initial Challenge, you will be considered in breach of Amendment 247, Article 6 of the Association's Constitution and will be subject to incarceration or extermination.

As a result of Mr. Bryn Lyons's involvement in your illegal use of magic, you are barred from any contact with him. Though Mr. Lyons has appealed the decision, until the matter is settled, you are expected to comply with the original verdict.

Sincerely,
Basil Glenn
Chief Secretary, Department of Justice—
   World Association of Magic
Senior Advisor to the Conclave

"What the Sam Houston? I wasn't told about any hearing."

"You weren't? Bryn Lyons said you had waived your right to be present."

"Oh." I cocked my head and frowned. "Well, I did tell him he could speak on my behalf to the what-do-you-call-it, the Conclave, but I didn't know it was like a trial. I would have gone and explained myself."

"Unfortunately, it's a bit late for that now."

"But did Bryn explain the special circumstances? That I had to put a zombie back in the ground after someone, against my will I might add, stole some blood and hair from me to do magic? And that I had to find a family heirloom to prevent the destruction of the soul of a very elegant former witch?"

"I didn't attend the hearing, so I'm not aware of what explanations were presented," he said.

Bryn's a lawyer and he'd gotten me out of trouble in the human court system last week, so I'd just assumed he would do the same in the magical one. But now I realized that Bryn might not have told them all the details about how my locket had gotten stolen. When I thought it over, it seemed pretty dumb of me to have sent him to tell my side of the story.

"Well, listen, I can't pay any fines. I'm flat broke. Actually, I'm unemployed." I bit my bottom lip thoughtfully. "Plus, this Initial Challenge thing sounds time-consuming, and if I can't get my old job back, I have to go job-hunting."

"Your nonmagical occupation is subordinate to your magical obligations. In the Initial Challenge, you'll face a difficult task that—"

"Hold on. I'm not a witch. I'm just a pastry chef. I had to use magic before on account of an emergency, but I don't want to join any magical world association or whatever, though I'm real honored to be asked. So you can just go back and tell them I'm going to stay a private citizen. And reassure them that I won't use magic again. I promise."

He smiled. "That isn't quite how things work. If you don't participate in the challenge by the allotted time, you'll face the consequences. Imprisonment or death."

"I'm a pastry chef!" I shouted. "Not a single one of the spells I cast last week turned out right. I tried astral projection and ended up half-possessed and drunk on magic. I tried to put the zombie back in the grave and gave a whole bunch of factory workers a deadly sleeping sickness. I'm not safe with magic. What I am is a magical menace!"

He grinned and gave me a sympathetic look that seemed designed to humor me. "You're just uninitiated. With proper training, you'll be quite effective, I'm sure."

Fury, red as my hair, exploded in my belly. "I don't think

so. As I said, there's something wrong with my magic. I'm pretty sure it's broken."

"That isn't at all likely. Now, I'm staying at the Yellow Rose Inn on Poplar Street. Do you know it?"

I took a deep breath and blew it out. Did he need me to translate American English to his language for him? "Yes, I know the Yellow Rose, but—"

"Excellent. Let's say seven thirty. By that time, your other instructor should have arrived, and we'll discuss things at greater length over drinks."

"Other instructor?" I echoed.

He tapped his finger under my chin. "Right. We're going to teach you what you need to know to survive the challenge."

I knocked his finger away, but he didn't react to that or the furious look I gave him.

"See you later, love," he said, strolling down to his car, a blue BMW convertible.

"My name is Tammy Jo!" I snapped.

He raised a hand to acknowledge that he'd heard me, but didn't bother to turn around and apologize for being overly familiar and more than a little patronizing.

I swung around and spotted Mercutio perched on top of the chest of drawers in the foyer. "Did you hear that?" I demanded.

He looked at me, and, since he had ears, I gathered that he had.

"Well, I don't know who they think they are," I said, slamming the door. "They can send ten more pretty-boy wizards with long eyelashes and Crest Whitestrips teeth. I don't have to be a witch if I don't want to! Now, let's get back to icing our darn cupcakes and planning our robbery."

2

MY DOORBELL RANG while I was in the middle of whipping the chocolate cream for mini–cream puffs. Miss Cookie has a special weakness for them, and I thought showing up with a big box, along with the key-lime cupcakes, would seal the deal.

The doorbell rang again, and I set the stainless steel bowl down. "I'm tempted to ignore that," I told Mercutio.

He circled the bowl with an expression that said he thought whipped cream looked every bit as interesting as regular cream.

"No more of that for you. You didn't eat your real food," I said, shoving the bowl into the fridge as whoever it was started knocking.

I walked down the hall and pulled the door open to find Bryn Lyons. He's got bright blue eyes, black hair, and a bank account that makes him way out of my league. If this were the Garden of Eden, he'd be the apple. You can guess who I'd be.

"I'm not allowed to see you," I blurted. And that wasn't just true because of what the Conclave had to say. My family had him on a special do-not-associate-with list.

"So you've said. Ready to tell me why?" he asked, stepping inside.

"Um. No."

He gave me a disapproving shake of his head before changing topics. "I smell chocolate."

"Good nose." *Good everything else, too,* I thought, looking him over in his dark designer suit.

"Anything that needs taste-testing?" he asked.

I was supposed to resist fraternizing with him, which was why I hadn't returned his calls or accepted his invitations to dinner over the past few days. But the thing is, I make food so people can eat it.

"Come on," I said with a roll of my eyes.

"Hello, Mercutio," Bryn said.

Bryn is the only one besides me who talks to Mercutio like he speaks human. It's just one more thing I wish we didn't have in common; Bryn's hard enough to resist as it is. Mercutio meowed a greeting, then sauntered off.

In the kitchen, I cut a puff in half and filled it with the whipped buttercream, then handed it to Bryn with a napkin. He ate it, closing his eyes to savor it halfway through.

"You're very talented," he said.

I smiled. Couldn't help myself.

"Actually, your baking skills are part of the reason I'm here. Jenson suggested that we solicit your services. Would you be interested in catering desserts for a party?"

"I, well, you know I can't come to—and the letter." I tried to untangle my tongue and my thoughts.

"How would a thousand dollars be? You can work out the specifics with Jenson."

A thousand dollars! I take it back. If this were the Garden, Bryn would be the snake, because he sure knew what to tempt me with. I grabbed the Conclave envelope off the counter and shoved it at him. He slid the letter out and skimmed it, then frowned and tossed it on the countertop like it was junk mail.

"I thought you were going to get me out of trouble with the wizard world," I said, waiting for an explanation.

"Things don't always go as planned."

Ain't that the truth!

My kitchen is open to the living room, and he turned and walked over to the couch. I shoved the bowl back in the fridge before I joined him.

"So," I said as I sat on the love seat. "What happened?"

"I didn't expect them to send anyone this soon," he said, then glanced over at me. "They're worried about you, Tamara."

"Me? I'm just fine," I said, pretending that I didn't know what he meant by that.

He smiled. "Not that kind of worried."

I sighed. "I tried to tell the guy who came that I wasn't going to do any more magic. Plus, hardly anything I did worked right. Honestly, what the heck do they have to be worried about?"

"Actually, I think it's the power of the spell I cast using our commingled magic. The one that I used to wound and drive out most of the werewolves that were attacking Duvall."

"The one on the night that we . . ." I trailed off, blushing. I'd gotten kind of drunk on magic and let him seduce me. Or maybe I'd seduced him. It was all as fuzzy as a peach, which was the way I preferred it. Good girls don't seduce dark wizards who might be dangerous to their families.

"Yes, the night that we . . ." he said, raising his eyebrows. He was teasing me. I folded my hands on my lap, determined not to get flustered.

"Well, shouldn't they be worried about you a lot more than me?"

"Oh, they're worried about me, but it's more difficult for them to manipulate me. I'm part of the establishment. Now, about this Initial Challenge, what did Perth tell you about it?"

"Nothing yet. He wants me to meet him tonight, but I'm not going."

"You have to go."

I pursed my lips. "This is America. Besides jury duty and jail, I don't *have* to go anywhere."

He smiled and leaned toward me, lowering his voice. "If I were the only one you had to deal with, maybe you could skip it. To me, you're so . . . appealing, sometimes I suspect I'd let you get away with anything."

My mouth dropped open in surprise. The man could convince a drowning woman to dive underwater.

"The trouble is it's not up to me, Tamara, and John Barrett, the president of the World Association of Magic, hasn't met you. All he knows is that you're a rogue witch. If you defy the Conclave's edict, he'll become even more determined and dangerous to you. I want you to promise me that you'll go to the meeting tonight and listen carefully."

"Well—"

Unbelievably, there was another knock at the door. Normally, I can go a whole week without ever getting an unexpected visitor. Today, though, it was like my driveway was the new Main Street.

Bryn stood up. "Given that I'm not supposed to be here and that I don't want to provoke them in a way that they could use against you, why don't I step outside?" He strode to my new sliding door that led to the backyard.

Mercutio bounded past me and climbed onto the bureau. "No jumping on the company!" I hissed as I got to the front door, but then I paused. Recently there'd been a lot of people trying to kill me and stuff. "Unless the company threatens me or seems dangerous."

Mercutio cocked his head.

I sighed. "Well, use your judgment I guess." I pulled the door open, and there was Zach, Marlboro Man meets Abercrombie ad.

"Hey, darlin'."

"Hey, yourself," I said with a smile. Though we fight more than those folks on reality TV, I'm still crazy about him. Plus, I'd nearly lost him to a werewolf bite and was still just plain happy to see him alive. "Where you been?"

He tipped his cowboy hat back and leaned down to give me a kiss. "Oh, around. Came by to see if you need money and to take you to dinner at TJ and Nadine's. They're grilling tonight. I picked up a case of Armadillo Ale and some steaks—"

Though Bryn never made a sound, I knew the moment he walked up behind me. I knew it because Zach went as still as Mercutio does when he sees a lizard he's gonna make short work of. Adrenaline kicked my heart into high gear.

"So you've got company," Zach said, taking a step back.

Uninvited company that was supposed to be in the yard out of sight!

I grabbed Zach's arm. I'm seriously attracted to Bryn, but Zach's been the candy apple of my eye since I was too little to know why I wanted to follow him to forever and back. "He was just going," I said.

"That right?" Zach said, still watching Bryn through narrowed eyes.

"We had some things to discuss," Bryn said from over my shoulder. "We weren't finished actually."

Bryn never makes things between me and Zach easy. I know it's because he wants me for himself. The trouble is, I'm not so sure why. Might be because Bryn thinks I'm pretty. Or it might be because he's able to siphon magical power out of me like some people steal sugar packets from restaurant tables.

I looked back at Bryn. "I'll take your advice about the meeting, but it's better if we don't see each other anymore, all things considered."

"The offer still stands for the catering assignment. You could deal directly with Jenson."

"Thanks. I'll think about it," I said, still holding tight to Zach's arm. I knew Zach could have pulled loose anytime, and I took it as a good sign that he didn't.

"I'll see you later, Tamara."

Zach stepped farther into the house to let Bryn leave. When the door was safely closed and we were alone, Zach said, "You're not working for him. Not today. Not next month. Not next year."

"Hang on now."

Zach yanked his arm free. "You're not working for the

guy you cheated on me with! I can forgive you once. I know you were out of your head drunk that night, but I don't expect to see you with him again—ever."

It hadn't exactly been cheating. Zach and I are divorced. Plus, I hadn't been myself. Or at least not *all* myself. I'd been part promiscuous flapper, on account of a spell gone wrong.

"You heard what I told him."

"I heard it. I also heard his answer to it. What you said didn't make a damn bit of difference to him. So here's what I think: from now on, when he shows up, you don't let him in. If he calls, you hang up. He'll get the message eventually, if you make him get it."

I had wanted to make up with Zach, but when he started using his police voice and telling me what to do, it reminded me of why our relationship was always on-again, off-again. I took a deep breath and blew it out slowly, trying not to lose my temper.

"I don't plan to get involved with him." But Bryn had helped me, and I wasn't going to slam my door in his face either. It wasn't good manners.

"What meeting did you say you'd go to? Is he going to be there?"

"No."

"What meeting?"

"Look, that's not something I can talk about."

Zach narrowed his eyes and his muscles tightened. "With me, you mean? 'Cause you were just talking about it with him."

"Well, it's complicated."

"Used to be you didn't have any secrets from me."

Things were getting trickier by the minute. If I wanted to be with Zach, could I really avoid talking to him about the supernatural stuff that was happening? I wrung my hands until I caught myself and then dropped them to my sides. "If you want to know, I'll tell you, but you won't like it."

He folded his arms across his chest.

"Edie's not the only messed-up thing about my family. The truth is that when I said Momma and Aunt Mel were kind of eccentric and whimsical, what I meant to say was that they're . . . they're—"

"Spit it out," he said.

"Witches. And it looks like I might be one, too."

"For the love of Christ! Your imagination just gets wilder every time I turn around. And I guess Lyons is feeding into this now? That damned letch. In Great-granddaddy's day, that guy would've been selling snake oil."

"You saw the werewolves. You know there's more to this world than—"

"Stop right there. I don't know what I saw. Whether it was men in horror-movie makeup or what, but I know there's no such thing as werewolves. Hell, I remember being half out of it and drinking some kind of bitter coffee at Lyons's house. Who the hell knows what was in it? Maybe LSD. And I'll tell you what's more, this kind of talk, you saying you're a . . ." He shook his head. "I'm taking you to church on Sunday. We'll sit down with the reverend."

"No."

"What do you mean 'no'?"

"What's hard to interpret about 'no'?" I put my fists on my hips. "I'm not going around talking to folks about this. It'll lead to trouble."

"You got that right."

"You know, just go on and go. Tell Nadine and TJ that I'm sorry I couldn't make it," I said.

"Don't do this, Tammy Jo."

"Look, I've got some stuff to figure out. I think it's best that I figure it out alone," I said softly.

He glanced away, frowning. "This is not right." He looked back at me. "Whatever you've got goin' on in your head, it's gonna pass, and I don't want you sitting here dwelling on it by yourself. You're coming with me. Let's get you fed on some Texas beef, and get you with some people that love you who aren't trying to mess your head up."

"I'd rather stay here."

Zach shook his head. "I don't want you here alone. You

can come with me, or I'll drive you to Chulley's tonight and tell him you're getting worse."

The blood plummeted to my feet, making me pale and panicked.

Chulley was the psychiatrist Zach had convinced me to see when I told him about Edie. After a session where Chulley and I really pissed each other off, I'd vowed never to go back. I found out later that Chulley had told Zach that he couldn't rule out that I'd need to be in a mental hospital one day. Straightjackets and padded rooms. Locked doors and needles and worse. It had happened to other witches in my family. And now Zach was threatening to give Chulley another shot at me.

No way! Not without the kind of fight that brings the neighbors out to their front lawns to watch the show.

"You're saying you'd tell him I've gone crazy?" I whispered. "Tell him I need to be locked up?" Saying it made it more real. Fear twisted my guts, and tears filled my eyes.

Zach winced. "Don't do that, darlin'. Don't cry," he said, pulling me into his arms and hugging me tight. "Whatever happens, you know I'm gonna take care of you."

But not the way I need, I thought unhappily. Confiding in him had been a big mistake.

After a couple minutes of watery protests, my head ached and my throat burned, but I did convince Zach that I was in no shape to go to his brother's for a cookout. He got the food and beer from his truck and called Nadine to say we couldn't make it. I lay on the couch while he broiled the steaks in the oven. Mercutio, who had caught the whole exchange from the top of the bureau, came to lie with me.

"I never should've told him," I said under my breath.

Mercutio licked my face.

"What should I do? Pretend that—"

From the kitchen, Zach said, "Jo, don't whisper to that cat. It's creepy as hell. In fact, why don't you put him in the yard for a while?"

The rift between Zach and me suddenly seemed wider than the Rio Grande.

I hugged Mercutio and set him on the floor. "Go play, Merc."

Merc looked at Zach, hissed, and then scampered over to the stairs and bounded up them.

"Lots of people talk to their cats. I saw it on a website."

Zach ignored this comment. "You want onions on your steak?"

"Okay," I said in a calm voice, though I was feeling more and more like a prisoner in my own house.

Just get through dinner. When he sees you eating and talking and acting normally, he'll decide you're not insane after all. Then he'll go home, and you can be as crazy as you want.

I got up and set the table while Zach finished cooking. It's never been in my nature to be sullen, but I was pretty darn quiet while we ate. Afterward, he turned the television on, and I realized that he wasn't going to leave. He planned to keep an eye on me all night, which made me feel like the walls were closing in. I wiped my clammy hands on the dish towel and took shallow breaths.

I was not going to give up control of my life without a fight. Plus, I was planning to meet those wizards because I hoped I'd have better luck convincing the second teacher to let me out of the challenge thing. I couldn't allow Zach to stand in the way of my getting there.

I needed an escape plan. Luckily, Zach wasn't some stranger, some guard at a mental hospital. I'd been married to him; I knew his weaknesses.

"You know, I got ESPN," I said as I rinsed a washcloth and my hands under cold water.

"You did? You didn't have to do that, darlin'," he said, but instantly hit the channel-changer button to take him there.

I laid the washcloth over the faucet and waited for him to get engrossed in some program analyzing football teams. That took about forty-five seconds from the time he turned it on.

"I'm gonna go wash my face," I said, discreetly grabbing my purse.

He nodded, eyes still on the commentators.

I walked calmly up the stairs, but as soon as I rounded the corner, I hurried to my room, shutting the door behind me. Mercutio sat on my bed, watching as I packed an overnight bag.

"We're getting out of here," I whispered, tossing two days' worth of clothes in the duffel.

I ripped a piece of paper from a notebook and snagged a marker to leave Zach a note. In big black letters, I wrote: "Dear Zach, You can consider us officially broken up. Love, Tammy Jo."

I taped the message to the mirror. Let him chew on that.

I grabbed the rest of what I would need to be out all night, then opened the window and hooked the fire ladder on the sill. The end of it landed on top of a bush.

"Okay, let's go," I said. "You want me to carry you?" I put my arms out. Merc ignored this offer and went to inspect the ladder situation.

"I'll go first," I said to encourage him. I slung the duffel strap over my shoulder and climbed out the window. Partway down, I stopped. "C'mon," I said, holding out an arm for him.

He yawned.

"I've got to go. With or without you!" I whispered fiercely and continued my descent. I was just climbing out from the bush when a blur of fur caught my eye. Merc came down the ladder in two bounds with his body nearly vertical, head facing the ground. He sprung from midladder to the lawn in a move that would've had me flossing my teeth with the grass. I stood openmouthed for a moment.

"That settles it. They should've named you 'Spidercat.' "

As cool as can be, Mercutio sauntered over to my little blue Ford Focus. In the spirit of great escapes, I rushed to the driver's side and got in. I started the car, wincing at the motor's noise, hoping ESPN in the house was loud enough to drown it out.

It wasn't until we were two blocks away that I started to relax. Not that Zach wouldn't track me down eventually, but

I hoped by then he'd be over the whole "drag Tammy Jo to a shrink" plan. Because if he wasn't, I would have to take steps.

Just because I loved him didn't mean I wouldn't go to court to get a temporary restraining order. Yeah, if I couldn't get out of the magical challenge, I'd have to work on becoming a witch in every sense of the word.

3

I TURNED OFF onto Duvall Trail Highway, which would take me to the Old Town area. Duvall was founded in 1874, and the historic part is protected from major development. As I ambled down the dusty roads, I passed Gruber's, the old textile mill, and some cottages that the Duvall Historical Society used for tours. They didn't have air-conditioning, so I'm not sure how much fun it was for tourists to stand inside them and get lectured to, but the iced tea and whiskey punch at the tour's end were always popular.

I would be a little early for the meeting, but I wanted to get done talking with Jordan as quickly as possible so I could plan my next move. My best friend Georgia's in-laws were in town so I couldn't stay there, and I couldn't really afford a hotel. Bryn's house was plenty big, but that would cause too much trouble. I really had nowhere to go. It's not easy to be homeless with a home, but I'd sort of managed it.

I got to Poplar Street and found the yellow and salmon pink Victorian that had been converted into the Yellow Rose Inn. I turned off my engine and eyed the big Harley Davidson motorcycle parked too near the fire hydrant. Whoever owned it might get a ticket if he wasn't careful.

I was halfway to the front porch when the door opened and the Harley's owner came out. I knew it was him by the worn black leather jacket, mirrored shades, and thick black hair that hung past his shoulders. He moved like he was a Mack truck that knew it was the biggest thing on the road.

He looked first at me, but then caught sight of Mercutio. *"¿Oce, qué tal?"*

That surprised me. I didn't realize that Merc knew Spanish. I took two semesters in high school, but I'm not what you'd call fluent. I did master the teacher's recipe for Mexican cookies right off, though.

"Ven aquí," he said, but Merc didn't come to him. Merc went straight up the nearest tree.

The guy stroked his goatee, sizing me up. I knew what he saw. Five and a half feet tall and a hundred and six pounds, wearing seven-dollar shoes with fuchsia roses on them. He probably thought he could huff and puff and blow me right down the street. I stood up straighter in my flip-flops.

"You the witch?" he asked.

"Well, actually, it's not real certain what I'm gonna do with my life."

He snorted. "I wouldn't worry about it. You've only got a few days left." He pointed to the tree. "That's my cat. When you leave, he doesn't."

"Like always, that's up to him," I countered.

"Think so?" he asked, then he murmured a few words and a branch on the tree burst into flames. Mercutio darted farther up a limb to avoid the blaze. The flaming branch burned brightly for a moment, then turned to ash and crumbled from the tree.

To Merc, he said, "When she leaves, you stay."

Mercutio swiped the air as the biker sauntered to his motorcycle and climbed astride. The engine roared to life, and he pulled away from the curb. I watched him drive down the block to the Whiskey Barrel, a bar and pool hall.

"You okay?" I asked.

Mercutio came down the tree trunk and pawed the ash before walking to me.

"Well, I don't like him."

Mercutio padded up the porch steps and sat on a wicker chair.

I squared my shoulders. Mercutio might act tough and nonchalant, but, at seven months, he was really still just a baby. "You don't have to stay if you don't want to."

Mercutio licked his paws as I went to the front door. "I'll be back in a couple minutes."

I walked into the cozy front parlor. It was chock-full of chintz-covered furniture and antique lamps. I found Jordan Perth sitting in a wingback chair with a crystal tumbler of liquor in his hand.

"Hello, Miss Trask. You just missed Incendio."

Incendio. That figured. "No, we met."

"Oh? Is he still outside?"

"He went down the street to the bar."

He frowned. "Did you introduce yourself?"

I sat in a chair next to his. "No, but he knew it was me. He asked if I was a witch."

"And what did you say?"

"Said I wasn't sold on the idea."

Jordan grimaced and leaned toward me. "Are you determined to end up dead?"

"Hmm. Let me think that over. That sure is a tough decision." I glanced at my nails. "I wouldn't say I'm determined to. No."

Jordan chuckled. "Very amusing." He took a swallow from his glass. "Would you like some brandy?"

"Nope."

"Please yourself," he said with a shrug. If that were my goal, I sure wouldn't have been meeting him to discuss magic lessons. "I assume you know you're from a long line of witches with earth magic. You remember the four elements, of course?"

"Earth, water, wind, and fire," I said.

"Exactly. The Conclave sent me because I'm skilled in earth, with sufficient talents in air and water. Incendio Maldaron is one of the world's most powerful fire warlocks. The two of us have to get you ready for a challenge that will utilize spells involving all of the elements. If the Conclave sent Incendio, it's because you'll need a complex fire spell to survive the challenge. You understand? You need him to teach you, but the man is a Class Eight warlock. If you act like you're not committed, he's not likely to invest himself, is he?"

"I haven't even decided yet that I'm going to do this challenge thing. I think I need to talk to the person in charge. To explain that I don't plan on being a witch as an occupation. Or even as a hobby."

"Are you trying to be thick? They don't care what you plan on doing. You've spell-cast, love. You're already a witch and subject to the laws of magic. You don't get to say that you don't want to play. If ordered to, Incendio can set fire to your house with you inside. Is that plain enough for you?"

Yep, plain enough to give me a major case of nerves. I picked up my purse and dug through it until I found a lone Special Dark miniature hiding under my sunglasses. I offered to split it with Jordan, who declined with an impatient wave of his hand.

"So, if I face the challenge and live, and *then* promise not to do magic, will they leave me alone?" I unwrapped the chocolate and popped it in my mouth.

"After a fashion, yes. A witch or wizard can go inactive once initial licensing has been completed."

"When are you supposed to start training me?"

"Tomorrow morning. You can join us for a drink tonight. Try to make a more favorable impression on Incendio."

I looked at my watch. "Can I meet up with you later? Give him a little time to settle in?" *And to have a few drinks, which will hopefully make him friendlier.* "I've got a couple of things I have to do first." *Like hide my ocelot from the wizard I'm supposed to suck up to.*

"Other things that you feel are more important than your own survival?"

I crumpled the wrapper. "When did I meet you?" I asked with mock curiosity. "Right, I believe it was today. So you'll give me a little stretch room, won't you? I was in the middle of my regularly scheduled and kind-of-in-a-crisis life when you showed up out of the blue and said I needed to drop everything. Before I can get down to witch training, I need to take care of a couple things."

"By all means, then," he said dryly.

He'd been way more cheerful when I first met him. Guess he didn't expect me to give him so much trouble, but trouble seems to be what I mostly get involved with these days. I left the inn, and Mercutio hopped down from the chair and walked with me to the car.

"Yeah, c'mon," I said and looked around to see if anyone was watching.

He stood at the passenger door. I let him in and hurried around to the other side. "You're going to have to lie low. I'm not sure what a Class Eight warlock can do, but it sounds pretty bad."

I drove across town to the new strip mall that was just completed. The tenants hadn't moved in yet, so the parking lot was deserted. It was only a couple blocks from Riverbank Park in Shoreside Oaks, the most affluent part of town. I parked my car behind the construction Dumpsters, so no one would spot it and tell Zach or mention it to out-of-towners. Yep, I was trying to hide things from my friends and neighbors because Duvall talks a lot, and it talks fast.

"C'mon, Mercutio," I said. Merc jumped out. "I sure would like to know more about how you hooked up with that Incendio guy. Did you start off friends?" I asked.

Mercutio batted his whiskers hard.

"No, huh?"

I kept us just inside the tree line and tried to be as quiet as Mercutio, who didn't make a sound as he padded through the woods. When we got to the park, it was dark. The metal tunnel-shaped shed that surrounds part of the dock was locked tight. Like a lot of stuff in town though, Zach's brothers' construction company had built it and they'd kept a key, since taking the paddleboats out at night was just their sort of fun. I reached under and behind the drain and found the tiny magnetic key holder that I'd seen them pull out one night when I'd been along for an after-hours paddleboat ride.

Once inside the shed, I found the big key for the chains around the paddleboats.

"You know I got the idea for this from you," I told Mercutio.

I went to the back door, which led to the far end of the dock. I flicked off the light and closed the door behind us. "Bryn said you floated down the river on a raft, and that's how you ended up at his house. I wonder how you came to be in Duvall in the first place though."

I unlocked the heavy chain, freeing one boat, then relocked it around the others. Merc and I dropped into the seats of the loose boat, and I uncurled the twine rope that was tied to a silver hook on the back. I wanted to have it ready to tie up to Bryn's dock when I got there.

I pedaled, and we backed up with a soft swishing sound. Then I turned the boat and pedaled forward. With the current, we moved quick as fish. We'd had a lot of rain in the past month, and the river was flowing fast.

We passed mansions. I checked out their beautifully manicured yards, full of big oaks and all kinds of flowering trees, rosebushes, and elegantly plotted patches of fall flowers. Some had statues and fountains. Some had tennis courts and swimming pools.

"In the summer there's a net that blocks the boats from getting this far downstream. But the paddleboat rental's closed now, so we can get through," I told Merc.

The property and houses got bigger the farther we went, and the river widened. I heard Cider Falls in the distance. We passed woods again on the right, and I thought we'd reached Bryn's property. As we whizzed forward, the forest came to an end and gave way to a beautiful lawn. I squinted, looking for his dock. It wasn't lit, but I could see some light from the outdoor floods bouncing off the reflectors on the side of his speedboat.

I pedaled toward the dock, which I could finally make out, but the current was dragging us sideways. Fast.

"Uh-oh." I gasped.

4

I PEDALED HARD. "The current's pulling us, Merc!" I whispered fiercely. We spun and I couldn't control it. I reversed my pedaling, and my legs burned. I knew I should've spent more time on that darn exercise bike at Georgia's.

"You jump and save yourself!" I said.

Mercutio hopped on the back, then leapt onto Bryn's dock. I bit my lip, terribly scared. Something jarred the boat, which jerked sideways, ramming into the side of Bryn's boat. Water sloshed in, wetting my feet and pant legs. I ignored the shock of the cold water and looked over to the dock.

Mercutio stood on the end, next to the metal hook used to anchor boats. He'd managed to loop the twine from the back of the paddleboat around the hook. Merc held it with his teeth and used his paws to flatten the line to the dock to help secure it.

"How the heck?" I sputtered, pulling on the rope hand-over-hand, dragging myself closer until I could hop onto the dock. I took the twine and secured it, then squatted next to Mercutio and kissed the top of his head.

"You're the smartest baby cat I ever heard of. If you decide you want to be famous, just say the word. You could headline in Las Vegas, I swear."

All of the sudden a bunch more lights came on. I looked over to where the paddleboat was banging up against Bryn's more expensive one.

"You think he heard us crash or you think he's got the dock rigged with security sensors?"

Merc stuck his tongue out rhythmically like he was tasting the air. He swatted the space in front of him and hissed softly.

"Or I guess he might have a protective ward around the property."

I heard a dog barking.

"Uh-oh. Angus! Quick, Merc!" I said, scooping him up. Angus, Bryn's full-grown rottweiler, had once attacked Mercutio. Merc still had the stitches from that fight. I just hate bullies.

"Angus is chained," Bryn said, stepping into the light from between a pair of oaks.

"Oh, good." I took a deep breath to steady myself and set Merc down. "Hey there."

"Hey, yourself. You're trespassing."

I widened my eyes. "You want me to go?"

Bryn didn't answer that. Instead, he strode over to me until he was too close. "You know, I'm a little tired of hearing that you're never going to see me again, only to have you turn up when you need something," he said.

I wrinkled my nose and hoped my face wasn't too flushed with embarrassment, since he did have a point. "Who says I need something?" I said, trying to seem innocent.

His gaze flicked to the stolen paddleboat, then back to me. He arched a brow.

"Well, actually . . ." I said.

He leaned closer. I smelled sandalwood and spices, and his power made my lips tingle.

"At your house, when Sutton showed up . . ." He shook his head. "I don't like being dismissed." Our mouths were almost touching. "You need to decide whether you and I are friends or not."

"It's not up to me," I said, exasperated.

I tilted my head, still feeling a current of power crackling between us. His uneven breaths were minty against my mouth. I needed to back away, but the chemistry between us was harder to resist than a chocolate éclair.

"Tamara," he whispered as his hands tangled in my hair. He held me still while his mouth covered mine.

I heard the rushing of the waterfall and tasted honey and magic. I slid my arms around him, my fingertips pressing the muscles of his back.

With my eyes closed, I barely registered the flash of light that signaled Edie's arrival. "You're turning into quite the biscuit," her disapproving voice said.

I jerked back from Bryn, leaving us both gasping for breath. He reached for me, but I batted his hand away in a classic Mercutio move.

"We're not alone," I said.

Bryn's gaze swiveled to Edie, and he said to her, "Ah, the family ghost, I presume. So that's what you look like, as stunning as all the Trask women."

"Can you see me, candylegger?" Edie moved closer, taking my spot.

"Only just," he said, catching his breath. "What's a candylegger?"

"A popular man about town, like you. With a useless but compelling kind of charm."

"Are you the one trying to keep Tamara and me apart? I can feel that this is fated, you know."

"Is that so? Are you star-crossed lovers kept apart by your selfish relations? A little old to play Romeo, aren't you?" she said and paused, looking him up and down. Then her voice turned as hard as the beads on her fancy dresses. "Before the year is out, she'll call you warlock," she hissed and sent a shiver up my spine.

"That is—" He paused. "Where did she go?" he asked, though she was still right in front of him. She leaned forward and pressed her phantom lips to his. He coughed and stepped back, blinking. "She's still here."

"Yes."

He looked at me. "I can't see her anymore."

I glanced at Edie. She toyed with the double strand of jawbreaker-sized pearls that hung from her neck. "He saw me with your power . . . from the kiss. When it faded, I did, too. He's not supposed to see me."

"I don't know what you meant," I said to her. "Why would I call him a warlock? Because he'll use dark magic?"

Bryn folded his arms across his chest and clenched his jaw, clearly not happy about being shut out of the conversation.

"No." She clucked her tongue. "Any witch or wizard can use white or dark magic. The true meaning of warlock is old. It comes from our history. Warlock means traitor, one who betrays his own kind."

"Well?" he asked. "What has she accused me of?"

"Nothing specific. She just doesn't trust you."

"The feeling's mutual. Vagrant spirits that interfere with the living are troublesome at best, and dangerous at worst. The latter seems to be the case here."

Edie stared at him. "He wants to wield the McKenna power through you, but he can't have it. Isn't that right, Tammy?"

I glanced at Bryn and wondered if and how he would earn the term *warlock*. I realized, too, that it was the second time I'd heard someone called by that title in the same day. I looked back to Edie. "There's a man in town. Incendio Maldaron. Jordan, the other wizard with him, called him a warlock. Jordan didn't say it like it was a bad thing. He said it like Incendio was a star running back who just scored the game-winning touchdown."

"Maldaron is here?" Bryn asked sharply.

Edie tilted her head. "I know that name. How do I know it?"

I nodded at Bryn. "He's my second instructor."

"The Conclave would never send Incendio Maldaron to teach spells to a novice. It would be like sending a death-row inmate to teach kindergartners how to fill squirt guns."

"What do you mean?"

"Since John Barrett took over, the Conclave has been using Maldaron as an enforcer . . . to punish or exterminate wizards who become dangerous. But, based on the things he's done over the years, Maldaron himself should be at the top of a hit list."

"Why? What's he done?"

"Assault. Probably murder, but he's never been convicted. Witnesses tend to disappear."

"Why would the Conclave hire him, then?"

Bryn smiled grimly. "He's effective at what he does."

I frowned. I'm no politician, but putting a killer on the payroll just didn't seem right. I guessed maybe the CIA did things like that, but the wizards' government shouldn't need to. They have magic on their side.

Mercutio meowed and sprung out from the dock. He landed on the paddleboat and stood looking upriver for a moment, then turned to see if we were paying attention.

"Your cat senses something," Bryn said.

"Merc knows Incendio Maldaron. Incendio says Mercutio belongs to him. It's why I came tonight. Merc doesn't like him. I wanted you to keep him here, to hide him until Incendio leaves town."

Edie snapped her fingers. "I remember now. 'Where there's smoke there's Ince.' That's what his friends used to say." She twirled her pearls at me. "Back in 1989, when Melanie had an affair with him."

"What!" I said with a gasp. My aunt Mel and a scary biker warlock?

"What?" Bryn asked, leaning forward. I held up a finger so I could listen to Edie, who continued unperturbed.

"Yes, she wrote to us from Mexico City, where she met him." Edie smiled. "He got very angry when she broke things off. He made threats, and I suspect he followed through on some of them, although she never said. Melanie always was too good at keeping secrets. You know what though? If you're worried about him, you should wear the earrings, the Colombian emeralds. Twin stones found together, set in white gold and cooled in white water. Melanie had someone famous help her do the protection spell." Edie paused. "She wore them every day for over a year. They were too flashy for day wear, and people around here made comments, but better to be overdressed than burned alive."

Edie dropped her pearls against her shimmering gown. "Finally Maldaron moved. To Spain I think. And with the ocean between them, she felt safe enough to put the emeralds away. She won't mind your wearing them."

I slapped a hand over my mouth, and Edie looked sharply at me.

"Heaven's sake, those weren't part of the jewelry you pawned, were they? The ones from the false-bottomed drawer?"

I felt ill. I guess it showed because she sighed.

"Don't panic," Edie said. Easy for her to say; she was already dead. "You may not need them. It's been twenty years. Perhaps he's mellowed with age."

I thought of his bad-to-the-bone look and put a hand to my head. I doubted he'd mellowed too much, but he was supposed to be my teacher. He'd been sent over on official business. So maybe I was safe.

"Let me go and check things out," she said as she faded to a pale green mist, then a faint orb of light that disappeared.

I turned to Bryn. "She's gone. I'm sorry I ignored you, but she had some really important stuff to say." My hands were shaky, so I clasped them together.

"Such as?"

"Can we talk about it in your house? My feet are wet, and it's kind of cold out here." I had to stall. I didn't know how much I should tell him about our family. He was on the forbidden list. Plus, now Edie had come forth with the alarming premonition about Bryn betraying me, just when I needed his help. With Georgia busy with her in-laws and Zach thinking I'd gone 'round the bend, I was running out of people I could count on. I sighed, trying to think positive. It was only October. We had two whole months before the year ended. Maybe Bryn wouldn't betray me until December.

5

BRYN OPENED THE back door to a big sunroom. Except for there being no sun, it was real nice. He turned on an overheard light, and I sat down on a tan-and-white-striped cushioned chair. I grabbed a small dark blue quilt that was thrown over the back of the seat next to me. As I spread it across my legs, I realized the squares had pictures of the constellations. *Perfect for nighttime.*

I glanced to a large wood and leather trunk sitting in front of a small couch. There were several fancy books stacked on top of it and a couple notebooks. I noticed a dirty dish and fork on a side table and a shiny coffeepot with a platinum-rimmed cup and saucer.

"Were you working out here?"

He nodded.

"You sure work long hours," I said, my eyes fixed on a thick binder that read *Yale Law* on the spine.

"Sometimes."

"I sort of know how that is. Some recipes have to be done over a couple days. Great pastry chefs have to be in the kitchen late. When I got to apprentice at Lampis, I used to be there 'til two or three in the morning sometimes."

"Lampis has excellent pastries. I've had dinner there often when I'm in the city. It's an impressive credit for your résumé. Why were you working at Cookie's bakery if you trained at Lampis?"

I shrugged, feeling my cheeks pink up. The head pastry chef at Lampis had wanted to know the same thing. He'd been mad as a hornet when I told him I was leaving to go back to Duvall. "I missed home." My gaze darted around the room, avoiding his eyes for a moment. "And you're one to talk. What are you doing in Duvall, Mr. Yale Law?"

He smiled. "This town has plenty to offer."

"Like a big magic tor?"

"There's that, too," he said, fixing me with one of those looks that could spark a forest fire.

I cleared my throat. "I came over for a couple of reasons besides dropping off Mercutio. I need to know if there's a spell to erase someone's memory for a specific conversation," I said, thinking I'd like to blot out my telling Zach I was a witch.

"Depends. Do you care if you erase other things? Random memories?"

Hmm. I wouldn't mind erasing all those dumb football facts he obsesses about. Who needed to remember every starting Super Bowl quarterback for the past forty years? Most of it happened before we were born. But what if I accidentally erased our first date or his brothers' weddings or something important? Couldn't risk that. "Yeah, I care. I'd need to be real accurate. I just want to erase a fifteen—or so—minute conversation. I can figure out the exact time if I need to."

"No," Bryn said with a short laugh. "The mind isn't like a VHS tape. There's no guarantee that you'd only erase the memories from that specific period of time."

Darn. "All right."

"Are you going to tell me what happened tonight? I thought you were going to the Sutton family barbeque."

"Yeah, change of plans. Now it turns out I've got to meet with those wizards for drinks. Earlier, Jordan didn't give me any details about the challenge, just that I'd need to use magic from the four elements to get through it. Does that narrow it down?"

"Not really."

I sighed.

"But don't worry," he said. "You can give me the details of the things they're teaching you. That will give me some idea. And I'll see what I can find out through other channels."

I looked at him closely. "What other channels?"

He smiled. "Barrett hasn't been in charge long enough to replace everyone at the upper levels of WAM—the World Association of Magic," he added. "I've still got some friends there."

Spies! Hurray! "That's great. Do you think they'll be able to find out before the day of the challenge?"

"That's the idea, but we'll see. Barrett's fairly paranoid. Normally, a simple challenge for a beginning witch wouldn't be the kind of thing that the president would be involved in at all. But since you know me, it's different."

"Why?"

"I'm not Barrett's favorite person," he said mildly.

"Why not?"

"Whenever he tries to grab too much power, I'm one of the people who stands in his way. Eleven times so far, I've done the research and prepared the briefs to oppose new policies he's tried to push through. Four times, when the vote was going to be close, I've gone to give the arguments in person."

"And you always win."

"Most of the time," he said with a nod.

"He must be pretty mad at you."

Bryn grinned. "He's never sent me a Happy Equinox card, so that's the conclusion I'd draw."

I sighed. "And you had to break the magic laws to help me with the werewolves. I bet that's not a good position for you to be in. I'm real sorry about that."

He shrugged.

"And here I am dragging you in again." I frowned. "It's

just I don't know what else to do with Mercutio. I can't see most folks in town handling him. I mean, he's great. But he can get a little wild with the furniture." Of course, nobody I knew had more expensive stuff than Bryn. I glanced around. Maybe Merc could roam the grounds and stay in the sunroom mostly.

"Mercutio can stay here, or he could stay with you. Maldaron has no claim on a cat like him. Animals of power are free to choose their own company. It's against the law to keep one against its will."

"Well, maybe so, but I can't really go up against Incendio, big-time fire warlock, can I? Especially since I need to learn some stuff he's supposed to teach me. Hey—" I cocked my head. "You said they wouldn't have sent Incendio here just to teach me spells. Do you think they sent him as a warning to you? So you'd stay out of things?"

"As a matter of fact, that's exactly what I think."

I shivered. It was dangerous for Bryn, but he was going to help me anyway. I didn't want to think about how much I already owed him, and I hoped he wasn't keeping track either.

"I take it that you came down the river so no one would see you drive up to the front gate? That was good thinking."

"Yeah, but I won't be able to battle that current to get back upstream tonight. I was thinking that you could take me in your car with the tinted windows and drop me off at my car when we're done here."

He nodded.

"Thanks for helping me, Bryn." I clasped my hands and took a deep breath. "I do need one more thing."

"You have my undivided attention, as is often the case," he said, catching me in that dark blue gaze of his.

"I wish you wouldn't look at me like that. I'm trying to be good, and you're always making me think about being anything but."

"Glad to hear it."

I sighed heavily, and he grinned.

"You know, things are only difficult because you fight your attraction," he said.

"Right, they'd be so easy if I had an all-out affair with you. Then our lives would be simple as meringue."

"Some trouble is worth it."

Probably. "So the thing I need from you is a strong protection spell. The spellbook I've got has one, but it calls for ingredients I don't have." Like medieval armor and knight's blood.

"I'm not supposed to provide you with spells. We've talked about the reasons."

"But when Incendio realizes that I took off with Mercutio, he might want revenge. How am I going to survive if one of the guys that's supposed to be teaching me is actually gunning for me?"

Bryn glanced up at the ceiling, thinking.

"I bet you've got lots of spellbooks," I continued. "You don't have to give me a spell from your best books. I'll take anything that you think will work."

He looked back at me for a moment and then got up and went to the stack on the trunk. He murmured something and waved his hand over them. The air shimmered and some of the covers changed. A few were still regular law books, but some had titles like *Conclave Precedent Rulings 1910–Present* and *World Association of Magic: Amendments.*

I shuffled over to the books, hoping to see a spellbook in the pile, but there wasn't one.

"You know what I'm working on out here?"

"What?"

"My appeal of the Conclave's decision to ban us from associating with each other. The only way a protection spell would even have a chance of blocking the magic of a Class Eight warlock would be if I reinforced it with my power. If I do that, they'll be able to prove I've ignored their ruling. It would give Barrett excellent ammunition against me."

I chewed on my lip, shifting my weight on the balls of my feet.

"If I were convinced that Maldaron was sent here to hurt you, I'd risk it. But he's bound by the Conclave's decisions, too, and they claim they've sent him to teach you. I would rather not break the law unless it's a definite matter of life and death, because breaking the law could be a matter of life and death for me. Barrett's made a motion to have my class raised to six because of the spell I cast on the wolves last week. If he succeeds and then I'm determined to have gone rogue by breaking the judgment from the recent hearing, the Conclave could send enforcers to eliminate me. And conveniently for Barrett, Incendio's already here."

"I remember Astrid saying at the witch's meeting that she thought you were more powerful than your level. Did you purposely pretend to be weaker than you are?"

"A Class Four wizard can break rules and not end up with a death sentence. The more power someone has, the more dangerous it is if he uses it without regard to the law, so there are harsher punishments."

"What class are you really?"

"If I told you, they could demand that you testify to what I've admitted."

"I wouldn't snitch," I said indignantly.

"Not willingly."

"Oh." What would they use? Truth spells? Torture? I wrinkled my nose and frowned. "I hate politics."

"It's the way of the worlds, I'm afraid. The key is to know how to work the system."

"Which I'm sure you do. Lawyers know the best loopholes, right?" I said, making him chuckle. "All right, so I'll try not to ask you for help until you win your appeal. Could you do me a favor, then, and win soon?"

"Of course. You know I live to grant you favors." He smiled to soften the blow of his teasing.

"Yeah, and it sure is sweet of you," I said with my own brand of sugar-laced sarcasm.

"I want something in return," he said, leaning close. Our eyes locked, and the attraction sizzled between us.

"A raspberry torte?"

"Something sweeter," he whispered, his lips brushing mine.

One kiss seemed a small price to pay, considering that all

his furniture would have to be reupholstered by the time Mercutio moved out. And considering that kissing Bryn was only about as terrible as winning the lottery, I closed my eyes.

His mouth was velvety soft as he drew my tongue into it. My toes curled and warmth swallowed me. Pretty soon, my whole body tingled, and I decided that it would be real comfortable to make love on one of the thick-cushioned chaises. That was about the time I knew I was in over my head . . . again.

I stumbled backward, pulling free of him and landing on a chair behind me. I gripped a cushion and concentrated on catching my breath. His blazing blue eyes sparkled, and he grinned, a little breathless, too.

"Tell me the truth. Have you ever felt anything remotely like that with anyone else?" he asked.

"Southern ladies don't kiss and tell." Except to their best girlfriends, their hairdressers, and sometimes their mommas. Definitely not to forbidden wizards who would use the information against them. "So I really need to be going. I've got to meet up with those teachers of mine."

"Why don't you come back here tonight? Mercutio will be calmer if you do, and it'll give us a chance to talk."

A chance to talk and a chance to kiss our way right into a big, fat, forbidden affair. "I'll see. One other thing."

"Yes?"

"I'll take the job of catering the party, and I'd really appreciate it if you could advance me the money. I'm nearly broke, and it looks like I won't have time for getting my old job back this week. I don't want the check for the mortgage payment to bounce."

Bryn pulled out his wallet and counted out a thousand dollars. Jiminy Crickets. His walking-around money was more than I'd ever had in my bank account.

Our fingers touched as he passed me the money, and that spark was there, like a flash of lightning in the distance. He reached for my hand, but I pulled it away and put both arms behind my back.

"It's not a good idea. We're like clothes that have been

too long in the dryer. I don't want any static-cling shocks, you know?"

"That's where we differ. I like our static cling and the shocks that go with it."

Yep, he was charming, all right. I smiled, then clamped my teeth together before I could take a bite out of one his candy legs. "C'mon, let's go." I nodded toward the door, anxious to get away. In some ways, I felt like I was way safer with Mr. Flamethrower and his threatening-me-with-death-if-I-didn't-play-along English sidekick. Sure, I knew I couldn't trust them either, but at least when I was with them, I could trust myself.

6

WHEN BRYN DROPPED me off at my car, he told me to be careful. He seemed as sincere as a diamond eternity band. Hard to see him betraying me, Edie's prophecy aside. Come to think of it, she'd gotten me into trouble plenty of times by not seeing things as the rest of the world would, like the time she encouraged me to run a credit card to the limit when I couldn't pay it off. Boy, had Zach and Chase Manhattan Bank been mad at me.

I needed gasoline, so I rolled into the Shell station. I was just through filling my tank when I spotted Jenna Reitgarten's silver Lexus pulling into the parking lot at De Marco's Italian restaurant across the street.

Boyd, Jenna's husband, reminds me of Wile E. Coyote's cleverer older brother. His sharp chin is covered with a pointed beard, his thin mustache is always perfectly trimmed, and his peppery hair, which used to be pleasantly scruffy, has been overcome for years now with some sort of oily gel that he took to using when he got promoted to bank president.

Boyd opened the door for Jenna, who wore a formal dress

that was cut lopsided with one puffy sleeve that tapered tight to the wrist. It looked like a homemade dress gone really wrong, but, in her case, it meant some salesperson at an expensive boutique had convinced her to go with it by showing her pictures in a fancy fashion magazine. In cities where the emperor's new clothes would've sold for more than a new car, Jenna's dress might have gotten compliments, even though the shade of pink made her skin look all pale and pasty, like freshly floured dough. In Duvall, though, people recognized silliness when they saw it and would be shaking their heads and laughing their lipstick off at Johnny's hair salon come Saturday afternoon.

I saw her body jerk a couple times and knew she still had the hiccups I'd semi-accidentally hexed her with on the day she'd been mean-spirited enough to buy the jewelry I'd pawned in a moment of desperation.

I wondered if the prolonged bout of hiccups might have tired her out. Maybe she'd be more susceptible to my asking to buy my jewelry back. If so, that would save me from robbing her house, which was something that I really didn't want to do.

I crossed Main Street, but by the time I got to De Marco's, they'd gone inside. I followed and was surrounded by warm air that smelled of bubbling tomato sauce and fresh-baked focaccia.

I'm hungrier than Zach after college football practice.

I frowned, knowing I didn't have time to eat. I watched the waiter go by with a tray of linguine with clams and felt like following them.

Shelby the hostess waved at me. She knew me partly because I liked to come in and eat the food there and partly because De Marco's had catered some receptions that I'd made wedding cakes for.

"Are you meeting someone?" she asked.

"Nope. I really wish I could have dinner, but I'm in a rush. I need to talk to Jenna Reitgarten for a minute."

"I just seated them," Shelby said, pointing to the right.

I zigzagged through the intimately arranged tables,

admiring the golden glow of the candlelight and licking my lips involuntarily at the grilled shrimp and angel hair pasta.

I found Boyd and Jenna in a cozy corner table.

"Hey there," I said, cheerful as a sunflower.

Jenna looked me over and wrinkled her nose, which I thought was pretty high and mighty for someone with mismatched sleeves. Her dignified disdain for me was somewhat undermined by her increasingly violent spasm of hiccups.

I bit the inside of my mouth hard to keep from smirking. "I heard you had a bad case of hiccups. You know, I've got a home remedy for them."

"They'll go away on their own," she said, her voice icy.

"Oh, sure," I said with a nod. "So, that dress is really something. Must be from a famous designer."

She flounced in her seat, maybe from pride, maybe from hiccups. But there was no mistaking her smile.

"Bialciano," she said and hiccupped. "You couldn't afford him."

"I'm sure you're right about that. But speaking of affording things, I would like to buy my jewelry back. I'll pay double what you paid Earl for it, and since you don't really wear much red or green, you'll never miss it."

Her smiled widened. "Would you really like them back?" she asked.

I nodded.

"And you'd actually pay double . . . even though you're out of work?"

"Even though," I said and nodded again.

"Well, you're right about the fact that I wouldn't miss them." She glanced around like she was thinking things over, but I could tell she wasn't. Still, my heart pounded with hope. She couldn't be all bad. She was human, not demon, after all. Well, so far as I knew. And maybe, just maybe, she might show some compassion to a fellow small-town girl.

"But I don't think so. I said I was going to teach you a lesson and I will."

My blood started to boil, and I had to stop myself from

trying to hex her with a nasty rash. My mouth was tight as I asked, "What lesson?"

"That you're not a good fit for this town. I don't want you here. If you don't move away, things will only get worse." She leaned forward. "I'll make them get worse," she hissed. Her eyes didn't turn red, but I swear I may have seen a little smoke flare out of her nostrils.

I blinked and took a step back, then I glanced at Boyd, who hadn't even bothered to look up from his menu. Slimy coward.

"Well, enjoy your hiccups—I mean, supper," I said. I hurried back out of the restaurant and across the street, wishing Merc had been there to hear what she'd said, because I was sure he'd have agreed that law-breaking was our only option. And not just an option, an imperative. If Jenna got away with stomping on me and driving me out of my home, who knew what she'd get it in her head to do next? After all, every tyrant had to start somewhere. Thinking back to Mrs. Neilson's high school world history class, I clenched my fists. What if my jewelry was Poland, and this was my chance to thwart a mini-Hitler in the making? I slapped my fist in my palm and nodded. No question. The hiccups weren't enough. Jenna had to be stopped. As soon as Edie got back, we were going to rob Jenna's house.

I DROVE BACK to Old Town and parked in the alley next to the Whiskey Barrel. It was dark, and while Duvall's not known for being crime-ridden, it'd been trying for an edgier reputation lately. I hurried to the cobbled walk.

The Whiskey Barrel's door is solid wood and hard to open. It sticks because the building's shifted in the years since it was built. I'd been inside the Barrel only a couple of times with Zach and his brothers because usually they didn't bother with Old Town. They liked Jammers better since it was a sports bar where every way you turned there was a big TV showing some game.

I gripped the brass bar on the door and pulled until it

finally creaked open. Willie Nelson crooned from the corner jukebox, and I stepped into the hazy room, blinking as cigarette smoke stung my eyes. There were about a dozen guys inside.

Incendio leaned over the pool table, and the cue slid through his fingers. The balls collided with a snap that sent the eight ball into the corner pocket. Incendio stood with a slow movement and reached for a stack of bills that sat on the table under a chalk cube.

He pocketed the money, took a drag on his cigarette, and eyed me. His faded black T-shirt with the Harley logo didn't taper in from shoulders to belly, so he wasn't made of perfect muscles like Zach or Bryn, but he wasn't flabby either. His torso was a lot like a barrel actually, big and solid.

He stubbed his spent cigarette out in a chipped ashtray. His thick left forearm had a tattoo of a skull with flames shooting from the eyes and mouth. I shivered.

He picked up the ashtray and walked to a small corner table. Jordan was sitting there with his arms folded, looking like his clothes were resisting the temptation to get wrinkled.

"Well, well. Out on your own again at night," someone said.

I turned to find my ex-friend Earl Stanton. Earl and I had recently had a difference of opinion. When I'd gone to Earl's to pawn my jewelry, he'd decided that I should stay at his house even though I wanted to go. So he'd tried to convince me not to leave by pinning me down on his couch. A few minutes later, I'd decided that the best way to change his mind was to hit him over the head with a heavy brass lamp.

"Hey, Earl," I said, wishing I'd thought to put a baseball bat in my pocketbook.

"Whyn't you come have a drink with me? There's some things I want to talk about with you," he said with well-whiskeyed breath. He grabbed my arm and pulled me to the bar. I didn't resist because there were several beer bottles on the bar that looked like they might serve my purpose in the case of another disagreement.

Jordan strolled over. "Miss Trask, so good of you to come. Who's your friend?"

I wanted to take exception to the term *friend*, but that wouldn't have been polite, and even if I did have to hit Earl over the head with a beer bottle later, I'd try to mind my manners at first.

"Earl Stanton. He owns the town pawnshop. Earl, this is Jordan Perth. He's visiting."

Earl let my arm go, and they shook hands.

"Mr. Stanton, a pleasure. Miss Trask, shall we?" Jordan asked, nodding toward his table.

"Sure," I said. Earl didn't object when I walked away with Jordan, which kind of surprised me.

At the table, there was a three-quarters-full bottle of tequila and three glasses. Two had golden liquor left in the bottom. One sat empty.

Incendio blew a perfect smoke ring as I sat down. "Red," he said with a nod of greeting.

"It's Tammy Jo, Mr. Maldaron."

"Where's my cat?"

"Since you're acquainted, you know Merc's his own kitty. He doesn't feel the need to consult me on his comings and goings."

Incendio shoved the three shot glasses together and tipped the open bottle over them. Tequila splashed down into all three and over their sides onto the table. He set the bottle down and reached into an inside pocket of his jacket and retrieved a little bottle of Tabasco sauce.

I said, "I don't drink." *With wizards. Especially if they have tattoos of fire-breathing skeletons.*

Incendio shook the Tabasco and eyed me through the smoke haze.

Trying to play peacekeeper, Jordan said, "Surely, you can manage one drink. Perhaps we'll have a toast."

Incendio tapped two drops of the hot sauce into each shot glass, and it shimmied into the gold liquid. He slid a glass in front of me.

"*A la verdad.* You give the toast, English."

Jordan leaned back, pursing his lips. "I think a simple toast is always best. As you said, to the truth."

Incendio shook his head. "You can do better, amigo. Give us some of that Anglo poetry." Incendio pulled a match free from a matchbook on the table. He whispered a couple words. There was a hiss, and flames danced on the tops of our tequila shots. He dropped the match in the ashtray, and I was startled to see that it hadn't been struck. The red flint was still perfect.

I guessed he'd pulled it out so that anyone nearby would assume he'd used a match, rather than a spell, to light those drinks. Momma and Aunt Mel had been good at that kind of thing, too. They said that people's minds would fill in what they expected to see, and all that a witch had to do to conceal her minor public spell-casting was to learn a little sleight of hand.

The flames on the liquor flickered and disappeared. Jordan licked his fingertip and touched the drops of tequila that had spilled on the table. He drew a small symbol in front of each of us. It was like a *Y* with an extra prong between the upper branches. Mine's tail was extra long and curly.

Jordan and Incendio lifted their glasses and waited. I fidgeted, knowing, sure as I'm twenty-three, that they were up to something.

"What's the point of having red hair, if you're as yellow as a stick of butter on the inside?" Incendio sneered.

"Pardon me?"

"You're from Texas, and you're too chicken to drink one tequila shot?" he challenged. "Maybe we need to get you a kiddie drink with a little pink umbrella."

I stuck my chin out. I knew he was goading me, and my pride made me want to pick up my drink, but I knew better. I forced a smile. "I'd like two pink umbrellas in my kiddie drink, thanks."

Incendio picked up the glass and set it down hard in front of me. "You'll drink with us or you're on your own with that challenge in a couple days."

I looked at Jordan.

"There's no harm in it, love. Have a drink with us."

I gritted my teeth, but picked up the glass.

Jordan smiled. "There's a good love." His voice was low and melodic as he said:

> *By the fire and the flame*
> *All truth speaks first*
> *From thy lips in thy shame*
> *All lies are cursed.*

Sure it was a spell. Sure I only had about eight days of experience with whatever little spark of power I have, compared to these guys who were trained up and dangerous. Sure I was in a dark bar full of men, at night, drinking with strangers. So, if I got into trouble, a lot of people might say I got what I had coming since I should have known better. But the truth spell was going to affect all of us, and I wanted answers.

I poured that tequila down my throat as fast as Incendio downed his. My throat felt like it was on fire, but I was pretty certain it wasn't, since no smoke came out of my mouth when I coughed.

"Just a sec," I said, hustling over to the bar. "Have any limes?" I asked the bartender.

He gave me a small dish full. I put a wedge between my teeth and bit down, swallowing the tangy juice as I walked back to the table. My glass was full again; so was Incendio's. He was ready to pour for Jordan, but Jordan put a hand over his glass.

"Three's my limit, mate. I don't even like tequila."

"Gringos," Incendio said with a roll of his eyes.

I discarded the lime wedge as Jordan said, "I'll just play a spot of pool." He got up.

"Hey, I thought we were gonna talk about the challenge thing," I said in a low voice.

"In a bit," Jordan said as he walked away.

"'Bout time he left. I'll drink two to your one. You think you can handle that, Red?" he asked.

Not for long. But now that the spell was already on us, how much difference would a couple more drinks make? From experience, I knew I could handle two or three tequila shots without getting sloppy drunk.

"I think I can, but if I lean over suddenly, you'd better mind your boots."

He laughed, and we both lifted our glasses. He tapped mine with his, and we drank them down. I coughed a little and chewed another lime wedge while he drank a shot alone. *Two to my one, and he started before I got here,* I thought. I didn't care how "bad to the bone" he was; I'd give a bottle of tequila the edge over a man every time. When he got good and drunk, I bet I could get a lot of information from him.

"What do you know about my cat? You know where he's from?" Incendio asked. There was already a slight slur at the edge of his words.

"No, where is he from?" I asked.

"We hooked up in Tijuana. He got in a fight with my hawk over a lizard. Jose never lost a fight 'til then."

"Yeah, Merc's a real good fighter."

"He's not the cat for a little girl. Few more months, he'll be tearing up everything in sight."

"I suppose who he lives with is up to him," I said, trying not to stick my chin out defiantly.

"Ain't hard to decide it's time to move on if your old house is a pile of ash."

"You burn my house down, and you'll be sorry," I said. I slapped a hand over my mouth, wondering why I'd said that.

"Why would I be sorry?"

I shook my head and licked my tingly lips. He filled our glasses again.

"Why would I be sorry? You think your boots are big enough to kick dirt on me? You been hiding your magic from the powers that be, and now you're going to unleash it?"

That surprised me. So WAM didn't believe that the reason I'd never used my powers before was because I hadn't had any? Did they think I'd been secretly training? If so, then Bryn was right. The guys in charge were paranoid.

"'Course not. But if you're here to cause trouble, don't expect me to just stand around and take it," I said. Sweat popped out on my forehead as he edged my drink to me. "Last one for me," I announced and swallowed it.

He drank, too.

"You know, Incendio Maldaron, I don't think that you're just here to teach me spells. Why are you in my town?"

He raised his eyebrows, then grinned. "Don't think too hard about it, Red."

"Are you here to—"

He reached across and covered my mouth with his palm. "You'll follow your next question to the grave."

Fear curled in my belly, and, for a moment, I saw flames dance in his eyes.

I leaned back and wiped my forehead. It was too hot in my seat. I kicked off my shoes, resting my toes in the sawdust on the floor.

"Where's Melanie? She still live here?" he asked.

"Yep, but she's out of town just now."

"You look like her."

"She's my aunt."

"You drink like her."

"Recklessly with strangers, you mean?"

He put a cigarette between his lips, and the end smoldered to life unaided by a match. He inclined his head. "Like fire doesn't scare you." He offered me a cigarette.

"I don't smoke."

"Not yet maybe."

Earl stomped over to the table. "Drinking tequila with Mexicans now?" Earl spat at me.

Incendio said, "I'm Colombian."

Like the emeralds. "But you lived in Mexico City, right?" I asked.

"There and a lot of other places. Wherever the money's good, and the power's easy."

"Enough of this. If you're finally through with Zach, it's about time. Now it's my turn," Earl said, grabbing my arm and yanking me out of my seat.

7

IN A MOTION as liquid as the tequila in my belly, I brought my knee up hard. Earl's breath went out of him in a whoosh and he stumbled back, clutching his groin. Incendio's laughter roared through the bar.

"You only had my oce a week, and you've already picked up his wildcat ways. Better give him back to me before he makes you think you can handle all the badness that can rain down, when you can't."

I leaned forward, my palms flat on the table. "Merc picked me, and I picked him. Unless he changes his mind, you can't have him back."

"Where is he?"

"That's none of your business."

I squeaked in surprise as an arm yanked me off the floor. My bare foot kicked my chair over. The crash echoed through the place, and everyone turned to stare at us. I looked over my shoulder at Earl's furious face.

"Earl, you'd better reconsider this!" I snapped.

He ignored the warning and dragged me toward the door. I thrashed and came free, falling on the floor. A couple guys stepped forward, I think to help me, but a wide section of the floor caught fire, blocking them.

I gaped at Incendio. "What are you doing?" I yelled, my breath coming short.

He smoked his cigarette casually. I felt fingers claw my arm and looked back at Earl, who was flushed and cursing. I planted my feet, trying to keep him from dragging me across the floor. My bare feet slid on the dirt and sawdust.

The bartender tossed water from a pitcher onto the flames. Steam sizzled up from it as Earl got me to the door. I caught sight of Jordan advancing on us, but Incendio called to him.

"No, English. Leave it," Incendio said.

Jordan frowned, but stopped walking.

My heart raced and adrenaline spilled into my veins. If Earl got me outside, I'd be in for whatever he had planned. I pictured myself on the ground with him pinning me down and ripping my clothes off.

"Let go!"

He ignored me, flinging the door open.

"No!" I screamed as he threw me outside. I rolled over the sidewalk and landed with a thump on the roots of a big tree.

I'd skinned my back, but I felt better on the small square of earth.

He reached for me.

"Stop, Earl!"

We struggled, and a thick branch cracked off the tree and fell right onto his bastard head. He fell backward, unconscious and bleeding over the cobbles. My whole body shook with the force of my revving emotions.

I climbed to a standing position, my back still against the bark, my bare feet planted on the dirt. The door opened, and the guys from the bar came out. Earl stirred and sat up, then put a hand to his bloody scalp.

"You bitch."

"Touch me again, and I'll kill you!" I yelled it so loud I

could hear it over the sound of my pulse pounding in my ears.

He staggered to his feet and came toward me, but one of the men grabbed him. "Time to sleep it off, Stanton." The guy forcefully guided Earl away from me. The crowd dispersed and then Incendio walked over to examine the branch. Jordan had my slip-on shoes in his hand.

"Thanks for the help," I snapped as I took my shoes from him.

"We wanted to see what you could do under pressure," Jordan said. "Which magic did you cast to drop the branch?"

"I didn't cast a spell," I said.

They both looked at me sharply. "I think she believes that," Jordan said quickly to Incendio.

"It's still a lie and cursed by the toast," Incendio replied.

A gust of wind shook leaves down on us as I glared at Jordan and Incendio. "Leave me alone!" I said, shoving my way between them as I passed. I moved down the path to the alley.

Cursed for lying even if I'd done it on accident? Not fair! Was it any wonder that I wanted to stay out of their crooked magical association?

I didn't think I'd cast a spell on the tree, but I'm not known for sensing magic, so maybe Jordan and Incendio had felt some that I couldn't. And thinking about it now, there had been a couple incidents over the past week when I might have done magic without using an incantation or mixing herbs. Once had been while we were under attack by werewolves at a witch's meeting, and Bryn claimed I'd sent his power back into him. But I just figured it went back where it was supposed to go without any help from me. The other time, I'd wished hiccups on Jenna Reitgarten, and she'd gotten them. Of course, that might have been a coincidence, but I was pretty sure it wasn't.

I stood by my car, feeling pretty . . . good. Maybe there was hope for me learning to use my magic after all. Plus the tequila had hit me. My lips tingled, and my head buzzed. I glanced at my car and knew I couldn't drive. It's only a little

Ford Focus, but it gets me around. I wasn't fixing to crash it to bits.

Who should I call to drive me home? I sure wasn't asking those rats, Jordan and Incendio. I could call Bryn, but then they might catch him giving me a ride and overreact by killing him.

I couldn't really walk home though. It was way too far. I could hitch, but, from the looks of Earl, the Duvall crime wave wasn't over. "What's it gonna be, Tammy Jo?" I whispered to myself.

As I tried to decide, I heard a cracking sound so loud it threatened to pop my eardrums and then a big crash and shattering glass. I ran around the corner and stopped, staring at the tree whose branch had knocked Earl on the head.

The tree had split down the middle, falling over and ripping up its roots. It had crashed through the roof of the Whiskey Barrel, smashing the street-side windows. The earth around the tree was blackened. The dirt that had been so soft under my feet was brownish black, too.

While I stood on the deserted street, something bit my ankle.

"Ouch." I slapped at my leg, stumbling onto the walkway for a better look at the tree. I heard a shriek and then was bitten again. I smacked my leg, making contact with something fuzzy.

I screamed and rushed toward a streetlight, my eyes darting over my shoulder, looking for a rabid squirrel or crazed chipmunk. And then I saw him. He wore a fuzzy animal skin, but unless they'd started carrying weapons, he was no squirrel.

My blood dripped from his spear. He was about two inches tall and poised to throw the spear at me like you'd throw a javelin. Well, like you'd throw a javelin if you were from the time of my spellbook, back when jousting was invented. I stared at his gnarled figure, and his dark eyes stared back at me from his scrunched face.

"What are you?" I asked.

It took me a moment to understand his high-pitched

squeak of a voice. "Foul witch usurper! You have destroyed our home. Prepare to die!"

"What in the name of all that's Hershey?" I mumbled.

Then I heard a chorus of shrieks and the rest of his tiny tribe swarmed over the path. They shook their daggers and spears and bared their pointy teeth as they raced toward me.

"Stop!" I yelled, but they didn't. I guess I could have tried to defend myself, but I couldn't imagine fighting back against toy-sized creatures, even if they were smudged with dirt and crazed with bloodlust. So I did the only thing that I could think of. I ran.

For having such short legs, they were surprisingly quick. A couple scrambled up trees and leapt from them to land on my shoulders. I managed to bat one off before he stabbed me in the neck, but his partner got tangled in my hair and swung from it, jabbing my upper back.

I screamed loud enough to pierce dogs' ears, shaking my head and swatting at my hair. This rendered me blind, which was probably why I ran shrieking into the night and slammed smack dab into the side of Zach's truck.

8

"OH MY GOD, girl," Zach said, when he sprung from the truck and bent over me.

"Get him off!" I yelled, rolling this way and that. Belatedly, I realized that I didn't feel anything poking me anymore.

Zach stared at me completely horrified.

Gasping for breath, I peered around. The army of mini-means seemed to have disappeared. Finally, when I was sure they weren't going to spill down on me from the back of the truck's flatbed, I sat up.

"Are you hurt?" Zach paused. "Did you break anything?"

He could have added, "besides my heart," because he looked stricken at my wild-eyed state.

"Um—" I felt my arms and legs with my hands. "Nope. I'm okay." I smoothed my hands over my hair, coming away with various bits of twigs and leaves. "A squirrel attacked me."

He raised his eyebrows. "A squirrel?"

"Yes," I said and remembered too late about Jordan's spell that was supposed to put a curse on us when we lied.

"I didn't see any squirrel," he said.

"Well, what do you think happened to my leg?" I

demanded, shoving my ankle up to his face. He looked at the small wound.

"I got a call that you had a problem with Earl Stanton."

"Yeah, but I took care of him."

Zach cocked his eyebrow as he lifted me to my feet. "You did, huh? The way I heard it, he slipped and knocked himself out, then a couple of his buddies dragged him off."

"Well, that's one version, I suppose." And it sounded better out loud than my version, in which I'd convinced a tree to commit suicide to help me defeat Earl.

I glanced down at my disheveled, dirty clothes and grimaced.

Zach ran a hand through his dark blond curls, surveying the street for a moment. "You want to tell me what the hell you're doing alone in Old Town, half drunk?"

No way to deal with that question without getting a whole new bunch of curses heaped on my head. "I'd rather do just about anything than tell you that."

He rubbed his jaw and shook his head. "If I was acting like you're acting, what would you do with me?"

As if any army of tiny men would get the best of Zach. He'd have stomped them into the cobbles. "I don't think it's too likely that this kind of thing would ever happen to you, Zach," I said with total honesty.

Between his curls and that handsome face scowling so fiercely, he looked just like those old paintings of the archangels, except he was missing an armored breastplate, some tights, and a big spear.

Zach leaned against the side of the truck, tipping his head back and looking up at the sky. He sighed. "You're wearing me out."

"Maybe you should go home and get some sleep."

He looked at me from the corner of his eye. "When we were married, I always knew where to find you. I never had to worry about you doing some fool thing, except maybe with a credit card. Now you're drinking and carrying on. What's happened to your good sense?"

"Lost it along with my job, I guess."

"Well, I've had enough," he said.

"Good thing I got us divorced, then. Saves you the trouble now that it's time for us to walk away."

"Is that it? You're giving me a taste of my own medicine? Hanging out in bars all night? Well, I've got news for you, darlin'. There's a big difference between what I can handle and what you can handle."

Considering Zach has about sixty pounds of solid muscle and a gun on his side, I didn't consider his announcement about being better equipped to handle trouble newsworthy at all. To my mind, my thwarting Earl was way more impressive. Plus, I'd taken out my share of werewolves the week before. I deserved a little bit of credit, for gumption at least. The belly full of tequila shots told me I should demand it.

"It's kind of embarrassing, huh?" I said. "Me running all over town, and you not being able to control me."

"Hang on a minute—"

"No, you hang on. My life is a mess, but it's my mess. Didn't you see the note I left? We're broken up."

"I saw it. You really think this breakup will stick when none of the others did?"

"What I think is that you didn't have to come looking for me tonight. I didn't want you to."

He winced, but I stood my ground.

"You can tell everyone I broke up with you again, and that you're fed up. You're washing your hands of me. Say it a few times, and people will believe it. Get yourself someone new." It nearly choked me to say the words, but it had to be said. Zach probably wouldn't be able to stand me living like I was, and I didn't seem to have a choice about the direction my life was headed.

"You want me to step aside?" He swallowed hard. "You think life as Bryn Lyons's trophy wife would be better, is that it?"

"This isn't about him. I loved you first and best, but you expect me to do whatever you say, like when we were kids. And tonight, you threatened to take me back to Chulley!

You really think I'd go along with that?" Furious tears filled my eyes. "The truth is I've got to be a lot tougher than I ever was, and I don't think you'll like it. Maybe it's time you let me go before either of us gets more hurt than we already are." I wiped the tears from my cheeks.

"That sounds like real good advice, darlin'. Too bad I'm not ready to take it." He clenched his jaw and walked around to the passenger door of his truck. He opened it and waited.

I climbed in, partly relieved and partly dreading the fights that were sure to come over the next week. Zach closed the door and went to the driver's side.

I'd said my piece so I sat quietly as he drove us back to the main part of town. He skipped the turnoff to his place, but didn't take the best road to get to my house either.

"Where are we going?" I asked.

"I gotta make a stop." Then he turned onto Earl's street.

"I said I took care of him."

"I heard you."

"So what are we doing here?"

"The way I heard it, you were screaming when he dragged you to the door of the Whiskey Barrel and threw you outside into the dirt."

"Oh." If somebody had told it to Zach that way, there was nothing in the world that would keep Zach from confronting Earl. I couldn't see any point wasting my breath on Earl's account, especially considering that my throat was sore from screaming all night, most of which had been his fault.

Zach pulled up to the curb and threw the truck in park. "Don't kill him."

Zach tossed his gun on the driver's seat and shut the door. I watched him walk to Earl's front door and kick it in. I shut my eyes and tried not to think about them fighting. I tried not to think about anything.

The tequila had helped numb my mind, but around the edges I still felt my anxiety. Starting in the morning, I'd be dipping into magic I couldn't control. I didn't want Zach caught in the cross fire, because, as tough as Zach was, he couldn't protect himself from supernatural trouble. I'd seen that with the werewolf bite.

I sighed. *That darn WAM. I'd like to wham them.*

A few minutes later, Zach got back into the truck's cab. His hair was mussed and his knuckles were scraped, but he looked fine. The splotch of blood on his shirt wasn't his.

At home, after I took a shower, he cleaned my cuts with peroxide and put Band-Aids on the deeper ones. I didn't tell him that I got some of them from tiny little spears, and he didn't ask for details.

Then I put peroxide on his skinned knuckles and taped some gauze pads on them for the night.

"You tired?" I asked. "I'm falling-down tired." I crawled into my bed.

He stripped and climbed in with me. I was too exhausted to argue about it.

He pulled me to him so I was lying along his side, his muscles all warm and solid, a comfort after my long, crazy night.

"You remember that time we were alone at my parents' house and TJ came home early? He dropped his key in the dark and couldn't find it, had to break in?"

"I remember you thought he was a burglar and almost killed him with your daddy's rifle."

"I was fourteen, and there was only one thought in my head: If he gets by me, he'll get to her. It's okay if I die, so long as I take him with me. So long as my girl's safe."

My body tightened in response. Zach would always be protective of me, and a part of me was glad. It was the same part that made a habit of kissing him whenever he said anything I liked, so I wanted to snuggle close to him until things took their natural course. But I knew I couldn't encourage that kind of intimacy. Instead, I gave him a quick kiss on the cheek.

"It's a real good thing I saw your back after I'd already been to Earl's house," he said. I heard his knuckles pop as he made his hands into fists. His breath went in and out in short, angry sighs. "I didn't kill him, but I ain't ruled out the possibility that I'll have to do it sometime soon."

"I'm glad to hear you say that, 'cause if he needs killin' this week, I'm going to be too busy to do it."

Zach laughed, and so did I. Deep down, though, the state of my life didn't seem funny at all.

9

WHEN I WOKE up the following morning on Tuesday, Zach had left for work. The room felt cozy and warm, and I curled the pillow to my face so I could inhale his scent. He was handsome, sexy, and completely loyal to me. I wished he hadn't gone; I'd have worked on saying good morning in the way I knew he liked best. Except . . . Except what?

I stopped the tumbling flow of my thoughts. My body felt extremely light, as if I might float off the mattress if I rolled over suddenly.

I heard kids laughing and realized my window must have been left open. I climbed from bed, hoping my neighbors wouldn't notice me pulling up the fire ladder. When I got to the window though, the ladder was rolled in a pile under the sill, and the window was shut and locked. I looked through the glass and saw kids in the driveway several houses down. Unless I'd gotten bionic ear surgery in my sleep, I couldn't have heard those children. I wandered away.

Looking in my dresser, I couldn't find any clothes I wanted to wear. I dug through the trunk at the end of my bed. I can't say why, on the twenty-eighth of October, I felt compelled to wear the jade green chiffon dress I'd bought for Georgia Sue's summer garden party. I had wedge sandals to match, but I couldn't make myself put them on.

"Bare feet are better," I said and knew it was true, the way I know my right hand from my left, the way I know if you don't use a double boiler, you've got to watch the temperature of melting chocolate like a hawk or you'll scorch it.

Something's changed. Then I remembered about Incendio and Jordan and their magical drinking game. I'd lied, more than once, after Jordan cast his truth spell.

My heart sped up a little, but I didn't feel sick or scared. I felt like I was a bottle of Sprite that someone had shaken up. Like I needed to be uncapped so I could bubble over onto the whole world. If this was being cursed, I should've tried it a long time ago.

I went downstairs and stopped at my back door. *Help.* I felt it, or maybe I heard it. I opened the door, and sunshine blazed in like a yellow Amtrak train. I blinked. The tree canopy looked like the leaves were made of green satin.

I stepped outside, and the dirt burned my soles. The ground was not right. Pain shot up my legs like hundreds of needles were being dragged along my skin.

The wind whispered through the leaves, and the tree talked in my head, telling me that I'd killed the plants and burned the ground very deeply. I already knew that I'd damaged the yard. I'd had to draw power from the earth the week before to rescue some people from a sleeping sickness. The aftermath of the spell had decimated Aunt Melanie's herb garden.

What I hadn't known before now was that the ground was still suffering. I knelt down and touched it, smelling soot and feeling the dry, barren soil. "Don't worry. I'll help you."

I came inside to the grating sound of the ringing phone. *Too loud.* I grabbed my ears as I raced toward it. The machine picked up just as I got there.

"This is Jordan, love. Meet Incendio and me on the Corsic Creek Bridge in an hour."

I unplugged the phone and the machine. Then I grabbed a tray of cupcakes and went out the front door.

BY AFTERNOON, MY house and yard were full. I licked honey off my fingers and kissed the jam off my four-year-old neighbor's cheek before I plopped her back down in front of the cartoons playing on the television.

I waved and smiled at the three school-aged children who passed by. They rolled a red wagon full of chrysanthemums and a plastic bucket of water through the living room on their way to the yard.

Bryn Lyons followed in their wake, stopping at my kitchen countertop.

"*What* is going on?" he asked.

"We're saving the earth. Want some of my homemade ice cream? I've got cherry chocolate chip and mint fudge. Though the mint fudge might not be all the way hardened yet," I said.

"Do you know there are children at the entrance of the neighborhood digging up plants and then rolling them over here in wheelbarrows? They're like ants marching in single file."

"Ants are perfectly within their rights to walk in single file if that's how they like it." I skipped around the counter and out to my yard, hopping over games and toys and children as I went.

"Make sure you pad the ropes, Matthew, so they don't cut into the tree," I instructed the boys, then turned back to Bryn. "I got cursed and now nature talks to me."

He stared at me. You so rarely see a lawyer at a loss for words. It's kind of nice.

The kids called for my attention to their work projects. I walked around, surveying. Rings of flowers organized by color. A castle painted in vibrant reds, blues, and yellows on the formerly white fence. Plants and garden art brimming from every nook. And from the older boys, a soon-to-be-completed massive hanging tree house. They already had the platform for its floor in place.

Matt dropped out of the tree and landed at my feet. He was tall and chubby, but an excellent climber.

"What do you think, Tammy?"

"It's wonderful," I said and kissed him on the cheek.

He grinned. "Okay, fellas, she likes it. Let's get the back wall up," Matt said and scaled the trunk.

"Does the construction union know there's a twelve-year-old foreman on the job here?" Bryn asked, his voice as dry as one of Edie's martinis.

"This doesn't concern them."

Abby, who was about eight years old, rushed into the yard, her dark brown hair streaming behind her. "Miss Tammy, Mrs. Packney's coming up the walk, and she's real mad about her rosebush."

I bent down. "Abby, I've got company. Would you like to take care of it for me?"

"Yes, ma'am!" She raced back inside.

"Only a pinch!" I called after her.

"A pinch of what?" Bryn said, gently pulling me back into the house. He avoided some muddy water that had sloshed onto the floor. I stepped onto a skateboard and, as he pulled me, I rolled through the house to the front hall.

"I don't believe this," he muttered as I hopped off the board and tugged him so that we were wedged in a corner behind the tall chest of drawers. When Mrs. Packney got to the door she wouldn't be able to see us.

Abby stood a couple feet away, peering out. The small box, still covered with dirt and weeds, stood at the ready near the front doorway. Abby opened it carefully and took a tiny pinch of the glittering gold dust. She closed the lid with just as much care and then stood, waiting.

"Tammy Jo Trask!" Mrs. Packney yelled through my screen door.

"I can explain, Mrs. Packney," Abby stammered.

"I doubt it!"

"I'll tell you if you'll listen," Abby said in a soft voice, sweet as peaches. She opened the door a crack so Mrs. Packney could bend down to listen. The woman leaned forward, her silver hair falling lightly around her round face. Abby blew the dust. "It's a beautiful day in Duvall. We're replanting the flowers together so none of them will be lonely," Abby said.

Mrs. Packney swooned a little before catching herself on the door frame. "I take very good care of my roses," she mumbled dazedly.

"And so will we. They'll be very happy here," Abby said with a smile that showed off the tiny dimple in her right cheek.

"Well, just see that you do. Those rosebushes came all the way from Houston."

"Would you like a cupcake or some biscuits for your walk home? We've got fresh honey from our very own hive. As Miss Tammy Jo says, there's no better bee than a Duvall bee."

"Good God," Bryn whispered fiercely.

"That would be nice, dear," Mrs. Packney said.

As Abby skipped past us on her way to the kitchen, she gave me an okay sign. I winked at her and squeezed Bryn's arm.

"C'mon. It's okay if Mrs. P sees us now." I grabbed the box of dust and skateboarded down the hall to the kitchen. Bryn followed me.

His eyebrows were somewhere up near his hairline as he looked around the house. "Welcome to Children of the Cupcakes, where your friends and neighbors can lead Stepford lives with only a single pinch of dirt," he said.

I sat down on my table, hugging my knees to my chest and playing with my chiffon hem, which was satisfyingly muddy.

Bryn lifted the wood box and looked inside.

"Close the lid. You scatter that around, and I'm not responsible for what happens."

"You're not responsible?" He shut the top. "Tamara, this is . . . I won't be able to get you out of this."

"Out of what?"

"You can't use magic like this. To do a spell of this power, controlling minds for something as trivial as stealing plants . . . The Conclave will lock you up. Or worse."

"Restoring nature isn't trivial, and it has nothing to do with your Conclave. That box isn't full of gold and herbs that I cast a spell on. I'm not a witch anymore."

"What are you saying?"

"I'm saying, turn a pumpkin into a coach and I'll ride to Rivendell." I smiled at him, waiting for a response. He stared blankly at me. "That tequila curse turned me into an elf. Or maybe it was the hobgoblins. Their spears could've had poison on them. Not saying that they did for sure, but . . ." I paused, thinking. "Honestly, I'm not certain how my turning elf happened. Only that it's as fabulous as fudge," I said, throwing my arms wide for emphasis.

"Hobgoblins?" he said, not even acknowledging my excitement. That's the trouble with some people, namely anyone who's suffered the serious misfortune of growing up.

"Yep, goblins. They attacked me 'cause I destroyed their home. Can't say I blame them. Damaging a tree . . . Well, I didn't know any better yesterday, but if I did something like that today, I'd have to take myself off frosting for a month as punishment."

I pulled the box gently from his hands and set it on the table next to me, patting the lid.

He stared at me, still looking bemused. Too bad he couldn't hear the trees. They're so good at explaining things.

"This dust is ground gold and dirt from under the hills. A prize from a pixie, passed to a knight, and buried here as a gift for my mother. Only she couldn't use it. Only children and the fae can see it for what it is. So says the tree." I pointed to the big ash tree in my yard.

Bryn glanced out and then back at me. "That box can't be what you think, if you found it out there. Faeries can be capricious, but they wouldn't leave a whole box of their dust in some witch's yard. Faeries and witches are, for the most part, adversaries. The fae don't believe we should perform magic."

"*We* believe you're not entitled to the earth's power because you don't respect the earth. Just look what I did to my yard back when I was a witch."

"You're still a witch. You don't just stop being a witch."

"Oh, no?" I lifted my hair to show him my ears. "See them."

"See what?"

Abby, who'd just given a dish of biscuits to Mrs. Packney, stopped at the table. "Her ears are pointed," she said helpfully.

"And my skin?" I said, stretching out my arms.

"Pink gold," she said with a theatrical twirl that made her shirt flare out.

Bryn turned to face Abby. "Does her skin look golden to you?"

"Yep. It shimmers like my mom's eye shadow."

"Okay, go play," he said, shooing her away. He turned back to me. "It's some kind of glamour that works on them because they're only human. It's not strong enough to affect me because I'm too powerful a wizard."

"It's not a spell. It's real, and they see the truth because they're children."

"Uh-huh. And what are you going to do with all these children?"

"What do you mean?"

"I mean, are they going home at the end of their whistle-while-they-work day?"

"They can go anywhere they like." I paused. "But if they want to live with me, they're welcome to."

The kids within earshot cheered.

"All right, Pixie Pan, that's enough. I'm getting you out of here. Whatever's bespelled your yard won't extend to my side of town."

"I'm not going," I said, grabbing my box, but he caught my arm and slid me off the table, making me furious. Bryn might be handsome, but he was not the boss of me, and if he tried to bend me to his will, he'd be sorry.

"Matt, you're in charge. Don't let anything happen to the other kids," Bryn yelled into the yard.

"If I tell them to, they'll stop you," I said as he pulled me toward the door, and indeed the kids rushed to block the hall. Bryn paused, letting go of my arm, and stared at my pint-sized warriors.

"What about Mercutio?" Bryn asked me.

Mercutio! My cat! The kids would flip over him. "Yes, drop him off. I'll protect him from the wizards now."

"No, you have to come get him. He's the reason I'm here. He was going crazy at the house, and Jenson had to call me out of a meeting with a client. He's been agitating my dog. Angus may very well break his chain."

I smiled. Bryn's ploy was as transparent as cellophane. On the other hand, I did want my cat back, and I wasn't afraid to go to Bryn's house. None of his mediocre mortal magic was a match for the power of faery. At least that was the way the trees told it.

"Okay, my darlings," I said to the kids. "I'm going to get a surprise, and I'll be home soon." They gave Bryn a superior smile that said they had complete faith in any- and everything I said. It was fun to be taken seriously. I don't know why I ever bothered to hang out with anyone over the age of thirteen before.

I pinched out a little dust and blew it into the room over their heads. They leapt off the ground, hovering over the floor before landing.

Bryn's jaw fell open in shock.

The kids chanted the word "surprise," tapping their forks on whatever was handy. They bounced off the walls, the bright colors of their clothes like streaming rainbows.

"That is extremely disturbing," he said.

"Jealous?" I asked with a smirk.

"Absolutely not. I have zero interest in being Lord of the Fireflies."

10

AS WE DROVE to his house, Bryn asked me questions about everything that had happened at the bar. I told him the verse that Jordan had used to cast the spell that cursed lying.

"He never said the nature of the curse? Never mentioned the fae?" Bryn asked for the second time.

"Nope."

"So it was random chance that the curse took this form. You could just as easily have ended up in a trance or have lost your memory. There are millions of possibilities. It was extremely reckless spell-casting. It doesn't make any sense for Perth to have left it random."

I shrugged.

The moment we drove through the gates, I regretted it. My window was rolled down, but all the sounds, the birds and trees, the grass and crickets, everything went silent the instant we crossed onto his property.

"Stop!" I yelled. "Let me out."

Bryn ignored me, but as soon as the car stopped, I bolted from it and ran to the front gate, which had already closed behind us. I buzzed security. "Open the gate, right now!"

"Don't open the gate, Steve," Bryn said, coming up behind me.

I looked at my arms. They still shimmered golden pink. I wasn't changed. It was only that his place was like some kind of graveyard for nature.

"What have you done? How come none of them is talking?"

"Who?"

"Let me out."

He shook his head.

I'll fix you! You'll see and believe and accept! I yanked the lid open and flung the dust at him.

He threw his hand out and shouted in Latin. A gust of wind blew hard, sending the dust away from him and out through the gates, onto the wind.

"Oh my God," he mumbled.

"Don't blame Him. You're the one who did it." I looked over at Bryn, whose hands were white from the grip he had on the wrought-iron rungs of the gate.

Iron. Yuck.

With clenched jaws, Bryn shook his head. Finally, he turned, narrowing his eyes at me. "How could you throw an entire box of what you believed to be faery dust at me? Had I been human, it could have driven me insane, permanently." He glanced out the gate, shaking his head. Then he scowled at me. "It's a reflex for me to protect myself. Now we've scattered whatever that was to the four winds. Can you tell me what you were thinking?"

I shrugged. "You made me mad."

He stared at me, his muscles tight enough to snap.

"I'm fae. We're capricious," I added.

"You're not a faery!"

I blinked. I'd never heard Bryn yell before. He was usually Mr. Cool. Mr. Calm. Mr. Control even in the face of attacking werewolf packs. Here I was, one little golden pink girl, and I'd gotten him shouting. And he claimed I didn't have faery magic.

He balled his fists and dragged air in and out of his lungs.

He leaned toward me, jaws clenched. "I'm a wizard, and I can taste your magic. I can feel and smell it. However distorted and misguided your magic is right now, I still recognize it. I'm a wizard. You're a witch. It's that simple."

"You're wrong. The tree told me I'm—"

"Someone put a spell on that tree! Can't you see that?" he said, his Irish accent as thick as I'd ever heard it. "I trained under the Polaris Wizards in Dublin for six weeks every year from the time I was seven until I was nineteen."

"Who?"

"And while I can't claim omnipotence, I do know more about the magic of a woman I've made love to than some bloody tree does."

He turned and stalked toward the house.

Kind of touchy about me changing teams. "When you get in, tell Steve to open the gate!" I called after him.

He turned and looked at me, walking backward. "You're not going anywhere until I figure out a way to unspell you."

"You can't undo this. I'm elven, I tell you."

He stretched his arms out with a nod. "Then welcome to your new home." He spun around and continued walking without breaking his stride.

"Is that right? Well, I've got one word for you."

He didn't turn back.

"You know the wizard's word for betrayer, don't you, Bryn?" He yanked the front door open just as I yelled, "Warlock!"

11

NO WONDER FAERIES *hate wizards,* I thought, marching to Bryn's house. "Mercutio!" I called. Bryn wasn't going to keep me prisoner. I'd go over Cider Falls if I had to.

Mercutio ran down the stairs, but stopped short.

"It's all right. It's me. C'mon, we're getting out of here. A little white water's nothing to us. We're indestructible."

Mercutio meowed.

"Yeah, I'm pretty sure about that. I'd say ninety-nine, well, ninety-five percent positive."

Mercutio darted down the hall, looking over his shoulder.

"What? You've got something to show me? A way out?"

He swiped the air with his paw. I jogged after him. He turned a corner, and I followed. Bryn's house was like a maze.

Merc stopped at a door and put his paw to it. I unlocked the door and opened it.

"Tamara, don't go out that door," Bryn said from behind me.

I saw a pillared-off inner courtyard with a fountain, swimming pool, flowering plants, and palm trees. On the far side, I could hear the falls and the river, where the stolen paddleboat waited to help me make my escape.

I stuck my tongue out at Bryn and darted out the door with Mercutio. I ran about five feet when I heard a pop. The air shimmered and when I got to the far side of the courtyard, I ran smack dab into an invisible wall.

I fell backward, landing on a chaise. Mercutio stopped short of the magical barrier and hopped up on the edge of the fountain. I looked down and saw a symbol drawn on the stone and marked with a drop of blood. I stood and walked around, finding the other symbols of the circle.

I paused and looked back at the door we'd come through. Bryn was leaning casually against the frame.

"Hubris," he said. "It's a big problem with the fae. If I didn't know better, your overconfidence, more than anything, would lend credibility to your story about being one of them."

He held up a piece of chalk in his right hand and licked blood off his left thumb.

Fury roared through my veins. I wanted to smash the whole world into tiny little pieces. "You tricked me! You trapped me."

"That I did."

I spun to face Mercutio. "And you helped? You're named for the wrong Shakespeare character! Mercutio was loyal to his friend to the end. From now on you're Brutus," I snapped.

I slammed against the barrier, testing my rage on it. It didn't give way, and I was left with trembling muscles and a cold fury that burned in my belly.

I walked to the edge of the circle, so that Bryn and I faced each other. I put my hands up. If there'd been no magical barrier, I could have touched his chest.

"Let me out now, and I might still forgive you," I whispered.

"No."

I leaned my mouth to the edge, puckered my lips, and closed my eyes. If he kissed me, it would break the circle and set me free. Moments passed while I waited. I felt him eyeing me like I was a raspberry truffle.

His voice was low and smooth. " 'So burns the god, consuming in desire. And feeding in his breast, a fruitless fire.' "

My eyes popped open. "Huh?"

He stared at my mouth and licked his lips. "From Ovid. It means I'm very tempted to kiss you, but I can't." He took a step back.

"Coward."

"So it seems," he said with a slight smile. "Stay out of trouble."

12

IT GOT LATER and later. I banged against the walls of the circle until my whole body ached. I was well and truly caught. Periodically, I felt the ground shake and knew that Bryn was amassing power for something.

I floated on the warm salt water of his pool, biding my time. Most people probably think faeries are basically harmless, like in those whitewashed, white-chocolate-sweet Disney movies. We're not. Actually, faery tales are bloody and dark, and, if I ever got free, I'd introduce Mr. "I'm a preternatural-prison-wielding wizard" to a real Tinker Hell.

Mercutio padded around the pool, occasionally meowing at me.

"I'm not talking to you," I said.

I ignored him for the most part, and, eventually, the sky turned as black and velvety as an Elvis cape.

"Let's trade," Bryn said when he appeared in the doorway.

I swam to the edge of the pool, resting my chin on my arms. "You don't have anything I want," I said, sounding much calmer than I felt.

"No, nothing much. Just your freedom."

"I don't think you'll leave me here forever. Eventually, you'll break this circle. What if you feel like swimming?"

"Are you willing to wait that long?" We studied each other for a moment. "If you're really fae, nothing I do will change that," he said.

"That's true enough."

"So there's no harm in allowing me to try to lift the spell I believe is on you."

No magic could affect what I was. The tree had sworn I'd be fae evermore.

I climbed out of the pool, and the cool night air chilled my skin. I wanted a bonfire or, better still, to be underhill in the land where the other faeries lived.

I walked to the doorway. Bryn stood straighter and looked me over. I glanced down. The wet dress was as transparent as a moth's wing. I folded my arms across my chest.

Looking at him, I felt a slight pang of regret. He might be a human wizard, but he was still utterly beautiful. There was even a sliver of his magic, a curl of power as silky as his hair, that I wanted to touch. But I didn't reach for him. He had captured me, and that made us enemies. If only things had been reversed. If I'd lured him underground and captured him . . . then maybe I could've kissed him as much as I wanted to.

"Try whatever spell you want." I walked to a cushioned lounger and lay down. "You've got five minutes, then I want something to eat. If I wasn't immortal, I'd be starved half to death by now."

He smiled. "I thought we were going to use a kiss to break the circle."

I was tempted, but I kept my voice as cold as the coming winter. "That offer expired when my stomach started growling." I wagged my finger for him to cross over.

He stepped past the threshold, and I heard the pop, feeling a faint tingle of power. He brought me a cup of hot chocolate.

"What's in this besides cocoa?"

"A piece of the stars."

"Right," I said, rolling my eyes. I drank the delicious cinnamon-spiced cocoa.

He took the cup and slid a piece of smooth stone into my hand. "Hold that for me." He closed his hands around mine and murmured something in Gaelic. The wind whipped around us and for a moment the heavens above seemed to pulse with bright light.

He kissed me and the power shot through me, knocking me back onto the cushions. My skin burned, and I jerked in pain. Two snakes coiled together inside me, sinking their fangs into each other's necks.

I screamed and screamed while they fought, their writhing bodies hopelessly tangled until they finally went limp.

After, I lay gasping for I don't know how long. Then I sat up dizzily and pulled my hands free of Bryn's and whipped the stone away from me.

"How do you feel?" he asked.

Some of the fae power was still coating my body, but it wasn't smoldering from within as it had been. And with every passing moment, I felt like I was fading away.

"What's happening?" I got up and pushed past him, staggering into the house. I stood under the hall light and examined my sweating skin. The golden pink had paled to my former creamy complexion. I leaned against the wall for support while the dizziness subsided.

Bryn stood in the doorway. "You're probably wondering what you're doing here," he said.

I cocked my head, confused and angry. He'd taken something precious from me, and I wanted to hurt him for it.

"You had an accident, and I brought you here to try to heal you."

I smiled bitterly. "If you tried to erase my memory with that spell, you better go back to wizard summer camp in Dublin."

He frowned. "What do you remember?"

"I remember, sure as Sunday, that you're now the permanent owner of an ocelot. I hope you'll be very happy together."

I stalked down the hall, my steps growing heavy. Gravity pressed down on me in the most irritating way.

"Tamara."

Strands of my wet hair kept falling in my face, and I shoved them back from my eyes.

"What about your neighbors' children?" Bryn asked. "Think about what you were doing."

I didn't want to talk to him. I wanted to get out. Perhaps if I got off his property, I'd breathe easier. The air was too thick indoors.

"You're angry that I undid the spell on you? You think it would've been better to let you keep a couple dozen children that didn't belong to you?"

I spun to face him, my temper blazing again. "That kind of spell wouldn't have been permanent. My spellbook says unstable spells don't last long, and you told me last week that magic dissipates."

"The spell on you was more expert than any I've ever felt. It totally changed you."

"Totally changed you, too! I never expected you to keep me prisoner," I snapped, rushing to the front door and flinging it open. A wave of compressive magic poured over me as it flowed into the house from the driveway.

Bastard! He'd closed a second circle.

"Imprisoning you was just temporary," he said.

"Then how come you have a second containment spell around the house?"

His eyes widened for a moment. "As a backup plan in case my first attempt to unspell you didn't work. I couldn't let you just walk out of here still under the influence of some dark magic. How do you know I've got a second circle?"

"I can feel it." I pushed the hair back from my face. "Yours is the only magic I can ever sense."

"Doesn't that strike you as interesting—"

"Nope," I said, cutting him off as I strode out onto the paving stones.

"Tamara, wait. You have to let me open it," he said, just before I stepped right across the circle. I knew where he'd closed it. It was like I'd made it myself. I'd known it wouldn't hold me now, though I couldn't say why.

I went to the security buzzer and pressed it.

"Steve, it's your old friend Tammy Jo. You better open the gate this minute, or I'll make a report and the police will come arrest you for kidnapping."

The gate slid open.

I didn't look back, and Bryn didn't call after me. Just like that, our brief friendship was over.

13

MY SATISFACTION AT escaping Bryn's property was fleeting. I was cold and wet and, with the last of the fake fae magic receding, I realized Bryn had been right to lock me up. What had I been thinking rounding up my neighbors' kids and turning them into my miniminions?

It had felt so right at the time. I shivered as I shuffled toward home. That trickster tree had seemed to have me all figured out, and I'd wanted to believe I was a faery who'd accidentally crossed over. For once, I'd felt like I knew exactly what I was doing outside a kitchen.

I passed the tor and heard music blaring in the distance. Hank Williams Jr. sang "Country Boy Can Survive." As I rounded the corner, I stopped and squinted at the scene before me in Magnolia Park. People danced around a huge bonfire. They were half naked with bottles hanging from their hands and little men, brownies, hanging from what was left of their clothes.

"Oh. My. Gosh."

People were obviously under the influence of more than alcohol. I should never have listened to that tree and unearthed the box.

"Where you been, Red?"

I turned to find Incendio walking toward me with his arm around a girl who couldn't have been older than sixteen. "Home mostly. I was real busy."

"So I see," he said, nodding at the park.

"No, this isn't my magic," I sputtered. *Liar, liar, pants on—oh, please don't set me on fire!*

"No? Well, someone invited the fae out to play. Wasn't me or English. Sure wouldn't have been Lyons. Who does that leave? Maybe the baby girl whose mother knows the way to the center of the Never?"

I waited for him to say more about Momma, but he just looked at me.

"If you want to know the truth," I said, "your curse-spell made me dig up some faery dust that did all this. Why would you do a random spell on me?"

"Who said it was random?" he countered.

"Wasn't it?"

He shook his head. "We took a taste of your power."

"But I heard the verse. It didn't say anything—"

"That's what the symbols on the table were for. What I'd like to know is how someone who's supposed to be new to the craft managed to counter that spell in less than twenty-four hours? Felt you recover your power. Who taught you such complicated magic?"

I sure wasn't going to tell the truth about Bryn unspelling me. The blank-faced girl snuggled against Incendio's chest, making me grimace.

"She's way too young for you," I said and grabbed the girl's arm, dragging her away from him.

"Hey," she complained. "Lemme go!"

"Come back here," Incendio said, holding his hand out to the girl.

I planted my feet and held on to her with all my might. She weighed at least ten pounds more than me, but I was determined.

"You can't have her. She's not legal," I said, trying to backpedal while holding on.

"Depends what laws you follow. Myself, I don't follow too many, *comprendes*?" he said, walking toward us. He jerked my arms off her waist and yanked her to him. She flung her arms around his neck as he swung her away from me. "Go wait on my bike," he told her.

I jumped in front of his path and put my hands out, slamming them into his chest. "You're not taking her."

He grabbed my hands, holding them flat against him. "You offering to come in her place?" he snarled.

"No."

"Then get lost," he said, shoving me aside. I stumbled back, and he turned, walking away from me. As I started forward, flames burst up in front of me. I ran and jumped over them just as they flared higher. I landed on his back with the hem of my dress smoking.

"What the fuck!" he shouted.

I clamped my arm across his throat, realizing that my feet had committed me to something that the rest of my non-action-hero body thought was a real dumb idea. It was going to hurt like crazy when he flung me off. I held tight, trying to postpone the landing as long as possible.

"If you take her, I'll report you to the police. They'll come and arrest you for statutory rape."

"She's eighteen," he growled as I dangled from him.

"If she's eighteen, I'm forty-five!"

He walked to a tree and spun, slamming me into it. Sharp pain vibrated through my back. I held on, but howled in his ear, raking my nails across his throat. He cursed and slammed me again, knocking the breath from my lungs.

"Incendio!" Jordan snapped.

"What?" Incendio asked, hauling me over his shoulder and dropping me on the ground at his feet. Despite the throbbing pain everywhere, I hadn't given up my suicidal determination to stop him. As he stepped over me, I grabbed his leg and held on with both hands. He dragged me along, but I'm pretty sure I slowed him down by at least a few seconds.

Jordan walked next to us, looking down at me. "What are you doing, love?"

I spit out the leaves and grass that had gotten nearer to my mouth than is strictly pleasant for a nonelf. "I'm stopping him," I said.

"Really?" Jordan asked, clearly skeptical.

"He's not taking some underage teenage girl off on his motorcycle."

Then, surprisingly, Incendio stopped walking. I rolled to a kneeling position, ready to clip him. We'd see how well he walked with only one good knee.

"Damn it!" Incendio grumbled.

I looked past him and saw the girl walking off with a boy in a Duvall High letter jacket.

Incendio raised his arm, but Jordan held out his hand. "Don't. The fae are here. Plus, so many human witnesses."

"Like I give a fuck about them or you." He glared at the flames of a lit barbeque, and they roared higher. Most people turned toward the grill. When they did, Incendio took advantage of the distraction and lobbed a ball of fire into the air toward the girl.

"Look out!" I screamed.

The couple turned their heads, spotted the blaze, and jumped back. It landed only a foot from them.

"Run!" I yelled, and they darted into the woods.

Incendio glared at me, bent down, and grabbed my arms. He flung me away from him and raised his hand like he was going to roast me.

"Incendio, for pity's sake, think about this!" Jordan said.

Fire raged in Incendio's eyes, but it slowly died out. He pointed a finger at me. "Not tonight, Red. But soon."

Incendio stalked away, and I stood up, trying to reclaim my dignity as I brushed off my dress. After my muddy yard, the saltwater swim, the flaming leap onto Incendio's back, and now sliding through the grass, I doubted even Oxiclean could put it right.

My body shook from the adrenaline rush as I looked around. I saw what Jordan had meant about the fae. It wasn't only the brownies playing with the people. There were hob-goblins in the trees and nymphs on the fall flowers. Small eyes sparkled and watched us from the darkness.

"Incendio's crazy. Do the people in charge at WAM know that?" I asked Jordan.

"He's never been this bad. Working for the Conclave has gone to his head. He thinks he's above the law, that they'll cover up whatever he does," Jordan muttered. "He's wrong."

"But they're not here. Do you have the power to stop him right now?" I asked.

His scowl grew harsher. "That's not your concern."

I kind of disagreed since he'd brought Mr. Torch and his taste for young girls to my town, but I decided not to argue, since it sounded like Jordan was going to talk to his bosses about Incendio. I had another problem. One that was all my fault . . .

"Jordan, some faery magic seems to have been let loose today while I was under the influence of your curse from last night. What spell can we cast to undo it?" I asked, point-ing to the wild-eyed people.

"This isn't witch magic. We're under no obligation to do anything about it," he said.

"But—"

"Concentrate on your own survival! You've lost Incen-dio's help for good, and a whole day has been wasted. We have a near-impossible task ahead. You have to prepare."

"What's the point if the fire part of the challenge is going to be so hard that only a Class Eight guy can get me ready for it?"

"The challenge can be adjusted, but you have to show some effort. No more skipping our training sessions."

"It was your spell to 'taste my magic' that messed things up. I was planning to come to train with you."

"We wanted to evaluate your power, to assess its nature. The spell shouldn't have affected your judgment."

"Well, it did. Around me, magic never works the way it's supposed to."

He raised his brows slightly, looking skeptical.

Then I got distracted when I spotted retired shrink Doc Barnaby. He's seventy-two, and, tonight, like Incendio, he was trying to romance a younger woman. But in the case of the Widow Potts, who was sixty-one, it was a better match. A week ago, the doc had been trying to raise his dead wife from the grave because he was so lonely. So actually I wasn't sorry to see him and the widow holding hands. Though I could've done without seeing them French kiss. Jiminy Crickets!

"Look, I'll train with you tomorrow, but tonight I have to break this up. See that woman over there? That's Arlene. See who she's dancing with? The man whose beer belly is hanging over his Aggie belt buckle? That's not her husband. Her husband's a Longhorn. This kind of thing can only end one way." I paused. "Yep, gunfire."

"Good Lord."

"Exactly. Can you please help me do something about this mess?" I said, waving my arm toward the park.

"I'm sorry, love. Even if I knew anything about faery magic, I'd never interfere with it. Everyone knows witchfolk who directly cross the fae end up with an arrow or a sword through the heart."

I shivered at the thought. "What if a witch unleashed some faery magic by accident? Wouldn't they want her to fix it?"

"I think not. The less meddling, the better."

"I'm sure that's not true." I clamped a hand over my mouth. Doc Barnaby had taken off his shirt and was two-stepping Mrs. Potts around the bonfire, nearly tripping over a bunch of mismatched couples who were lying in the grass, kissing like they were warming up for prom night.

Oh boy.

Raised voices made me narrow my eyes. A pair of guys across the park was arguing loudly about whether Coach Cal was to blame for the high school football team's losing streak. Punches erupted, and I started toward them, but the scuffle ended before I got there. I heaved a sigh, but knew this was only the beginning. With people's inhibitions gone, there would be trouble. It was only a matter of time before someone got hurt.

"All right, I'll see you tomorrow," I said, turning to the street.

"Where are you going?" Jordan called.

"To eat some crow," I grumbled and broke into a run.

When I got to Bryn's house I was doubled over, rubbing a stitch in my side. I pressed the buzzer, sucking air.

"Yes?"

"Steve?"

"Tammy Jo?"

"Yep, turns out I'm back," I said between gasps.

"Are you hurt?"

"Only my pride. Can you open the gate?"

"No."

"No what?"

"No, I can't open the gate."

"But I'm on the list. Bryn's list of people you're supposed to let in automatically."

"Not anymore."

I leaned against the iron bars and shook my head. Well, this was a fine how-do-you-do. One little fight and Bryn had told his security guy that I couldn't set foot on his property? And speaking of feet, I'd run all the way from the park without shoes. My soles were stinging along with my ego.

"Tell him I'm here to say I'm sorry."

"I can't do that. I'm not allowed to tell him when or if you show up."

My jaw dropped open. "What if I was bleeding to death or something?"

"I'd call nine-one-one."

I rested my forehead against the nearest bar and squeezed my eyes shut. I couldn't believe this. People did occasionally get mad at me, but nobody had ever locked me out before. "Look, Steve, this is an emergency. The town has lost its mind, and I need Mr. Lyons's help to put things right."

"Sorry."

This was not good. I had a spellbook of my own that I'd

acquired the week before, and I'd flipped through it more than once. Faery folk were mentioned very briefly, along with some other magical creatures, but there were no spells directed at them or their magic. I definitely needed access to Bryn's library and his brain.

"Steve!"

"I've been working for him for almost two years, Tammy Jo, and I've never seen him so pissed," Steve's voice said from the intercom. "I overheard the way you talked to him. No one talks to him that way. *Ever.*"

Zach talks to him that way. Of course, without a warrant, Zach probably couldn't get past the security gate either.

My heart sank to my ankles. I could see it from Bryn's point of view. He had been helping me a lot over the past couple weeks. I owed him probably a half dozen favors. And it had been ungrateful of me to mouth off to him, but I'd been under the influence of a magical curse, for pete's sake.

Anyone would've gotten angry about being trapped and kept prisoner. I know I'd never have let him spell-cast on me otherwise, but he could've tricked me instead of trapping me. What was the point of him being so brilliant if he didn't use it to manipulate his friends into agreeing to stuff that was for their own good?

Besides, Bryn's differences with me aside, Duvall was his home, too.

"Okay then, don't tell him I was here, but tell him the town's in trouble. Maybe he'll come out and see for himself. And can you see if Mercutio will come to the gate? I want to talk to him."

"Your cat left right after you did."

"Where'd he go?"

"Remember how he's a cat? He didn't say."

"Yeah, they like their privacy."

He barked out a laugh. "Yeah, right. Well, your secretive cat made a helluva racket in front of the gate, and Mr. Lyons said to let him out, so I did."

Merc was out and hadn't followed me to the park? I hung my head. All my friends were furious with me. An image of the shirtless Doc Barnaby popped into my head. They were probably only going to get madder before the night was out.

BY THE TIME I got back to the park, there were police cars parked with their flashers on. I glanced around. The faeries had all gone back into hiding, but the people hadn't recovered. Zach and the other deputies were arresting anyone who refused to get dressed.

I guessed the dust hadn't blown over to the police station because the cops were acting normal. That at least was one thing to be grateful for.

I didn't approach Zach since it looked like he had his hands full. I did knock on the window of Doc Barnaby's Oldsmobile. Doc rolled it down, and I saw that he had his shirt on and Mrs. Potts snuggled up next to him.

"Hello, Tammy Jo."

"Hey there. Can I get a ride home?"

"Oh, sure. With two beautiful women in my car, I'll be the envy of the whole town."

Oh boy. I got in the backseat.

As he pulled away from the curb, Doc Barnaby said, "Now, Tammy, I've been wanting to talk to you about those magical powers."

For the love of Hershey! "Um, Doc Barnaby? Remember how everything we talked about is confidential? Doctor-patient confidential?"

"Oh, I was already retired by the time we had our session. I let my license expire several years ago, of course. Besides, there's no reason for us to keep it from Lela here. She and I don't have any secrets."

Hellfire and biscuits.

Twelve generations of witches were probably rolling over in their graves. In one foolish moment I'd exposed a line that had been secret for three hundred years.

Maybe I deserve to be cursed. They'd probably think so.

"You know, I'm pretty worn-out. Can we talk about this stuff some other time?"

"I don't see why not," he said.

"Would you like a malt, dear? We'll be making some chocolate ones, just like in the old days," Lela Potts said.

"I guess," I said, about as thrilled as a girl offered a nickel to take a day trip with the devil. For once, it was going to take more than chocolate to cheer me up.

14

ON THE WAY home, I remembered that my car was still in Old Town, and I had Doc Barnaby drop me off there to pick it up. When I got back to my street, I tried to ignore my rowdy neighbors who, under the influence of the faery dust, were having a block party like it was Times Square on New Year's Eve. I shook my head at their offers to drink rum punch straight from the three-gallon bowl. Reba came on the stereo, and everyone went back to dancing around their lawns. I spotted various children asleep in lawn chairs. *No bedtime tonight.*

I was so focused on getting in the house that I was completely startled when Mercutio jumped down from the front tree. I clutched my chest until my heart remembered how to beat.

"Hey there," I said.

He cocked his head.

"I'm sorry about acting all stuck-up earlier. Being an elf went right to my head. I don't know why they say, 'He was down-to-earth' for humble people. I couldn't have been any further in the dirt than I was today and look what happened. 'Down-to-earth' should mean 'Thinks she invented flowers and gave them perfume.'"

I took a deep breath and waited for him to swipe a paw at me or to give me a hiss, but he didn't. "If I ever act like I don't need your help, maybe you'd better just go ahead and bite me. Help to remind me what's what."

Mercutio darted up the steps and waited. Yep, that's a true friend. Totally gracious in the face of an apology. He didn't stay in the tree . . . or lock any gates, pretending he'd never heard of someone called Tammy Jo Trask.

I bent down and hugged Mercutio's neck. "Thanks."

He purred in my ear and put a paw on the door.

"You're right. No time for sugar. Well, not that kind of sugar," I said, opening the door.

I glanced around my filthy house, trying not to look too hard. In the kitchen, I tore open a new bag of miniatures and ate a handful while telling Merc about the faery dust situation.

I went out into the backyard, grimacing at all the stolen plants and flowers. What a mess it was going to be to return them.

Later. After the other priorities of saving my life and the town's sanity are taken care of.

I put my hand on the tree, hoping that there was still a drop of faery magic left inside me, so that I could hear him.

"Hey there." I waited. "I need some more advice and information, Mr. Tree."

Nothing. All day long I couldn't get the tree to hush up. Now I needed him to talk and what did he do?

I walked back in the house, leaving the sliding door open in case the tree decided to get chatty later.

"I don't know what to do," I told Merc as I filled a bucket with soap and water and washed the floor. "I'm trying to remember everything Momma said about faeries, but she didn't say much stuff that's practical to us right now. She mostly told stories, you know?" I sighed as I scrubbed.

Merc sat on the couch licking his paws. I dumped the water and refilled the bucket, squeezing a little lemon juice in it.

"Jordan said witches shouldn't mess with fae magic. And the tree said Momma couldn't use the dust as a witch, so now that I'm back to being a witch—sort of—there's probably no chance that I'll be able to control it again. You know what we need? A pixie. One of them would know how to turn off the dust effects. Only how do I get in touch with one? I can't see the hobgoblins taking a message."

I finished the linoleum and went to work on the countertops, appliances, and glass door.

"I saw some wood nymphs at the park before the police broke up the party." I wrinkled my nose at the smell of ammonia. The chemicals burned my throat more than usual, and I opened the kitchen window to air things out.

I looked at the living room carpeting. Mud, grass, jam, honey, and more fruit juice than you'd find at a Welch's factory were ground in, soaked in, and probably there to stay forever. "I guess I'm going to have to spring for new wall-to-wall." I leaned against the counter, feeling plumb tuckered out, but I could afford to relax like I could afford a marble floor, so not so much.

"I'll just have a shower, then we'll go try to find us some pixies."

MERC AND I searched for them, but the mission was a bust. In fact, not a single member of the fae came out to talk to me, despite my rustling the plants and leaves and sending Merc up in the trees to have a look around while I asked them to come out for a chat. I even offered them cookies. Nada. The honey snaps I brought were pretty insulted.

Back at home, I got a message from Zach. He was calling to check on me. Apparently, they'd made a record number of arrests, even after letting more people go with a warning than they probably should have. All the deputies would be on overtime until further notice.

I sighed heavily and left Zach a message in return, telling him I was fine. Luckily there wasn't a lying curse on me anymore, or by morning I would've been sporting pointed ears again. Then I got out my spellbook and started rereading it. Unfortunately, it's not written like a storybook. It's more like a recipe book, which explains why trying to read it in the middle of the night put me right to sleep.

I WOKE UP on Wednesday the twenty-ninth to find Merc standing on my chest, dangling a piece of paper an inch above my face.

"Wha?" I mumbled, rubbing my eyes and pulling the paper off the claw he'd speared it with. I turned the crayon drawing right side up and squinted. It was a map of Duvall that one of the miniminions had drawn the day before.

"You want I should put it on the fridge?" I asked, closing my eyes. Merc bopped my nose with his paw. My garbled response had a couple of four-letter words I hoped that, as a baby, he didn't know yet.

I sat up and blinked until my eyes were focused, then looked more closely at the picture. Yep, definitely Duvall. In the northwest corner, there was Old Town, and, following Corsic Creek as it headed south, Glenfiddle Whiskey's faux-castle factory was on the east bank and Armadillo Ale across the water was on the southwest.

I smiled at the detail. On the opposite side of Duvall, on its eastern border, were the tor and the Amanos River. The map wasn't exactly to scale though. Some of the neighborhoods weren't drawn, but there were smatterings of trees and flower gardens and a bunch of squirrels, rabbits, and birds.

Hold on.

I brought the map nearly to my nose and gasped. Brownies, pixies, water nymphs, goblins, and a troll under the bridge. In the corner, scrawled in crayon, the artist had signed her work, "Abby."

I looked at Mercutio. "If I've thought it once, I've thought it a hundred times. Merc, you're a genius."

I shuffled to the fridge and pulled out a small carton of heavy cream. I filled a bowl to the top and set it on the floor. Merc darted up and went to town on it.

"You know, I don't think we can rule out the possibility

that you should be in charge. I could put the utilities in your name and get one of those little chauffeur's caps for when I drive you around."

Merc, in his characteristically cool approach to life, didn't show any enthusiasm for lording it over me. I stroked his sleek fur for a couple minutes, then had scrambled eggs for breakfast to keep my strength up.

"Abby's at school this morning," I said, munching a piece of bacon and giving half to Mercutio. "I think I better go learn some stuff from Jordan Perth while I've got time. Hopefully, the town will sleep and stay out of trouble until I can find out what to do about the faery dust. You think that's likely?" I asked.

Merc batted the air with his paw.

"Nope, me either. Well, we could go back to bed and hide under the covers, but that's not really the Texas way, is it? You from Texas, Merc?" I asked.

He just blinked.

"You sure act like it. I guess if you're not, you got here as soon as you could. Davy Crockett wasn't born here either, you know, and look what a hero he was at the Alamo." I munched before adding, "Yep, I guess if we're going down, we'll go down fighting."

I DIDN'T MAKE it more than two steps outside my front door before my feet stopped, shocked still. The first time I made a chocolate ganache I charred the chocolate pretty darn bad, and that was what my front yard smelled like. My neighbors on either side of me used to have trees centered perfectly on the plots of grass across the sidewalk from their front yards. But now, like a smile with missing front teeth, there was a startling gap. I walked closer to where Jolene's maple tree used to be. There wasn't even a stump left. Only smoky-smelling soot and ash in a perfect ring where the tree had been. None of the grass had been burned. So not a regular fire, then. A magical one.

I glanced back at the houses that were only twenty or

thirty feet from the site. The houses could have been next, and I'm sure that was just what Incendio wanted me to catch on to with his act of horticultural terrorism. I balled my fists in fury. If he thought he could intimidate me by roasting the local foliage, well, he was kind of right, but that didn't make me any less mad about it. I couldn't talk to the trees at the moment, but that didn't mean I was going to stand by and let him level them with his flaming trigger finger.

I opened my car door and gagged at the rank metallic smell. The seat was covered in congealed blood, and painted on the seat back was a five-letter word beginning with *B* and ending in *itch*, which I'd rather not use. I staggered back, noticing a bit of grayish white fur on the door frame.

Every muscle seemed to seize up with fear. I stumbled onto my front lawn, retching, and landed on my side. I rolled onto my back and lay there, staring up at the light blue sky, taking deep breaths. If the body of what was probably a rabbit was somewhere in my car, there was no way I could stand to be the one to find it. I might have to junk my car and ride a bike. I ran my hands over the grass, trying to calm down. It worked. Kind of.

If he killed a bunny to vandalize my car, I'm going to make him pay. No matter how long it takes or how much work and magical training, I'm going to make him sorry.

And, while I wasn't normally one to tattle on people, if I ever came across Incendio's boss, I was going to tell him that Incendio needed some serious help, like a nice long prison term.

I wiped the sweat off my forehead and got up, glad that I'd decided to leave Mercutio home to sleep while I went to my magic lesson. Bloody graffiti was the last thing anyone needed to see. I used my fingertips to close my car door. I shuddered and walked away from my house.

I paused outside Doc Barnaby's place because I could hear Willie Nelson music coming from behind the fence. I opened the gate and peeked into his backyard, my mouth dropping open. There were about thirty people, wearing pajamas and bathrobes, reclining on blankets and pillows.

They ate coffee cake and fruit between doing the two-step. It was like an ad for Bed, Bath & Beyond the Bend.

Barefoot children chased each other innocently, and I thought about the scalded trees and the fear-o-gram in the front seat of my car that was way too close to them. What if they'd seen Incendio while he was up to no good? They could've been scarred for life, like I was likely to be, or maybe he would've done something to them so there wouldn't have been any witnesses left behind. I clenched my jaw and marched away. Yep, something was going to have to be done about that warlock.

I walked to the entrance of my neighborhood and flipped my phone open. I told Jordan in a flat voice that there was a problem with my car and that I needed him to pick me up for our tutoring session, then I sat down on the cold curb to wait.

I noticed a dark blue Chevy TrailBlazer across the road. As I stared, my cell rang and I flipped it open.

"Hello."

"Not driving your car today?" the muffled male voice said.

If my hair hadn't already been piled on top of my head in a tortoiseshell clip, it would've stood straight up on the back of my neck.

"Who is this?" I asked, standing up.

"I'm going to make you sorry," he said in a low voice. The connection went silent.

The truck pulled out from the curb and squealed its tires as it drove away. Unfortunately, I couldn't see the license plate number. My hands shook as I closed the phone, and I sunk back down to the curb.

I didn't think the voice had been Incendio's. It had sounded a little like Earl's, but he didn't drive a TrailBlazer. Also, the trees had been burned with paper-cutter precision, which was definitely, almost positively, Incendio's handiwork.

Still, I knew, sure I was sitting there, that the driver of

the TrailBlazer had messed up my car, which meant there had been two dangerous overnight visitors trying to put the fear of homicidal maniacs into me. A totally unnecessary and redundant thing to do, I might add.

15

I CALLED ZACH to tell him about my car being vandalized, but my call went straight to voicemail. I grimaced. He'd probably worked all night handling the dust-crazed people. *My fault.* I decided not to say that I needed him. I just asked him to call me back when he got a chance. I closed the phone and tried to figure out how to deal with the jerk from the TrailBlazer myself.

When my phone rang, the Martina McBride ringtone startled me so badly, I swear my butt rose two feet off the curb when I jumped. I banged my bottom upon landing and winced. I didn't recognize the number of the incoming call.

I flipped it open, hesitating for a moment before answering. I felt like shouting, "I don't care how psychotic you are; a killer would never get away with an insanity plea in Duvall, Texas!" Instead, I went with a quiet, "Hello."

"Miss Tamara?"

"Um, who's this?"

"Mr. Jenson."

My spine melted with relief. Mr. Jenson, Bryn's butler, put the *gentle* in English gentleman.

"Hi, Mr. Jenson. What can I do for you?"

"It was Mr. Lyons's intention to hire you to provide dessert for a party he's having tomorrow night."

"Oh, that's right. That's tomorrow, huh?"

"Quite. Did he speak to you about it?"

"He sure did, but when was the last time he talked to *you* about it?"

"Yesterday morning."

"Yeah. Kind of a lot's happened since then." *Like my being banned from Casa Lyons.* "You'll probably want to talk to him to see whether he still wants me helping out with that party."

"Have you been paid?" he asked.

"Yep, but I'll give the money back. No hard feelings."

Mr. Jenson cleared his throat. "My dear, I would not dream of troubling Mr. Lyons with domestic details. That is, after all, why he employs me. We will proceed as previously planned. There will be roughly forty guests, and our kitchen, which I believe you have admired in the past, will be at your complete disposal, with the exception of the one hour directly preceding the party when the caterers from Dallas will need to make use of it for their preparations."

"That sounds real good, except for the fact that I can't get past the gate. See, we had a little—"

"Your pardon, Miss Tamara."

"Um, yes?"

"I shall manage everything. It will be most convenient for you to come in through the kitchen entrance."

Through a back door. I couldn't believe Mr. Jenson was going to sneak me in. Did he really think that much of my baking? Maybe so. It is my one talent. But going against Bryn's direct orders? Couldn't they kick him out of the butlers' union for that?

"Mr. Jenson, if you say you want me, I'll be there. I've got a full day today, but I can start work in the evening. Will you be there tonight?"

"Certainly. Ring this number just prior to your arrival."

"Okay. See you then."

"Have a pleasant day, Miss Tamara."

Not possible. I closed the phone. I was a little nervous about going to Bryn's house when I knew he didn't want me there, but I couldn't let Mr. Jenson down. Also, maybe Bryn and I would bump into each other. And maybe if I said I was sorry, we could go back to the way things had been earlier in the week. Except—was that a good idea?

After all, I was supposed to stay away from Bryn. And now, for the first time since Georgia Sue's Halloween party, he was leaving me alone. I chewed on my lip. I kept saying I wanted him to stay away from me. So how come I wasn't happy about it now that he was?

It was about ten more minutes before Jordan Perth showed up in his rented BMW. With the convertible top down, he looked like he'd just escaped the set of a pop music video. Justin Timberlake played helpfully from the stereo.

I got in the passenger seat. "What did they say?"

"Who and about what?" Jordan asked.

"The Conclave about Incendio."

"Oh. No word yet."

"Did you tell them it was urgent? Because I think he came by and burned down some trees in my neighborhood, trying to scare me. The scaring me part worked, by the way."

Jordan frowned.

"I don't suppose if he tries to kill me, you'd be able to stop him."

Jordan turned red, and I had my answer. "I'll speak to him. The Conclave hasn't ordered him to kill anyone, so if he does, he'll have broken the law and will have to face the consequences."

"No offense, but since I'll be dead, that's not very helpful."

"Listen, just try to stay away from him. And if you do see him, don't provoke him. Incendio gets carried away in the heat of the moment. No pun intended."

I clenched my jaw. That was it? That was all the help I could expect from Jordan? Lousy advice?

He continued. "Incendio's got a bad temper, and you seem to push his buttons. You remind him of someone—"

"Not my fault!"

"Agreed. But what I was going to say is that once he's cooled off, he's reasonable enough. I bet by now he's nursing a hangover and thinking better of causing trouble for you. Just avoid him, and you'll be fine."

We drove in silence for a few minutes, then he said, "Now, as to your magical education, are you ready to begin?"

"I guess so."

"That's what I like. Unbridled enthusiasm."

I fought not to roll my eyes.

"I noticed you didn't bring a notebook. So you've got a photographic memory, then?"

"Not exactly," I said. If he'd wanted me to bring a notebook, why hadn't he said so?

He reached beside his seat and handed across a small binder. I opened it and found a pen and white pad of paper.

"Thank you," I said.

"There are three main components to the success of any spell, but one of them is absolutely essential."

"Oh. Okay," I said, yanking the cap off my pen. The cap slipped from my hand and flew out of the car. In the side mirror, I watched it bounce off the concrete. "Whoops."

"Control. One must have absolute control over one's power."

He glanced at my hand, holding the now capless pen. "Write that down, love. In fact, you might want to underline it. Several times."

I frowned. As I wrote and underlined, I had to ask, "Is it important to be able to feel the amount of power you put into a spell in order to control it?"

"It's indispensable."

I was afraid he was going to say that. It was the key problem I'd been having since coming into my powers the week before. Whether my powers were tepid or boiling enough to bubble over, I couldn't tell at all. For the most part, I was numb to magic. Except when I came into contact with a certain blue-eyed wizard whose kitchen I was going to hijack.

"Why did you ask about being able to sense magic? Have you found that challenging?"

"Kind of. Is there a trick to it?"

"No. Most can easily feel their own power or lack of it. It's a constant source of frustration for those who are unsuccessfully trying to grow their powers."

"You said *most*. What about the people who can't feel magic?"

He glanced at me. "You mean who can't feel it at all?"

I shrugged.

"That would be a disaster. Better not to do any spells than to try to spell-cast without a sense of one's magic."

"Well then, can you flunk me from basic training or whatever?"

"I beg your pardon?"

"I mean, if this was the army, I'd have flat feet and they wouldn't let me enlist. I don't feel magic." *Except for Bryn's.*

"That's pretty implausible." He studied me through narrowed eyes. "It sounds like the kind of thing you decided to say to get out of the Initial Challenge."

I sighed. "Okay. If you want to be the driver's ed teacher with a blind student, it's up to you. Just don't say I didn't warn you."

16

NONE OF THE small spells I tried made anything happen. It was like I was fourteen all over again, except instead of feeling like crying and riding my bike over to Zach's to avoid magic lessons, I felt like bopping Jordan Perth in the nose and eating a handful of chocolate-covered almonds.

I sat at the edge of Lover's Lake swimming hole because Jordan had decided it was the best place to focus energy and to get in touch with the elements. It made sense. The wind-mills are across Corsic Creek, so we had three of the four elements covered, namely wind, water, and earth.

I was supposed to be concentrating on sensing my magic. What I sensed was that I needed to get to work on my to-do list. I needed to steal my family jewelry back, to get Abby to lead me to some pixies, and to make sweets for Bryn's party. I also needed to find out who in town that owned a TrailBlazer had been watching too many horror movies. I'd looked through my incoming-call log, but the TrailBlazer number wasn't listed. It just said *restricted*, which was ironic, since I *wished* someone would restrict the nasty guy's calls, but they obviously hadn't yet.

The only other person, besides Incendio and Bryn, that

I'd had a big fight with lately was Earl, but his car was some little black foreign thing. He also sometimes drove a van that read *Stanton Antiques* on the side when he was hauling big items to his pawnshop or his momma's antique store. But maybe he'd borrowed the truck? Then again, maybe someone I'd never suspect had inhaled a big clump of pixie dust and had gone crazy. If so, it could be anyone. I shuddered at the thought, which brought me back to my to-do list and finding a pixie to help me counterspell the dust.

"Hello!" Jordan snapped.

I looked up. "Yes?"

"Any progress sensing your power?"

If I said no, he would probably make me sit around on the moss all morning.

"You know, I do think I felt something."

"Excellent. Let's try another earth spell. All you need to do is tell me what direction the energy is flowing while I cast."

He brought out a wand and flicked it several times from right to left as he praised the earth for being the earth. Yep, that was the whole spell.

"What direction?" he asked.

I had a one in four chance, and I had seen him move the wand, which seemed like a pretty good clue. "East."

"Very good. Now you'll try. Use my wand to focus energy. You can use my verse if you'd like or come up with one of your own. Over time, you'll select your words very carefully. It's important that they have meaning and texture for you."

"Texture?" I asked, taking his wand.

"Yes. Some words are slippery, some hearty. Some bring a color or a feeling to mind. You'll need to begin keeping lists."

"What words are slippery? Besides slippery itself, I mean. Like slick? Slimy?"

He sighed. "No, it's not their actual meaning. It's a feeling they conjure."

Being that we'd already established that I'm feeling-impaired, magically speaking, I wasn't too glad to hear that words don't mean what they mean. I pursed my lips and tightened my grip on the wand.

"Nice Earth, thanks for being solid and round. Now, it'd be great if you could move the ground," I said.

I didn't think anything happened, but wasn't sure until Jordan said in a disgusted voice, "Sodding hell."

"What's sodding?"

"Look, you must try harder. We've got loads of material to cover. Surely, you can do better. I've experienced your power and can sense it now. You have more than enough to perform these simple spells."

I slapped my fist in my palm angrily. He could feel my power, and I couldn't? So darn unfair! What was wrong with me?

"This is what always happens. You think you're the first one to try to teach me magic? I lived eighteen years with two great witches." And the ghost of a third. "They were determined. We tried all sorts of stuff. None of it worked."

"But you did spell-cast last week."

I shrugged. Magic had happened, but, for the most part, not what I'd intended. Plus, Bryn and his father, Lennox, had been spell-casting a lot, and I'd used some of Momma's memorabilia and Aunt Mel's plants. I wasn't at all sure that I hadn't somehow tapped into someone else's power and hijacked a little of it.

"Maybe it was some fluke. Some phase of the moon or something that made magic work for me that time."

"You're not a lunar witch."

"How do you know?"

"Did you invoke the moon in your spells?" he demanded.

"Nope, but I was out at night plenty. Maybe the moon decided to help me out."

"What about the tor? Did you cast any spells from there?"

Yeah, some that had turned out really scary. I nodded.

"Let's go. I had thought to start small, but given that you don't appear to have any talent whatsoever for connecting to your power, we need all the help we can get."

I looked at my watch. "Okay, but if nothing happens there, I'd like to get dropped back off at home. I've got a lot of stuff to do, and if I'm dying at the end of the week, I'm kind of pressed for time, you know."

He smiled, though I didn't think that was especially amusing.

"All joking aside, they are going to let me out of this challenge when you tell them that I can't cast even the most basic spell, right?" I asked.

"I don't know that they'll believe it. I'm not even sure that I do."

I folded my arms across my chest and glared at him. Couldn't he tell that I'd tried my best . . . Well, that I'd tried my best at first, before all the daydreaming?

We were halfway back to the car when I spotted several women having a picnic with their kids. I glanced back to the spot where Jordan and I had been, wondering if they'd seen us. I was pretty sure they could've if they'd been looking. I studied the group, and my stomach knotted. Standing and staring in my direction was none other than the one person in town who'd sworn to run me out of it. Jenna Reitgarten.

I DECIDED TO tell everyone that Jordan was a part-time symphony conductor. It was the only thing I could think of, other than the truth, that I could say if Jenna started telling people about what she'd seen us doing at the lake. Anybody who'd ever heard me sing knew I wasn't musical, but a lot of singers can't sing and that doesn't stop them from being on the radio.

I stomped my foot on the floor of the car. Why did Jenna have to pick that spot for a picnic? All my luck lately had been bad, and it seemed like she was always around to take advantage of that. Case in point, when I'd pawned the family jewelry. It was meant to be temporary, but Earl had been mad when I didn't let him rape me on his couch, so he'd sold the jewelry to Jenna, my least favorite person in town. And naturally, she hadn't let me buy it back. And naturally, she had the all-important emerald earrings that I really needed to get my hands on.

"What's on your mind?" Jordan asked as he drove us up Macon Hill.

"It's not fair that Incendio got so much power and some of us who wouldn't burn anyone's house down didn't get enough."

"I know," Jordan muttered. "But what I want you to concentrate on is your magic, love. I really believe that you have potential."

"Thanks. I'll try," I said and smiled to let him know I appreciated his support.

Halfway to the top, he parked, and we got out and walked on the grass just off the path. He stood with his arms a few inches out from his sides, his palms down and fingers spread as if trying to absorb the tor's energy.

"Well, this is a more impressive ley center than I expected. And you have it all to yourself in this little town. No wonder Lyons is here."

I shrugged. "I don't feel its magic."

"Well, it's here, and I sense your connection to it. Let me try to help you feel it. Give me possession of your hold on the tor."

"I don't have a hold on it."

"Indulge me. Say: 'Jordan Robert Perth, I convey my share of the Duvall Tor to you.' "

"Hmm. Sounds kind of formal. Do I need to consult a lawyer? Oh right, I'm not allowed to talk to the only lawyer I know."

Jordan waited. "You mentioned being in a hurry."

"It's not that I've got any share in the tor. My personal property is pretty darn limited, if you want to know the truth, but I don't like saying anything that says I'm giving up a piece of Duvall. I'm sure you've got some real nice tors all your own in England."

"There is Glastonbury, though it can hardly compare to this," he said, as sarcastic as Edie whenever she's bored or tired or in the vicinity. Speaking of Edie, where was she? I needed her help to rob Jenna. And it would've been nice if she'd been around after the faery dust spill. I could've used her advice about it. She'd promised to check things out with Incendio and come back. Of all the times for her to desert me, this was the worst.

"If you please," Jordan said.

"No, I'm not gonna say that. Just give me a spell to try."

He threw his hands in the air impatiently. "November first is only three days away. Try anything."

I dropped to the grass and pulled off my boots and socks. "I'm better in bare feet," I explained. I stood and stretched my arms out. "I'll try that earth spell again, but if nothing happens, I'm going to quit for the day." I squared my shoulders and concentrated hard. Then I repeated my call for the earth to move. The grass didn't even ripple. I glanced at Jordan, who shook his head. I stomped my foot angrily, and tried once more. Still nothing.

Damn broken magic.

I grabbed my boots and socks, and we went to the car in silence. I wouldn't say I was totally screwed, but just because I didn't say it, didn't mean it wasn't true.

17

WHEN I GOT home, I went to Abby's, hoping to talk to her, but she was over at a friend's house for dinner and to play dolls. So I went to work on cleaning my car. Thankfully, I didn't find any murdered bunnies.

I used a blanket as a makeshift seat cover, then I went to the grocery store to pick up a bunch of ingredients, and called Mr. Jenson to tell him I'd be over. I wasn't supposed to go to Bryn's house according to the Conclave, so I should've been more sneaky about it, but I wasn't lugging all those bags through Riverside Park to the paddleboats. Plus, to hell with the Conclave.

I buzzed the security intercom and talked to Steve's unfriendly counterpart, who'd never told me his name. What he did say was that I was supposed to confine myself to the kitchen or he'd personally toss me off the property.

If Mr. Jenson hadn't been waiting, I would have turned around and gone home. Instead, I took the back drive and stood under the tan awning until he opened the door and welcomed me inside.

Mr. Jenson's wrinkles have wrinkles, but they're all very dignified. I washed my hands and arranged my supplies. He insisted on helping me, though I didn't need it. To be friendly, I let him wash the fruit and shell the pistachios.

"You've been with Mr. Lyons a long time?"

"Since he was a boy."

"Did he tell you we had a fight?"

"I don't recall him mentioning it."

I smiled. "No, you wouldn't when you're talking to me." I opened the cupboards to get the lay of the land and to get out the equipment I wanted. Everything was top-of-the-line and like new. "Still, I bet if you tried to remember, you might. He probably said a few choice words."

Mr. Jenson moved the black marble pastry board aside so I could plug in the mixer.

"We used to see quite a bit of Mr. Lyons's Irish temper, but it's been some years ago now. It was at its worst when he began boarding school in England. He often engaged in what the lads referred to as 'scrapping.' But then one year, he came home from a holiday in Dublin and we found him quite changed. I commented over the Christmas break that we had received no notices of disciplinary action for fighting or other acts of frank rebellion. I said I presumed that things were going well in the current school term. He said, 'There's no advantage to losing control, Jenson. In fact, there's a definite disadvantage to it.'"

"How old was he?"

"Eleven."

"What was he like before then?"

"A prankster with quite the ability to charm any member of the household staff into turning a blind eye to his antics. Had his upbringing been left entirely in my wife's hands, he should have run wild and then become a film star or a drunkard. She was herself Irish and extremely fond of him. She never forgave Master Lennox for sending him away to school."

"Well, didn't she change her mind when she saw how he turned out? Yale law school and all that?" I mixed cocoa and flour and added a teaspoon of baking soda.

"He was still in law school when we lost her, but he did make her quite happy in the end."

I whisked some egg whites and started melting the chocolate. It smelled delectable, and I was happier than a kid with a gift card for a new video game. This might not have been my house, but the kitchen was my domain, where I didn't have to think about earth, wind, water, and fire for magic spells. I could think sweet, spicy, savory, and pungent. Those were my elements.

"How did Bryn make her happy? I bet he made good grades."

"He was always an excellent student, but his marks meant very little to her. Those last six months, he flew home every weekend. When she was very weak, he had tea in her room and read her Irish stories and poems, resurrecting his boyhood accent, giving her a piece of Ireland here in the middle of—" Mr. Jenson waved a hand. "Well, not her home certainly."

I stirred the chocolate, then dipped my finger in for a taste. Dark and sweet, just the way I liked it.

"He wouldn't hear any praise for doing it, but it's quite something for a clever young man to abandon his school chums and the fun to be had with them in order to be shut up in a sickroom with an old woman."

I digested that for a minute. It hit home somewhere in the vicinity of my heart, just like Mr. Jenson meant it to. "I bet it surprised Lennox. He can't have raised Bryn to think much about taking care of other people."

"You are most perceptive, Miss Tamara." Mr. Jenson poured me a glass of water from a crystal pitcher and set it near my hand. "But the younger Mr. Lyons has always been his own man."

I took a sip of water, then folded the liquid chocolate into the fluffy egg whites. "Well, I'll try to do right by him with this," I said, waving my hand over the counter.

"Yes, I'm certain you will."

I WORKED FOR several hours more. When Bryn got home from his office, Mr. Jenson took him his dinner in the dining room, and I couldn't help but wonder whether he'd even been told I was there. I kept working and tried not to think about him and how much I wanted to see him.

"I said I'll take it," Bryn's voice said, just before the kitchen door swung open. He had a dinner dish in his hand that he was apparently determined to dispose of himself. He stopped just inside, surveyed things, then turned and looked pointedly at Mr. Jenson. "Care to explain this?"

I tensed. He was still very mad at me. He dropped the china plate in the sink, and it clattered, making me wince. I was surprised it didn't break.

"The menu is my responsibility," Mr. Jenson said calmly. "I have always had leave to hire the most exceptional culinary talent, sparing no expense by your own instructions. Am I now to be undermined in my efforts?"

"Did you really believe that you could have her in my house without me realizing it?"

"You had no cause to enter the kitchen. Mrs. Freet would have cleared the dining table, per our usual routine."

"Winley had to cooperate for her to get past the gate."

"Clearly. If it is your intent to release him from service, I shall tender my resignation as well. It was my affair."

There was the briefest hesitation on Bryn's part before he answered. "Fine. Despite this 'affair,' as you call it, I'll be happy to give you a reference for your next position."

I gasped.

"I shall not need it. I will, of course, retire. I intend to travel. I should very much like to see the Grand Canyon, and perhaps Las Vegas." He gave a slight bow before he left the kitchen.

I frowned at Bryn. "Mr. Jenson's too old for Las Vegas. Not that I've been there, but even their commercials could shock a senior citizen into a heart attack."

"What are you doing here?"

I narrowed my eyes at him. "I'm tap-dancing." I was so mad at him for the way he'd treated Mr. Jenson. Being angry with me was one thing. I knew I deserved it. But taking it out on an old man? After all their years together? I didn't care if Mr. Jenson had gone against orders by smuggling me in; Bryn should've treated him with more respect. Where was that loyal kid from the stories now?

I put the two bourbon pecan pies into the fridge next to the pair of pistachio layer cakes. When I turned, Bryn was standing in front of me.

"You shouldn't fire him because you're mad at me," I said, moving around him to pick up the trays of cherry tartlets.

"I didn't fire him. He resigned."

"You pushed him into it!"

"I'm not the one doing the pushing. Jenson has an excellent budget. He could have found a local business to allow you to use their kitchen. In fact, he could have hired a car to take you to Dallas, rented a space for you to prepare everything, and had you and the food brought back."

"Maybe he didn't think of it. Not everyone plans things out twenty steps ahead like you do," I snapped, feeling my heart race. I took a deep breath and lowered my voice. "Sometimes people aren't thinking straight, and they make mistakes."

He folded his arms across his chest, but at least he wasn't clenching his jaw anymore. His voice was smooth, but not cold. "I suppose they do, but I can promise you that Jenson thought of the alternatives. He chose to go around my instructions because he wanted you here."

"Maybe he did." I chewed my lip for a moment as I put the trays away. "But you still can't fire him. He cares a lot about you. You wouldn't want to lose him. That would be bad judgment on your part."

He raised an eyebrow.

"And besides," I said, looking directly into his eyes so I'd be convincing. "He only let me come over because I told him that I wanted to apologize for yesterday and that I wanted to make it up to you by helping with the desserts for your party." Nothing in the kitchen could've matched my tone for sweetness.

Bryn tipped his head back and laughed. I guess he's pretty good at spotting lies, being something of an expert in them as a lawyer.

"I really am sorry for how rude I was last night," I added sincerely. I saw his face soften and knew he didn't want to stay mad at me. "Plus, when you taste that bourbon pecan pie, you won't be sorry they let me in." I stepped around him, hanging the spare white apron on the hook when I reached the door. "Good night."

"Tamara."

I paused with my hand on the knob.

"How'd it go today with Perth?"

I didn't ask how he knew where I'd been. "My hair got real messed up riding around in that convertible he rented. Next time I'll carry a comb."

"How did the spells work out?"

I sighed. "They didn't. Whatever the challenge is, I'm going to fail it."

"Have you eaten?"

"Yep." I cocked my head as I turned to face him. "The last time was lunch."

"You could have dinner here. I was in the middle of some research. There are a couple more things I need to find, then I'd like to show it to you. I think I know why your power doesn't respond to conventional training."

For me, the answer to that question ranked up there with, "Why does God let bad things happen to good people?" and "What's the meaning of life?"

My heart banged against my ribs, but I tried not to get my hopes up. Discovering the reason for my defective magic seemed like too big a miracle even for someone like Bryn to pull off.

"If you've figured that out, I don't think I'll be able to eat while I'm waiting to hear."

"Not even grilled swordfish?"

My stomach growled. "Well, no use starving."

Bryn smiled.

"And on your way to your library, you'll talk to Mr. Jenson, right? Tell him he can't resign?"

Bryn nodded, walking toward the door. "We would've worked it out, you know."

"Good," I said.

"What I'm saying is that you don't have to fight for everyone. You'll wear yourself out if you try to fix the whole world."

"I know it. That's why I just stick to Duvall."

18

AFTER I ATE, I washed my dish and stood around the kitchen for at least thirty whole seconds before I went down the hall looking for trouble. I mean Bryn.

I'd only opened two doors before Security Steve appeared in the hall. He was dressed in a navy blue blazer that made me think about Bryn's boarding school days.

"Hey, you relieved the day guy, huh?"

Steve glanced around, rubbing a hand over his brush cut. "What are you doing here?" he said, taking my arm and trying to lead me toward the kitchen.

"I didn't break in. He knows I'm in the house."

Steve looked me over, and I laid a hand over my heart for emphasis.

"I was just looking for him."

"Come with me," he said, leading the way down the hall.

"You saw me on the monitor?" I asked.

"Yeah." He let go of my arm, and we walked side by side. He knocked on a heavy carved door.

Bryn opened it, and Steve scrunched his eyebrows up. "Sorry to interrupt you. I noticed Miss Trask wandering and thought I should help her find you."

Bryn nodded and stepped out of the doorway, waving me in. Steve headed back down the hall, but stopped and turned immediately when Bryn spoke. "Steve, the daytime security post is vacant. If you want to switch to days, you can. And I'll interview your cousin tomorrow afternoon. Two o'clock if he can manage it."

"I can do a double if you need me to cover the day shift, but I'll keep nights if it's okay with you. And he'll be here at two."

Bryn nodded, and Steve disappeared down the hall.

"You fired the daytime security man?"

"Have a seat, and don't touch anything."

I frowned. I didn't like people getting fired over me, even if they were kind of rude to me on a semiregular basis.

The study had floor-to-ceiling bookshelves. Some of them had doors with fancy crisscrossing metalwork and stained-glass images of the planets and stars. The doors were open, with a key hanging from one of the locks.

I sat down on a dark brown leather couch. "Mr. Jenson's staying, right?"

"Right," Bryn said, scanning the bookshelves.

"So how come the security guy gets the ax?"

"Jenson brought you here in a misguided attempt at matchmaking. Winley, on the other hand, helped Jenson because Jenson paid him to. If Winley would take money from one man to betray me, he'd take money from another."

"What if Mr. Jenson quits because you fired him?"

Bryn ran a hand over the spines of some books, peering at them. "I'll acquaint Jenson with the skeletons from Winley's past. After which, Jenson's only question will be why I hired the man in the first place."

"Why did you?"

"What is this? You planning to hire a household staff?"

"Absolutely. I've been needing someone tall to stack the pots and pans on the top shelves for me for the longest time. Getting that step stool out all the time is a pain in the behind."

"Right, because you couldn't find anyone tall to volunteer

to do that for you," he said. "There's never a traffic jam of men wanting to help you with whatever you require," he said, pulling a book from the shelf and flipping through it before he put it back.

I rolled my eyes. "You're sure right. I get offers from guys to organize my canned food all the time. And there are never any strings attached."

"It's the strings that make life interesting," he said, looking at me in that hungry way that makes me want to rush toward him and run away at the same time.

Needing a distraction, I leaned forward to look at a newsletter on the coffee table. The fancy lettering at the top had *W. U.* centered and in bold. It had been printed from a computer and the whole front page was an article about a missing man from Austin named Tom Brick. Next to a column of symbols, it said he'd last been seen October fourteenth and had been identified as a missing person on the twentieth when he didn't return to work after his vacation.

"What's W.U.?"

Bryn paused. "Can I trust you? With a dangerous secret?"

I bit my lip and nodded. "You can trust me to keep secrets."

"W.U. stands for Wizard's Underground, and it's a banned publication. It contains stories and facts that aren't available elsewhere because they've been suppressed. WAM's current administration wants absolute control over the flow of information."

"That's not right. Haven't they heard of freedom of speech?"

He smiled wryly. "They've heard of it."

"Do you know the man who's missing?"

"We've met." Bryn slid a rolling ladder over and climbed halfway up to get a book off a high shelf. He thumbed through it.

"Where do you think he is?"

"I don't know."

"Says here he was on vacation. Maybe he stayed an extra week in Acapulco or something?"

Bryn came down the ladder with a book. "I'm sure they checked that out before reporting him missing."

Bryn took the newsletter and tossed it in the fireplace. He said a few foreign words, and the paper caught fire, burning to ash.

Wow. "You can do fire magic, too?"

"Some." He nodded. "We need to look at this outside."

He handed me the book and led me out of the room. He stopped at a utility closet to get a flashlight, then I followed him through the sunroom and outside to the dock. We climbed onto the stolen paddleboat and sat down.

"How come we're out here?"

"I'll tell you in a minute." He opened the book, shining the flashlight on the page. "What do you see?"

"It's a spell." I read the verse. "Sounds like maybe it's for finding stuff that's locked away."

"Do you see anything else? Look closely."

"You mean the gilding?"

"What do you mean by 'gilding'?"

"The gold swirls in the margin, and—" I cocked my head. "There's something golden, a shape, coming out of the page. Like you'd see with 3-D glasses."

"What kind of shape is it? Can you tell?"

"No, it's just kind of a blob." I stared at it, then shook my head. "I can't tell."

"I bet I can help you see it better."

"How?"

"Kiss me."

I folded my hands on my lap, studying them. We were barely back to being friends. I didn't think complicating things was a good idea, even though kissing him is like the Fourth of July.

"This is just a magical experiment. I won't take advantage of the moment."

My heart pitter-pattered. What he said should have put me at ease, but instead it bugged me. I'm not some lab rat.

"I don't kiss except for kissing's sake."

"Oh? Should I seduce you into it?" he whispered. "Then we might not stop."

My cheeks burned. "Thought you were mad at me."

"I was."

"Not anymore?"

His dark blue eyes glittered. "No."

"Still, it's lucky that I didn't agree to be your apprentice back when you asked last week. Then you would've been stuck with me."

"Yeah, that would have been terrible," he said, but it didn't sound like he thought so. He slanted his mouth over mine, and we kissed. The power sparked to life, and I felt him draw some of it off.

When he leaned back, he asked, "What do you see?"

My lips tingled and burned in a cozy, sitting-by-the-fireplace-drinking-eggnog kind of way. I dragged my eyes away from his handsome face and looked at the book. A shimmering golden lion roared and leapt from the page. It circled me and pounced back onto the book, roaring again.

"I see it! It's a lion," I said, putting my fingertip out. My finger fell through it, the gold swirling around my hand. I pulled my hand back, and the lion re-formed. After a few moments, he faded again to a shimmering blob.

"I haven't been able to see that lion since I was twelve," Bryn said.

"Could you see him after we kissed?"

"I could make out a shape."

"Why can't we see him all the time?"

"In my case, it's because I block the magic that put him there. When I kiss you, some of your magic disrupts my ability to do it."

"Why do you block it?"

"Because I'm a wizard, and it's fae magic."

"Oh." I stared at the book.

"I think you were right, Tamara. You are part faery. I suspect the two magicks don't mesh well. When you were under the curse, your witch magic was suppressed, and the fae emerged unopposed. When I lifted the spell and the mixed nature of your magic was restored, you were changed on a fundamental level. That's why the second containment spell I'd cast earlier couldn't hold you. You were not the same creature, and the circle didn't recognize you anymore."

"My witch magic wasn't suppressed. Some of it was temporarily stolen." I explained about the symbols on the table and how the spell hadn't been random. "But you said you could still feel my magic when I was under the witch-power-drainage spell, so it couldn't be fae."

"I know what I said."

"But how could you feel it? If you block faery magic?"

"I don't know." He glanced back at his house. "I can't find anything in the books to explain it." He looked back at me. "My theory is that it has to do with the way we seem to be connected. The attraction, the physical contact, pulls down the barriers between us."

"If you're right about me, what does it mean? The powers don't work because they cancel each other out?"

A sudden loud crack and huge splash twenty feet away startled us and nearly tipped the boat.

"What the Sam Houston?"

Bryn swung the flashlight onto the water in the direction of the crash. The river's surface rippled.

"Was it the faeries?"

"I don't think—" he began, but then I heard a crack and saw something flying toward us. I grabbed him and yanked, tipping us into the river. Even underwater, I felt the explosion. It threw us against his boat, and we came up sputtering.

19

"FOR THE LOVE of Saint Patrick," Bryn spat, looking upstream. "C'mon, let's get out of the water quickly." We swam, and the current tried to drag us under. I couldn't quite reach the dock, but Bryn caught my arm and hauled me to it. I grabbed one of the metal struts and held tight. The current was so strong.

"We lost the book!"

"Never mind about that now," he said, climbing onto the dock. He pulled me out of the water.

At the next loud whistling sound, I winced and ducked. "What is it?"

"Cannonballs. George Miller has a collection of antique cannons. Apparently he's decided to fire them."

"What? Why?"

Bryn tugged me along with him toward the lawn. "Samhain is the beginning of the dark season. It's the time when the walls between worlds are the thinnest. The Unseelie open their doors on All Hallows' Eve. Normally, I spell-cast to reinforce the doors in Duvall. But this year, a few days before the feast, you and I scattered a whole chest of faery dust, coating the town and the tor with it."

"Oh boy."

"Right. What's more, people are under its influence. Last night, besides all the vandalism and drunk-and-disorderly conduct, there were apparently two robberies and three assaults. It'll get worse every night. I expect Halloween to be very interesting."

"We have to stop it."

"I wish I'd thought of that," he said dryly.

"Bryn!"

"Well, how do you suggest we do that? Because my power doesn't touch the fae."

I swallowed hard, not thrilled with what I was about to suggest. "Maybe you'll have to curse me so I can be mostly faery again. Then they'll talk to me and tell me how to stop it."

He shook his head.

"Why not?"

"Faeries can't be trusted."

"I know, but we have to try."

"Not that way. Not by cursing you to become one of them. You'll know too much now, and, in that form, you'll never agree to let me unspell you. I won't risk it."

I cocked my head. "Risk what?"

"Losing you to them."

It was sweet of him to say, but I didn't understand why he was so worried. "But if you cast the spell to curse me, can't you just cast a counterspell?"

"If I get your permission as part of the initial spell, then I'll need your permission as part of the counterspell."

"Then don't ask my permission."

"You don't—"

A cannonball crashed onto the deck of his boat. "Down!" Bryn shouted, knocking me to the grass and covering my head with his arms. The explosion rocked the night and debris rained down on us.

A few moments later, we sat up as his pretty little boat tipped sideways and sank.

"I'm not really keen on having to wash two inches of mud

off my floors again, but I don't see that we've got too much choice. It's me or the town."

"Look, the spell would have to be complicated and powerful, and since there's nothing in the books to guide me, I'd have to write it new, meaning it would be untested until I cast it. That kind of spell could easily go wrong, even if you cooperated. If I forced it on you, you'd fight it, making the likelihood of disaster exponentially higher."

"I wouldn't fight."

"Tamara, listen to me. You *would* fight."

His tone made my muscles tighten with fear. "Why? Does it hurt?" I remembered the pain of the witch power being restored. It had been excruciating, but I could take it again. Of course, he'd asked my permission that time, so I guess that meant it could be even worse, which scared me.

"It's more than painful. Let's leave it at that."

I blinked.

"Besides," he added, "there's no guarantee that you'll even want to undo all this and restore the town to normal when your fae side resurfaces. You used that dust recklessly and without remorse, remember?"

He had a small point there.

"I'll come up with a strategy to deal with this. I just need time to do more research," he said.

"Time, huh? Tell that to your boat." We got up and walked to the house. "Maybe Jordan could help. It was his spell—"

"Absolutely not. If Perth or Maldaron believed for a moment that you were part faery, with access to fae power, and still capable of spell-casting in the witch world, the Conclave would kill you."

I stopped walking. "You're sure?"

"Yes."

"It's a law or something?"

He nodded. "The Conclave would never risk that you'd learn to use powers beyond their control."

"But you'd risk it? By keeping my secret?"

He nodded.

"Because you like me? Or because you know that you've been able to borrow my power in the past and you're willing to take a chance, so you can use it again?"

"While I don't deny that I enjoy the way our magicks mix, I don't need your power, Tamara. I can draw far more than I need in other ways."

"So you're protecting me from the Conclave because it's the right thing to do?"

"You could put it that way."

"I *did* put it that way. Is that how you would put it?"

He smiled, but didn't answer.

Lawyers! Can't live with 'em. Can't shoot 'em in the foot to make 'em talk!

I clucked my tongue at him and started walking again. "Couldn't you just say you're one of the good guys? Just to, you know, ease my mind. Because I've got a lot to worry about at the moment without adding your ulterior motives to the list."

I marched ahead of him to my car that was still parked on the back drive.

"Where are you going?" he asked.

"I know someone who might be able to get a faery to talk to her."

"I'll come with you."

"No. The fae don't like adults, and they don't like witch-folk. You're both, so you stay here. Keep reading your books. There might be something in them that will help us."

Another cannonball exploded over the water.

"And maybe get Robert E. Lee over there to do something besides cannon practice," I added.

20

THE DU-FALL PARADE had come early to my neighborhood. My "dust drunk" neighbors had stolen a float of Snoopy on his doghouse wearing a cowboy hat and lassoing a papier-mâché steer. Rodeo Snoopy? That was a new one on me, but I guess like Barbie he's tried plenty of careers over the years.

I needed to talk to Abby, and I spotted her sitting like a princess at the end of the truck, wearing a pink ruffled dress and a large pink rose on her head.

"Y'all better sit down before you fall off that thing!" I called to the six adults standing at the edges as the driver zoomed down the street at speeds that were in keeping with Snoopy's Red Baron days—and far exceeding usual parade standards. If they fell off the flatbed trailer, they were likely to crack their skulls. My next-door neighbor Jolene was still wearing her bathrobe from the morning, but she'd wrapped the tie like a sash and waved to me like a demented prom queen.

As I drew closer, she hiked the robe up to her chubby knees and eyed the bull like it was her next steak dinner. Then she lifted her leg to climb on.

"I don't think that's gonna work," I said.

Sure enough, as she tried to mount him, the bull pitched sideways. She hung there, arms around its collapsing neck, dangling like a plus-sized party favor.

As the driver slowed and maneuvered to turn around, I raced to the float and scooped Abby up. I was real glad she was the only child to rescue from it.

"Miss Jolene, you need help getting down from there?" I said, dropping Abby on the grass.

"Yee haw!" Jolene shouted.

I decided to take that as a yes.

I rushed toward her. "Come on down, Miss Jolene," I said, grabbing her arm. "Before you fall."

She yanked the rope, ripping Snoopy from his house and launching him on top of her and the bull, which teetered for a second and then crashed off the trailer onto the street, knocking me down along with them.

"Miss Jolene?" I gasped, crawling over to her. "Are you okay?"

"Move," she said, shoving me aside and rolling free. She snapped the rope authoritatively from Snoopy's paws and wrapped the legs of the now pancake-shaped bull. She tied them off expertly and slapped the ground.

"Time!" she said triumphantly, standing over her flattened but completely hog-tied bull.

"Well, that'll teach him," I mumbled.

Abby dissolved into giggles, and the other adults on the flatbed cheered and congratulated Jolene.

The driver of the truck gunned the engine and started down the block again with a Snoopy-less doghouse and five happy, but pretty much crazy, people.

"How are you doing?" I asked Abby.

"This is fun."

"Uh-huh," I said, thinking this was about as much fun as cleaning a kitchen after someone forgot to put the top on a blender before hitting the start button. "You want to help me out with something?"

"Like what?"

"I've got to see if I can find a pixie in the forest. I saw the picture you drew. I thought you might know where to look."

She smiled. "I do."

"Oh, good."

"Let me get my stuff. You have to have some bait to lure them out."

"What kind of bait?" I asked as she darted away.

"Mostly I use Gummi bears, Jelly Bellies, or Sweethearts. Let me get my bag," she called over her shoulder before she skip-raced to her house while I waited.

When she came out, she was carrying an impressive-looking backpack, like we were about to be Girl Scouts on wilderness training. As I led her to my car I realized the adults were stripping to Merle Haggard. I slapped a hand over her eyes and rushed her into the passenger seat.

"Keep your eyes closed," I said, getting in. I zoomed past the float, just as one of the guys launched a beer mug through Jolene's front window. Jolene, understandably annoyed, tackled him. That might have settled things if a couple other people hadn't decided to dive into the tussle. I grimaced, dragging my eyes away from the rearview mirror. I was tempted to try to break things up. But I knew in my heart that it wouldn't do any good.

I stared uneasily as I saw Charlie Buckland coming out of a neighbor's house carrying a flat-screen television with the cords dangling. I stomped on my brake and rolled the window down.

"Charlie, you put that back!"

He grinned at me and ran across the lawn to his own house.

Abby, in the passenger seat, giggled. "He left the door open. We should see what kind of sparkly things they have. I like earrings that dangle."

"We can't do that. It would be stealing."

"Wasn't taking other people's plants stealing, Miss Tammy?" she asked with an innocent, curious little face.

I grimaced and took a deep breath. "Yeah, that was, and it was wrong. I wasn't thinking straight, and now I'll have to make up for what I did." I glanced in my rearview mirror. "Lately, plenty of people aren't themselves."

"Nope, they're a lot more fun."

I sighed. At least she hadn't spotted the fight, which her own momma had jumped into.

"Let's go to Magnolia Park," I said.

"No, the best place to find pixies is in the woods by Macon Hill."

"The woods by Macon Hill? There aren't even any trails there."

"No people trails. That's why the faeries like it. It's one of their favorite places."

"But what were you doing there? You could've gotten lost."

She smiled. "Someone would've found me. Duvall's not so big."

I drove to the west side of the tor and parked on a small, unmarked road that she pointed me to. We got out near a patch of evergreens, and I saw a truck a couple hundred feet away. The sun was setting, and I didn't feel that good about tramping around in the dark. One of us could trip and break a leg. As I got closer to the truck, I froze. It was the TrailBlazer.

It seemed to be empty, and I really wanted to get the license plate number so Zach could look up the owner.

"Stay here," I whispered to Abby.

My heart banged in my chest as I snuck closer. When I started to pass the passenger side, I peered in the window. I could just make out the mailing label on a box in the seat. Earl Stanton. The bastard.

I turned, walking quickly back to my car. "C'mon," I said. "Now's not a good time."

"This way," Abby said, darting between two trees.

"No!" I shouted in a whisper as she disappeared behind them.

What in the world?

My stomach knotted with dread. I didn't want to go into the woods and run into Earl, but I certainly couldn't leave her.

"Abby! Come back here right now!"

She didn't come out. I balled my fists furiously. Sometimes I regret that I never got pregnant when Zach and I were married, but some days, like now, I'm not sorry I don't have kids.

I ducked into the woods and spotted her.

"Abigail Farmer, get back here."

She ignored me and I had to hurry to follow as she ran along the edge of forest. *C'mon! Get back here!*

I heard men's voices, and my breath caught. I raced to catch her and did, grabbing her arm and pulling her back.

They must've heard us crunching on the leaves and needles because one of the men turned, and I saw his swollen, bruised face. I realized it was Earl, his lip crusted with dried blood and twice its normal size. Zach had really done a number on him.

"Shoot!" I whispered. "We have to go back," I said as he stomped toward us. "Hide!" I shoved her away from me and crouched behind a tree trunk. In the dark, he wouldn't be able to see me. All I needed was to stay still. I waited, holding my breath as he got closer.

Suddenly there was a burst of light and flame above me. A branch blazed overhead. *Incendio,* I thought, filled with dread. I hadn't been able to see him because Earl's body had blocked my view, but now I knew. When I dropped my gaze from the tree limb, it was just in time to see Earl's meaty hand grab for me.

Oh, God!

I stumbled backward, but he bore down on me. I had to get away.

"You!" he spat, yanking me up by the arm. He marched farther into the woods, dragging me.

"Let me go," I yelled. "You let me go right now!"

"Little tease, I'll teach you."

I hauled off and slapped his bruised face with all my might. He growled and flung me to the ground.

"You want it? Right now?" he sneered, dropping to his knees and pinning me.

My heart hammered and besides being afraid for myself, I couldn't stand that Abby might see whatever he did to me.

"Earl Stanton, you stop right now!" Where the heck was Incendio? Would he just stand by and let it happen? "You don't want to do this. You're better than this," I said, hoping maybe he'd find some part of himself that had once been my friend.

"Oh, I'm doin' this. Zach ain't here now, is he? Mr. All-American thinks he's the only one who's got a right to you. Well, I'm gonna do this, and he's gonna know it. And the next time he shows his face at my house, I'll blow it off with a shotgun. He'll go to his grave knowing what I did to you out here in the dirt."

I was so shocked, I couldn't even speak. It was like all the fear in the world had shoved its way into my body, and it made my skin feel too tight. Bile threatened to roar up my throat, but I swallowed it back down. My hands clawed the ground, trying to drag me away, but he had me.

As he reached for his zipper, a part of me knew that fighting would mean more violence and more pain for me. Maybe he'd lose control and beat me to death.

If you can't get away, be quiet and still so it'll be over faster.

But, smart or not, it wasn't in me to just lie there and take it. The sounds of the woods fell away, and all I heard was my own heartbeat.

I grabbed a handful of dirt and flung it into his eyes. I rolled my face away as his fist crashed down with a thump. He shook me by the shoulders until my teeth rattled and my eyes blurred with tears. He was blinking himself, trying to get the grit out, and then I saw Abby's little face behind him. She bent, and I felt her press a rock into my palm.

When he leaned forward, I cracked him in the temple with it. His eyes rolled back, and he fell onto me. I shoved him off, kicking wildly at his motionless body.

I staggered to my feet, shaking, relieved and furious at the same time. The rock was there on the ground, and my fingers itched to pick it up, to use it on his skull. I heard my ragged breathing, felt the tears drip from my jaw, but it was like I wasn't completely in my body . . . like I could use that stone and it wouldn't be my hand holding it.

I remembered what I had liked about being fae. The utter lack of conscience.

In the distance, I heard a motorcycle engine. The familiar sound brought me back to myself. I noticed the soft noises of the woods around me and felt the cool air. Slowly, I stepped back from the rock.

I shivered as I surveyed Earl's body. Blood ran from his temple to the hard ground. I heard him breathing and knew that he might never wake up again. *Good.* Or he might wake up any second. *Not good.*

Sniffling, I took Abby's hand and led her silently away. "I'm sorry you had to see that," I said, rubbing the tears from my face.

"The faeries are this way," she said, skipping ahead.

I took a gulp of air and blinked my burning eyes. Abby wasn't upset, which seemed strange. I realized she must not have understood what Earl had been about to do. I was glad she didn't.

By the time we got to the edge of the stream a minute later, I was steadier on my feet but still wanted to get out of the woods and back to my car, which had locks and was big enough to run Earl over seventeen times if he came anywhere near it.

Which way is the car?

I wasn't sure. I'd followed Abby because she seemed to know the way, but nothing looked familiar.

"Where are we?"

She knelt down and opened her bag. She pulled out a pack of Gummi bears. "Eat some. You'll feel better."

I took a few and popped them in my mouth. She dropped some Gummies into the water and onto the ground and then put a few in her mouth.

"What do you want to talk to the pixies about?"

"I spilled some of their dust," I said.

"I know. I've seen it swirling in the air."

"You have? I thought once it blew away, people would get back to normal, but they haven't. I need to know how to get rid of the effects."

"It would wear off if the dust wasn't still blowing around town."

"It ought to have settled by now."

"Oh, no. Not here. Duvall's got the four winds. The dust goes in figure-eights. It'll never settle."

"How do you know? Someone told you that?"

"I see how it rides the winds." She bent over her bag again. I didn't feel like eating more candy and hoped whatever she pulled out next would lure the pixies because the Gummies didn't seem to be working. "Someone will have to re-collect the dust. Later, after the fall," she said.

"The fall?"

"The fall of Duvall." She giggled. "It rhymes," she said as she stood and turned around. She held a crossbow, and it was pointed right at me.

"What are you doing?" I stammered, my heart clenching.

"It's better this way. When the gates open, she'll send them for you. She'll make them do worse than kill you. They'll toy with you," she hissed.

I stared at her, my mouth agape.

She said, "You're a traitor." It was eerie to hear a high-pitched child's voice full of malice, and my heart seemed to tumble around in my chest.

"Abby, I gave your momma presents for you at your baby shower."

Her laughter was like shattering glass, and I took a step back.

"I'm not human, silly. I came last year." She smiled and I got a glimpse of pointed teeth. Suddenly there was a faint greenish cast to her skin, and it glimmered as though she were a lantern lit from within.

"I don't understand," I said, taking another step back.

"I'm a changeling. I thought you were one, too, but you're not. You're just a mixed-blood mongrel. Still, we would've welcomed you since you understood Treespeak, but you abandoned the life of fae. You spit on us," she snarled, flashing needlelike teeth.

I bolted. I heard her high-pitched laughter as she chased me. For someone small, she ran much too fast. And then I felt a sharp pinch and fell forward.

Pain blossomed as I landed, a hot lance piercing my back and shoulder.

I shrieked, grabbing my arm as I rolled onto my side. I felt blood trickle down my back as I saw her sneakers.

"A poisoned tip for the witch and an iron shaft for the faery." She laughed again. "You were easy peasy, and I'll get a special prize from the queen and be in her favor now." She bent down so that her small face danced over mine. "You can go ahead and cry now. I like hearing people cry. Sometimes I say enough mean things to Abby's mother to make her cry in front of me. She tries not to—"

I gasped at the thought of a centuries-old creature tormenting an innocent and unsuspecting mortal woman.

"You're a wretched little thing, aren't you?"

"Humans get their feelings hurt so easily. It's fun."

My good arm shot forward and propelled my fist into her belly. The move jarred my shoulder, making me groan in pain, but it also knocked her down.

"Get away from me," I said.

She laughed as she stood up. "You'd better hope you die before your fat, ugly admirer wakes up. The dust has brought out his true nature, and he'll use you if he gets the chance. He thinks you're so pretty." She ran a finger over my cheek. I jerked my head away and tried to get to my knees, but my head swam, and I fell back to the ground, wrenching my shoulder. I whimpered, hating for her to see my pain.

She circled around me, jeering. I closed my eyes and pretended to be unconscious. She tugged the arrow several times, making me scream until the pain was so white-hot that I saw a bright light. Then I really did faint.

21

IT WAS DARK when I woke. My shoulder ached, I couldn't feel my legs, and my side was soaked. I struggled to get my bearings. From my hips down, I was in water. I vaguely remembered stumbling and falling into the stream.

In the distance, I heard a yowl that sounded like Mercutio. I tried to cry out, but my voice was soft, like it was muffled under a pillow. It didn't matter if he found me anyway. I could feel that I was dying. All I wanted was to melt into the water like a lump of sugar. No pain. No fear.

As time passed, the arrow in my back didn't hurt anymore. The numbness seeped along me by inches. My hands, my belly, the tip of my nose. Soon I'd be a bit of frost floating on the stream, pretty as the snowflakes you see in pictures.

The next time I woke, I heard Bryn's smooth voice above the sound of the creek. "What's happened to you?" Then he cursed. "You've been stabbed? What is—is this an arrow?"

"'Xactly," I slurred, my tongue heavy and thick.

"Who shot you?"

"Abble. Not axshually—" My words sounded like I had a mouthful of taffy.

"All right. Don't talk, Tamara." He picked me up and

carried me through the woods to a clearing where he'd parked his car.

"She's like ice, Mercutio. Stay close to her. Keep her warm," Bryn said, when he laid the passenger seat back and put me on it. Mercutio climbed next to me and lay against my belly. "This damned arrow," Bryn growled, repositioning me, curling me forward so he could close the door.

I woke up again at his house, lying on a bed with my body propped up at a forty-five-degree angle to keep the bed from driving the arrow in deeper. He had cut my top off and was examining the tented skin where the arrowhead had almost broken through the front of my chest just above my collarbone. I pushed his hand away.

"Tip's poison. Don't hurt yourself," I tried to say, but my words were so garbled, I wasn't sure he could understand me.

"You're not going to die. Do you hear me, Tamara?" he said fiercely. "Talk to me. Stay awake."

I felt the tug at my shoulder as he touched the shaft, but there was hardly any pain.

Body feels so strange.

"I'll try not to hurt you more than I have to, but I have to get this out. The tip's undoubtedly barbed. I'll need to—"

"Don't care what you do." I closed my eyes. I wanted to sleep. I could tell that whatever he was doing would be too late. But what the hell? If it made him feel better, that was fine by me. Edie's locket lay cold and heavy against my chest. I hoped to see her soon.

I drifted until I felt a pinch. I grimaced as the arrowhead tore through the skin in front.

"Will this do?" I heard Mr. Jenson ask.

"Yes," Bryn said.

Then I felt the metal shaft held tight and heard a snap. Something hit the floor with a thud. My eyes flew open as he gripped the arrow with pliers and pulled it from my upper chest.

"The shaft's intact. I got it all," Bryn said.

I closed my eyes, not caring. He rolled me onto my stomach and poured something hot on my upper back.

"Soak the cloth in it, Jenson," he said and then he draped a wet cloth over my shoulder blade, covering the wound before he rolled me on my back. Mercutio licked my face as Bryn poured what smelled like hot herb tea on me and then put another soaking wet rag over the front wound.

I opened my eyes and saw the anguish in his. "It's all right. Doesn't hurt," I slurred.

"That's what worries me." He pushed a strand of hair off my face. "I'll call you if I need anything else, Jenson. Close the door."

My lids drifted down as Bryn yanked off his shirt.

"Tamara, you're not leaving this world. Do you hear me?"

"Have to go." My whole body was numb, and it was pressed against the bed as if gravity were three times stronger than usual. My chest seemed too heavy to even lift enough to get a breath in. My lips tingled, and my lids dropped shut.

"No. Stay with me." His voice was soft in my ear and then faded.

I drifted away, floating above the bed, looking down at my body. My dusky skin turned blue, and Bryn pulled me to him. He put my Edie locket over my good shoulder and out of his way before he slid a smooth black stone between our chests. The words of a spell shattered the quiet.

He kissed me, and his magic sizzled, a hot tendril of smoke curling inside my frozen mouth. I shivered, wanting to go. It was calm and cool and nice where my spirit was headed.

He forced his breath and his magic into my lungs, and, a moment later, I was back in my body. It hurt as it thawed. Pins and needles. I squirmed, trying to escape it, but he held me against him, a furnace of coursing magical heat.

Minutes passed before he drew back. His lips and the tip of his nose were blue, too, his breath cold against my cheek. He coughed a couple of times and licked his lips. Frost tipped his gleaming black hair as though we were walking through an arctic winter.

"Look at me," he said.

I stared up at him. His blue eyes glittered darkly, and I saw the whole universe in them.

"Tamara."

"I want eyes as pretty as yours," I mumbled.

He sighed with a slight smile and let his forehead rest against mine. "You hardly need my eyes. Even as blue and cold as death, you're more beautiful than midnight."

As the feeling came back, my shoulder throbbed. I let out a hiss of pain. "It hurts now," I said, biting my lip and trying not to cry.

He shivered. "I know. I'm sorry."

"You're cold."

He poured some steaming tea from a pot into a cup and gulped it down. Shaking, he pulled the covers over us.

"Why are you cold, Bryn?"

"I divided the poison between us."

"How?"

"By casting a spell that never should have worked."

"But it did, and now you're poisoned, too?"

"So it seems," he said, finding my hand with his and interlacing our fingers.

"You shouldn't have done that."

He squeezed my hand, and I sighed. *Men. Can't live with 'em. Can't die without 'em.*

22

BY THE NEXT morning, my shoulder hurt so badly that I wished I had died. October thirtieth, only two days until the challenge. Not that I was in any kind of shape for a magical pentathlon or whatever WAM had planned for me.

"Stop that," I complained as Bryn cuddled closer to me. His cool body actually felt nice, but whenever he moved, the mattress shifted under me, which sent sharp pains through my chest and back.

"You're warm," he said.

"I'm feverish. Hey, cut that out," I said, using my good hand to block his naked body parts from getting too close to my own. I pushed at him.

"Tamara, I'm freezing. And I got in this condition by saving your life."

"Who asked you to? My shoulder was as numb as Novocain last night. I felt way better."

"Sweetheart, please. I swear I'll never save your life without your permission again. Just let me—"

"No, you be still! I'll do it."

I slid my thigh between his and leaned against his chest. "Better?"

He sighed. "Much. You know what else are extremely cold? My lips."

"Bryn, my shoulder feels like someone is shoving a red-hot poker through it."

"I bet. Why don't you kiss me, and I'll cast a spell to see if I can divide the pain between us."

"Think that would work?"

"Shouldn't, but it probably will."

"We'd better not. You're already sick enough."

The edges of his mouth twitched up. "Tamara, I know you can't be bought, but if I could bribe you into kissing me, how much would that cost? Would ten thousand dollars be enough?"

I laughed in spite of myself, and the pain made me groan. "Ow. Don't make me laugh."

"Sorry," he said.

I sighed. "No, it's not your fault." I paused. "Do you promise to keep still?"

He arched an eyebrow and murmured, "As if my life depended on it."

I edged my mouth closer and kissed him. The power sparked between us, but not as strong as it usually did. I felt him mumble against my lips, and I gasped as he pushed magic into me.

I broke out into a sweat, and the pain flared white-hot and then cooled. My body tingled.

"Did you just give me poisoned magic?"

"Only a little. Did it help your shoulder?"

I moved my arm experimentally. There was soreness, but the pain was so blunted that I could lift my arm all the way up. "Wow."

"Good. Kiss me some more." Someone knocked, and Bryn frowned. "Can't a man die in peace?" he grumbled.

I checked to be sure that I was totally covered before I said, "Come in." I blinked as Mercutio's spots caught my eye. He'd raised his head, and I could see it over Bryn's body. He'd apparently slept on the bed with us all night.

Over my shoulder, the door opened. I blushed when I

realized it was Mr. Jenson, who'd gotten quite an eyeful of me the night before.

"What is it, Jenson?" Bryn asked.

"The police."

"What about them?"

"They're here and insisted that I check to be sure that Miss Tamara is not in the house. I assured them that she was not."

"Why are they looking for her?"

"Something to do with a body."

"A what?" I gasped.

"Shh," Bryn said. "Get rid of them."

"Of course. Shall I cancel the party tonight?"

"No, that'll arouse suspicions."

"Whose body?" I asked.

"A person called Earl Stanton," Mr. Jenson said.

Uh-oh. "Did he die from a blow to the head with a rock-like object?"

"That wasn't mentioned and is of course of no consequence to us since we are utterly uninvolved," Mr. Jenson said with emphasis. I was grateful to him for wanting to protect me, but worried about how many of Bryn's habits had worn off on him. Bryn was smooth enough to never get tripped up by the police, but I didn't want Mr. Jenson getting caught lying for me. "Breakfast will be ready in thirty minutes," he said and left before I had time to protest.

"I'm not sure they'll be able to tell what killed him since the body was completely charred," Bryn said.

"His body was burned up?"

Bryn nodded.

"How do you know?"

Bryn surprised by me by smiling. Then he said, "The president of the Shoreside Oaks Homeowners Association called last night while you were asleep. He's furious that a dead body was found in the woods so close to the neighborhood since that will be counted in our crime statistics."

My mouth dropped open for a second in shock. "That's the thing to get upset about? How many feet the body was found from the neighborhood because property values could go down?" I snapped. "Rich people are crazy!" I paused. "No offense."

"None taken."

I sighed heavily, then my thoughts went back to the more important matter. "I wonder why Incendio killed him."

"Can you move your thigh an inch higher?"

I poked him in the rib. "No. I really need you to be brilliant lawyer guy right now."

"Then move your thigh. I'm sure my concentration will improve when sensitive parts of my body don't feel like they're packed in dry ice."

"Hush," I said, sliding my leg higher. "No, don't hush. Tell me what you think about Incendio."

"I think I wish I had his powers. I'd set this room on fire to warm up."

"I'm going to get up and see what I can find out."

"No," Bryn said, grabbing me. "Don't go."

"Then help me think this out. Why would Incendio meet Earl in the middle of the night? And why would Incendio come back to kill Earl after leaving? Maybe I interrupted them, and they had unfinished business? Incendio came back and they argued and then Incendio killed him?" I liked that scenario. I didn't mind Earl being dead, but it would be nice if I wasn't a murderer. "I think maybe Incendio and Earl were together the night before last, too. Incendio burned down some trees in my neighborhood, and Earl trashed my car.

"I think the first time they met was at the Whiskey Barrel," I continued. "And Earl was pretty nasty to Incendio, acting all mean and racist. Incendio doesn't seem like the type to forgive that kind of thing—or any type of thing for that matter. So how could they have become friends?"

"I don't know."

I edged away from him.

"For the love of Saint Patrick, how am I supposed to know that?" Bryn said.

"You're not, but shouldn't one of us be out there trying to figure things out? And trying to rescue the town?" I thought of Imposter Abby's "Fall of Duvall" comment and shivered. "Tomorrow's Halloween. Did you already cast the spell to reinforce the doors between our world and the faery one?"

"Yeah, I cast it yesterday."

"I sure hope it holds," I said, knowing that the circulating pixie dust would make it less likely to. Big cities think smog is the biggest air pollution problem. Little do they know! "So, I should go. Mercutio can stay here and keep you warm."

"I want you, Tamara. Not your cat. No offense, Mercutio."

Merc licked a paw unperturbed.

"Besides, you can't go out," Bryn continued. "The police are looking for you."

"I know. I've got a plan."

"What's that?"

"I'm gonna avoid them."

"Brilliant. From now on, you're in charge of strategy."

"If you've got a better idea, let's hear it. I can't stay in this bed forever."

"Why not?"

I laughed. Though I'm always attracted to him, this playful side of Bryn was even more irresistible than usual.

Sleep had flattened his glossy hair against his head, and I slipped my fingers through it to smooth it back into place. "I'm afraid some of that frost has settled into your brain."

"You might be right. Why don't you kiss me? That seems to heat me up better than anything."

23

IT TOOK ME another half hour to extract myself from Bryn. I took a shower and crookedly slapped a couple of gauze pads on the wounds, which throbbed.

Mr. Jenson had laid out some clothes for me that must have belonged to one of Bryn's former girlfriends. The knit shirt was a little oversized and a weird yellow-green color that I suspected would clash with some skin tones, like any that occurred in nature. The pants were off-white, a color I didn't have a lot of confidence I'd be able to maintain with my presently rough-and-tumble life. They were also too long for me, but with a few safety pins, I created a hem and was ready for the world. Sort of.

I thought I'd head out, but I was distracted by a delivery that Steve signed for at the gate and brought to the front hall. Two heavy boxes that seemed to have been overnight mailed by FedEx from the Witches' Brew.

"Tell the boss his books are here from Austin," Steve said to Mr. Jenson.

"Let me see those," I said, putting out a hand. Answers that I needed might be in those books.

He moved them beyond my reach. "You'll have to ask Mr. Lyons," Steve said, taking the boxes down the hall.

I ventured upstairs to Bryn's room and knocked. He called for me to come in. Inside, steam billowed from the master bathroom, where he'd recently showered. I looked him over. He'd dressed like we were in for a freak snowstorm, wearing a heavy sweater, jeans, wool socks, black gloves, and a blue-and-white-striped scarf wrapped twice around his neck and partially covering his stubbled jaw.

I smiled at him. "That's a real interesting look. I think *Gentlemen's Quarterly* might take you off their—"

"Is making fun of my wardrobe really the best use of your time?"

I chuckled. "Sorry. It's just that there's never anything good to tease you about normally. This might be my only chance."

"I didn't mind the way you teased me last week. You're free to do that whenever you like."

Oh boy. Remembering the night when we'd gone too far curled my toes, but it also made me think of the aftermath, how I'd been hungover, how it had hurt Zach. The pang of guilt brought a flush to my cheeks. I was even more caught between Bryn and Zach now than I had been last week.

"You got a delivery of books from Austin," I said, in a hurry to avoid thinking about my personal life.

"Good. I didn't have much in my library specifically about the fae. I bought out the reference section on them from the Brew."

"Can I look through them with you?"

He nodded, dragging his fancy down-filled duvet from the bed. It trailed behind him as he left the room.

We went downstairs, and he lay on the couch under the thick cloud of bedding, while I opened the boxes and looked at the expensive collection of books.

"Why don't you lie here with me, and we'll look at them together?" he said.

I perched on the low table across from him and shook my head. "You rest."

"I'll rest better if you come closer." He raised the edge of the duvet.

"Bryn, you know Zach and I are still involved. I don't . . ." I tucked my hair behind my ears. "I don't want anyone to get hurt."

He let the duvet drop. "Your relationship with Sutton has already been proven a failure. It's time for you to move on."

I blinked, feeling the sentences stab at my heart. I didn't like Bryn saying with such confidence that my relationship with Zach couldn't work, even though I did have my own doubts about it, especially now.

"He and I got together too young is all."

"First love gets its hooks in deep, but that doesn't mean it's supposed to last forever," he said, his voice smooth and utterly confident, but not harsh. "Sutton needs someone to stand in his shadow. You're not that woman anymore, Tamara. Your potential shouldn't be squandered."

I cleared my throat, my emotions all jumbled. I liked hearing that he thought I had potential, but I wasn't ready to deal with the rest.

"Let's see what these books know about faery dust."

"You read. I'll rest my eyes," he said, closing them.

I read aloud until he fell asleep, then scoured the books silently. Unfortunately, I didn't find any information about how to re-collect pixie dust. I started flipping through books on witchcraft, too, looking for a spell that might help me break into Jenna's house undetected.

Mercutio sat next to me, licking his paws.

"Listen to this, Merc. Says here some witches and wizards have something called magical synergy. Each one's power feeds the other's and enhances it. One plus one equals three. Says it's really rare to have that happen. Only a dozen reported cases in the last four hundred years." I glanced at Bryn, who was sound asleep, and then back to Merc. "You know, I've been thinking. When did my power spark to life? When I came into contact with he-who-shall-not-be-kissed over there," I said, nodding at the couch. "Yep, and it works best after I've just seen him, or when you're around and I go barefoot. If I'm going to try to fix the town and survive the challenge, I'll bet that's the key somehow." I nodded to myself. "And you know who knows the trick to re-collecting the dust? That little two-faced Abby imposter. Maybe I can trap her in a circle and make her tell."

I moved closer to Bryn, whose lips were bluish despite the fact that he was well bundled. I sat on the edge of the couch and nudged him. It took a few firm pokes before his eyelids rose.

"Hey there," I said.

"I'm cold. Lie down with me," he said, the words slower and less crisp than usual.

My muscles tightened anxiously. "Why don't you sit up? That's enough sleeping for now."

"I'm cold," he mumbled, his lids drifting shut.

My heart thudded in my chest. I didn't like this one little bit. I nudged him. "Bryn, wake up."

He didn't respond. I jumped up and darted down the hall, calling for Mr. Jenson.

"What is it?" Mr. Jenson asked when I found him in the kitchen.

"He's worse. Can you make some more of that tea he had you brew last night? We need to keep him awake and drinking hot stuff. Maybe we can turn up the thermostat, too."

"Yes, of course."

I chewed my lip. "I thought he'd be better by now."

"He said his chills were not as severe when you were nearby," Mr. Jenson said, giving me a pointed look for several seconds. "And you realize that last night when you were ill, he was quite adamant about staying with you."

"Yeah, I know he saved me," I said, turning to hurry back down the hall. In the study, I slipped under the covers with Bryn and lay on top of him. Even through the clothes I could feel his body leeching heat from me. I raised my shirt up partway and his, too, so we were belly to belly, skin touching. Then I kissed him. His lips were cold and almost rubbery beneath mine. The magic between us was so faint that I almost couldn't sense it. Worry was quickly turning to panic.

I moved up and down, sliding my skin over his, creating some friction. "Bryn, wake up," I mumbled against his mouth. He exhaled slowly, and I drew his icy breath into my lungs, warming it, and gave it back to him.

His lids fluttered open, and his cool lips softened under mine.

"Give me back some of that poison," I said. He didn't answer. "You hear? My shoulder's throbbing something fierce," I lied. "Gimme some of that stuff back to make it numb again. Do your spell."

"I'm tired," he slurred.

I poked his ribs and kissed him some more. The power flared a little stronger. I felt his arms slide around me.

"That's it. Give me some poisoned magic."

He mumbled against my mouth, kissing me, and I felt the chill in my spine. I shivered, but was happy to see his pupils constrict, and his gaze sharpen.

The numbness tingled through my body, making my hands ache.

"You stay up. Mr. Jenson's bringing you some hot tea, and you're gonna drink every bit of it." I waited for him to answer, but he just looked at me. "You hear me about the tea?"

"I heard you. If you kiss me again, I'll do anything you say."

I took the flirting as a very good sign and bent closer, kissing the side of his face gently and whispering near his ear. "Please try not to let the poison win out. If you die, I don't think Mr. Jenson will be my friend anymore."

I crawled off him and stood up, then tucked him in tighter against his protests.

"Stay," he said.

I was torn. He did seem to need me, but us snuggling together wasn't going to save the town from having a meltdown on Halloween and it wasn't going to help me face the challenge or get Aunt Mcl's earrings back. I couldn't work on those things from Bryn's couch. And maybe Bryn's system would fight off the poison, if I just let him rest. Then I had a sudden brainstorm.

"Bryn, do you think that spring that we used last week to cure the werewolf bites for Lennox and Zach would save you from an elfish poison?"

"Might." Bryn closed his eyes, shivering.

"Sit up," I said, pulling him as Mr. Jenson came with the tea. "Mr. Jenson, I've got an idea that might work. Will you help me get him in the car?"

"I don't need help getting in the car," Bryn said, through chattering teeth. "Just get her the keys to the Mercedes."

24

WE WERE A few miles out of town when Mercutio seemed to want me to turn left onto a dirt road. "That's not the way, Merc. We've got to take care of Bryn."

Merc stood with his front paws on the dashboard, watching the road go by.

I drove another mile and spotted Jordan's rented convertible behind us.

Shoot! "What's he doing back there?"

Bryn licked his lips and pulled the blanket around him tighter.

"Who?"

"Jordan Perth."

Bryn checked his side mirror. "He either suspects you're in the car, or he wants to talk to me."

"With the tinted windows, he can't know I'm in here. I'm going to ignore him."

"If we're going to Leon's Spring, he'll see you when we get out. Why don't you take me back? I'll have Steve drive me."

"No, I don't want to waste any more time. I want you back to normal so you can do research and make strategies and, more importantly, so that if we need to share power to cast some save-the-town spells, you're up for it."

The corner of his mouth edged up. "So you're just defying the Conclave to save me, so I can be a power source for you? Thought you were one of the good guys."

I laughed softly, recognizing my own complaint. "Well, now you know better." I parked near the path that led to the spring.

"Stay in the car for a minute," I said, thinking Bryn looked exhausted and would be better off keeping warm under the blanket.

"No. Let me talk to him alone. He may not be looking for you, and I might be able to get rid of him."

"But—"

He held out a hand to silence me. "When things settle down, I'm going to teach you to play chess."

"Huh?"

"The game helps train the mind to think several steps ahead of what's happening. Strategic planning is key in this life."

"Hmm. Was it you or was it me who thought of bringing you to the spring to fix you?"

He smiled. "Fair enough." He slid a hand over and pulled my head to his. The kiss was brief, but I was glad to feel the power arc between us. "You're chewing through small doses of poison very fast," he said. "The bit I gave you at the house, I can't even taste it." He pushed his door open and got out, leaving it ajar. "What can I do for you?" Bryn said to Jordan, who was out of his car and approaching us. Bryn raised his hand.

"That's close enough," he said. "What do you want?"

"What are you doing out here, Lyons?"

"I left something out here a few nights ago. I'm here to retrieve it. And you?"

"Who's your driver?"

I saw Jordan slide his wand out in a subtle move that Bryn, on the opposite side of the car, probably couldn't see. Was he going to attack Bryn? That seemed extreme and unlikely, but should I let him get the chance? Bryn *had* said that strategic planning was a good thing.

In a couple of steps, Jordan was next to my door and I flung it open, knocking him flat. The wand bounced a foot from his hand, and I scrambled out to get it before he did.

"What precisely are you doing?" Jordan asked, his voice sending a chill through me.

"This here is Texas, and when someone pulls a weapon it's usually 'cause they're thinking of using it."

He stood up and held out his hand. "I suggest you return my wand. You're in an unimaginable amount of trouble already," he said, nodding toward Bryn.

"Well, seeing as I'm already in all that trouble, I'll just hang on to this until we finish our business here." I moved around the car to Bryn, who had leaned up against it and was shaking his head.

"She's new to all this," Bryn said to Jordan.

"*She* is. What's your excuse?"

Bryn's gaze slid to me for a moment and then back to Jordan. "I'll save that for court."

"Bryn, c'mon," I said, tugging his arm. Jordan followed us, staying about ten feet back. I kept a firm grip on his wand. We got to Leon's Spring, but the water was gone. The hole in the ground was dry and cracked like we were in the middle of the desert and it had evaporated a hundred years before.

"What happened to it?" I mumbled.

Bryn sighed, his lips blue-tinged from the frigid poison consuming him again. "This is . . . disappointing."

Jordan approached us. "Problem?" he asked in a tone way too cheerful for my taste.

I squared my shoulders and faced him, holding the two ends of his wand in each hand. "I may not be much of a witch, but I could break this wand into a couple of pieces without any trouble at all. If you want it back safe and sound, you'll go on back to your car."

"Love, please. You're signing up for a death sentence," Jordan said. "Give me back my wand, and distance yourself from him right now." When I didn't respond, he looked at Bryn. "Lyons, I'm going to retrieve my wand. If I cast, will you interfere?"

My heart thumped in my chest. Bryn didn't answer Jordan, but Jordan didn't wait long. He raised a hand toward me.

Bryn raised a hand, too, and shook his head at Jordan. "She'll return your wand intact unless you attack us."

Jordan narrowed his eyes, scowling. "You're in violation of the law. Both of you!"

Bryn shrugged. "I'll answer for it when the time comes. Now go back to your car." Bryn held himself starch-stiff, but I saw him shudder involuntarily.

Jordan saw it, too. His eyes widened for a second as he realized that Bryn was weaker than usual.

"Bryn—"

Before I could get out a warning, Jordan spewed a spell. I reached for Bryn to knock him out of the way, but Bryn yelled in Gaelic and flung his hand toward Jordan.

Jordan and Bryn both fell backward as their energies crashed into each other. My skin burned, and I looked down to see a slice along my forearm where the splintering magic had cut me.

I rushed over to Bryn and was plenty relieved when he licked his chapped lips.

"Are you okay?" I asked.

His teeth chattered. "No, I don't think I'd characterize how I am as okay."

"I meant other than being poisoned."

"Oh, then yes, I'm just great," he said, shivering as he rolled onto his hands and knees. He ignored me trying to hurry him and took several long seconds to stand. I paced, anxiously eyeing Jordan's unconscious body a few feet away.

"Let's hurry," I said, clutching Bryn's arm.

Bryn looked at Jordan as we passed him. "As negotiations go, the outcome of that one was suboptimal. Let's try not to get into any more duels with the Conclave's representatives."

"He started it."

Bryn smiled, stopping to lean on me for a moment. "Rules from the playground don't always fly in a court of law. Who started it will likely be beside the point."

"If you ask me, the rules of this Conclave are kind of dumb." I opened the passenger door.

"Let's keep that opinion to ourselves, too." Bryn dropped into the passenger seat and I covered him with the blanket, tucking it around his shoulders.

"Where's Merc?" I said, realizing for the first time that he hadn't come with us to the hole formerly known as a spring. I spotted Mercutio a few hundred yards away on the road we'd driven in on. Nice place for him.

"Mercutio," I called. He didn't come. I got in the car and started it up. I U-turned to get it on the road and tossed Jordan's wand out the window as I pulled away.

25

"I THINK YOU'RE going to have to give me all that poison back," I said.

Bryn's eyes were closed, and he didn't bother to answer me. The dull ache in my shoulder was nothing compared to how worried I was about him falling asleep in the middle of our getaway. Turns out, maintaining consciousness is a basic skill I value in my partners in crime.

I zoomed down the road, with one eye on the rearview mirror. Mercutio, up ahead, turned and ran down the road he'd wanted me to take earlier.

"What? Is it some kind of cure for Bryn?" I mumbled. I swung the steering wheel, kicking up gravel and fishtailing, but managing to make the turn. Bryn's head bounced off the passenger window and he groaned, opening his eyes.

He looked around, lids only halfway up. "Do I even want to know?"

"Um, slight detour. Mercutio insisted."

Bryn's body shook with chills as he looked in the side mirror. "This road is very narrow, Tamara."

"So?"

"If this is a dead end and Perth pulls in behind us, we'll

be boxed in," he said, his voice slow and slurry. He cleared his throat.

"Well, then Mercutio will have to bite him or something. We'll manage."

"I've seen the way you two manage things."

"You know, if you don't have anything helpful to say, you can just go on back to being quiet. Merc and I like to keep a positive attitude when we're in the middle of getting chased."

His lids drifted down. Even though I'd told him to hush, I didn't really want him sleeping. That was too darn close to comatose for my taste.

"How come some wizards use wands and others don't?" I asked, trying to engage him.

"A lot of children are trained using wands because wands help the user to concentrate power. In the beginning, you can do more powerful spells if you use one."

"But you don't use a wand."

"No."

"So what's the downside?"

"Using a wand beyond Class Two becomes a habit that's almost impossible to break. Like a spellbook, a wand will hold power that goes unused. They have some terrific properties, but in the company of human beings you wouldn't want to have to pull out your wand to do a spell. It lacks a certain subtlety." His voice trailed off for a moment, and he seemed to have to force his eyes open to look at me. "Also, if you use a wand, you never learn to concentrate power within yourself and to withstand the pain of doing that. So if someone gets your wand, your power is cut down to size. Once it was explained to me in those terms, it was an easy decision."

I nodded.

"Where are we?" Bryn murmured, leaning his head against the passenger window and staring out at the ranch house we were fast approaching.

"Heck if I know," I said before I realized he was talking more to himself than to me.

"This looks familiar." He licked his lips. "I've been here before."

"Was it a long time ago? This place looks deserted." I glanced at the overgrown grass and weeds and the rusted gate that was almost falling off its hinges. I stopped and jumped out to open the gate. I drove through, glancing several times in the rearview mirror. No sign of Jordan yet.

"I don't remember exactly when it was," Bryn said. "Must have been when we first moved to Texas. The woman who owned the place was a witch, but she died." Bryn nodded. "Lennox took me to her funeral about a decade ago. Your mother was there, too. She smelled like confederate jasmine," he said wistfully.

"My momma or the dead woman?" I asked sharply.

"Never mind."

I narrowed my eyes, looking around as I rolled to a stop behind the large red-brick ranch house. Momma's pretty as a picture and does always smell like flowers. "Did you flirt with her?" I asked, frowning.

The edge of his mouth turned up. "Not successfully."

"Well, that's too bad," I said, though I didn't think it was.

"Not really. All things considered."

"What things?"

"This inevitable . . . love affair between you and me."

"It's not a love affair," I said, shoving my door open. "It was a one-night stand, and a mistake."

He opened his eyes to slits and frowned at me.

"Not that it wasn't a nice mistake. From what I remember of it, it was real nice."

He rolled his eyes before closing them. "Tell your cat to hurry at whatever he's doing. I want to get back to my bed."

"I'll be back in a minute." I walked around the corner of the house and crossed through some tall wildflowers. As the breeze picked up, I got a whiff of something nasty. It smelled like spoiled meat.

"Merc?" I called. I slapped my way through some overgrown grass and weeds, moving toward an old red-and-white barn that could've used a couple coats of paint. I heard water and when I stumbled into a clearing, I saw what must have been the Amanos River on my left.

Merc's soft yowl from the barn made me run toward it. I pushed the door open wide as I rushed in. I froze at the rancid smell and at the sight of Mercutio dodging Incendio's attempts to grab him. My heart clenched.

Incendio looked at me, malice flaming in his dark eyes. His gaze flickered to a lump in the charred hay.

"What's going on?" I said, edging around the barn's perimeter toward the hay. Mercutio hadn't come here for Incendio, so what had he wanted me to see?

"Get out of here, Red," Incendio snarled.

"What are you doing here?" I asked, as I got close enough to realize what I was looking at. *Oh, no!* The partially charred and rotting body of a man. My belly lodged a big complaint as heaps of insects did their business on the corpse. I gagged, breaking into a sweat. I saw the unburned part of the man's face. Tom Brick, the missing wizard.

"Just couldn't leave it alone, huh?"

I backpedaled as Incendio raised his arm. I was about to become a lump of charcoal, and I screamed a protest. In that instant, Merc leapt forward and bit Incendio's leg. The blast of fire went wide as Incendio staggered. He kicked outward, and Merc sailed through the air, but landed as he always does on the pads of his feet.

Merc ran from the barn, and I followed his lead as fast as I could. I darted back and forth as balls of fire exploded around me, then dove into the tall flowers, happy for the cover. I got to my feet, but ran hunched over so he wouldn't see me. The flowers caught fire with the next burst of magic from Incendio, but I ran ahead of the blaze, coughing as the smoke swallowed me.

I tripped and skidded out of the tall grass and ran to the car. Merc was waiting for me at the driver's door. I flung it open, and we both got in

A huge wall of flame roared behind us as I threw the car in gear.

"Bryn!" I yelled, shoving his shoulder.

He murmured, but didn't wake. I slammed my foot down on the gas pedal as flames licked the back of the car and danced on the trunk.

"Please don't explode," I begged the car. More balls of fire rained down from the sky, and I swerved, barreling toward the river.

"Hang on, Merc!" I yelled. I hit the power button to bring the windows down just as I launched the car off the bank. We slammed into the surface of the water, the impact jarring us. The current caught us and spun us around. Incendio continued hurling fire, but we were already halfway submerged, and the flaming car just sizzled.

Water poured in the windows, but Bryn never stirred.

26

I SLAPPED BRYN'S face, trying to get him up. The car's weight dragged us down suddenly, and the air bubbled out the open windows in seconds.

Now completely underwater, I fought my panic. My watery vision was blurry, and I blinked several times as I fumbled to drag Bryn from his seat. I tried to get us both out the passenger window, but we got stuck.

C'mon!

My heart slammed against my chest as I thrashed, scraping my back and wounded shoulder.

I can't! God, help!

I felt a sharp pain in my good shoulder and realized it was Mercutio's claws pushing me. I arched backward out the window, kicking my legs hard and banging against the frame as I got loose.

I kept hold of Bryn, hoping he wasn't drowned already. I broke the surface, gasping. I pulled Bryn's head up, noticing his skin was a scary pale color.

"No!" I said, trying to jostle him awake.

Merc's head bobbed above the water as the current dragged us downstream over rocks and past branches. I turned Bryn's face and kissed his icy mouth. I felt nothing as I blew my breath into him.

"Help me, Merc," I sobbed as we tumbled over some shallow rapids. "There," I shouted, spotting a big tree branch hanging low over the water. Mercutio, with his teeth buried in Bryn's arm, helped me swim to it. I caught the branch, and it nearly yanked my arm out of its socket to hold on.

Then my knee banged on the ground, and I realized it was shallow at the water's edge. I stood, bracing myself against the fast-running water, and Merc and I yanked Bryn onto the shore. I dug my toes into the dirt and flung myself on top of his cold body.

"Think!" I hissed at myself, but fear had my mind as blank as freshly rolled dough.

"Okay. Okay. Okay!" I snapped, digging my nails into my palms to focus as I leaned over him and chanted:

You will not die before you wake,
I give you my power now to take.
Let poison and water flow to me,
Quick as the river by the tree.

I sealed the verse with a kiss and felt the power arc from my body into his. I choked and sputtered, falling back with the poison coursing through me, my skin tingling.

I heard Bryn gasp and felt his body shudder against mine. *Yes!*

"Thank you, God," I whispered. "But why does my magic only seem to work when I'm in a dead panic?" I mumbled as Mercutio licked the water from his fur.

"What happened?" Bryn rasped.

"You halfway drowned," I said, staring at the sky.

"Jenson would say that isn't possible."

"What?" I asked, looking over at him.

"Nothing. What happened?" Bryn's brow was creased with worry.

"We're in so much trouble," I mumbled.

Merc padded across the grass and tapped the water with his paw.

"What, Mercutio?" Bryn asked.

"He's crazy. You're crazy, Merc!" To Bryn, I said, "Your house will be downstream a few miles. He thinks we should swim home. Right, Merc?"

Merc purred.

"I think Incendio killed Tom Brick. I think Mercutio was there to see it and the river's how Mercutio escaped. He must've jumped in the water and swam, found a raft, and ended up at your dock."

"Incendio killed Tom Brick?"

I nodded. "I saw his body." My teeth chattered. "It was partly charred, which I think means Incendio killed him. I don't know what Incendio was doing there today. Maybe he decided to burn the place down to get rid of the evidence?"

"Why would Maldaron kill Brick?" Bryn wondered aloud. "Brick was a minor wizard. He'd only achieved Class Three status, despite being Lennox's age. Definitely not a threat to anyone powerful enough to be in the Conclave."

"Maybe he did something they didn't like? I mean, they're after me, and I'm not even Class One yet."

"It's so hard to concentrate," he said and pulled me close to his body. "Why is your skin colder than mine? What have you done?"

"I took the poison back. I tried to get it all, but I don't think I did. Your lips still look blueberry-stained."

He scowled. "You shouldn't be drawing the poison back into yourself. It took considerable effort on my part to get it out of you."

"You were dying! Besides, I think I'm getting immune to the poison. Whenever I get some of it, my body's cold and tingles for a while and then goes back to normal," I said, shivering. "Anyway, I got us into all this. If one of us has to die, it should probably be me."

Bryn clenched his jaw. "It's not going to be one or the other of us. I'll cast a spell that sees to that. I don't care if it drains me dry of power for months. I'll go underground afterward, if I have to. No elf magic is going to kill us."

Bryn pulled me to my feet. I felt his arms quiver and knew the poison was still wearing him down.

"Let go. You have to save your strength."

"C'mon. Mercutio's right about letting the current do the work to get us home." He stepped into the water.

"The water's cold," I pointed out, though the wind against my wet skin felt just as freezing at the moment.

"It'll be all right. We don't have far to go."

We sunk into the streaming water, and it pulled us along. Mercutio didn't get back in the water, but ran along the bank parallel to us, occasionally slowing down when we did, watching over us like a feline guardian angel.

"I love that cat," I said.

"I know." Bryn cast a glance at Mercutio. "Angus may have to live with my father."

"Where is Lennox?"

"Out of touch. He's trying to negotiate peace with the more reasonable of the wolf packs in the region. They're angry about last week."

"Oh." I chewed on that thought, glad that someone else was handling putting things right with the shape-shifters. "And what does Mercutio have to do with your dog? You can keep Angus chained if we come to visit. Not that I think I'll be coming over much once we get this stuff straightened out."

"No?" Bryn asked skeptically, his arm tightening around my waist and pulling me close so we were pressed together like two slices of bread in a peanut butter sandwich. "Past experience suggests otherwise," he said. "Besides, there's that thing at my house that you want."

His book collection? "What?"

"Me."

My jaw dropped. "Good grief," I snapped.

"Don't be angry. It works out well since I want you, too."

"There are rules against us being together."

"So you keep saying. Why don't you give me the details? Don't you know that lawyers are experts in loopholes?"

"Nobody gets what they want all the time, Bryn."

"Who told you that?" he asked with a smile.

Considering how often we'd been having to save each other's lives lately, he seemed downright overconfident. I frowned, pushing against him, trying to get some distance between us. He eased his grip, and I floated a few inches away. I was pleased, though, with how strong his arms felt around me and that his lips had pinked up, too. Maybe I'd drawn enough poison out for his body to fight off the rest.

"The current's slowed down. Should we swim a little?" I asked.

He pulled me to him for a second and brushed his lips over mine before I could escape. Then he let go of me and turned. His arms cleaved the water in smooth strokes. In moments, he was several feet in front of me and pulling away. Then he looked back, realizing he'd left me behind. He paused until I came up beside him.

"Stay close to me, Tamara."

As if I ever have a choice, I thought grumpily.

27

WE HIT A couple of tangles over shallow rapids, which would have been fun if we'd been inner-tubing on a hot day as opposed to freezing our behinds off after an already exhausting week.

I banged over the rocks, sputtering and cursing, pretty darn annoyed that Bryn took bouncing around like a pinball in stride. We finally saw the golf course, and I knew we'd hit the northeast edge of town.

I'd lost sight of Merc, but guessed he'd decided we were okay to float downstream without his help. The current had picked up again, and as soon as we got into Shoreside Oaks, I swam to the bank and climbed out. Bryn came to the edge, too. With his hair slicked back and his eyes glittering that dark blue, he looked as handsome as ever, and I didn't think it was a great thing that I was noticing again.

"What are you doing?" he asked.

"This is where I get off," I said, pointing myself in the general direction of where my car was parked by the Macon Hill woods.

"Incendio and Jordan will probably comb the town for you. They can't get onto my property. It's fortified."

"I don't care. I want a hot shower and clean, dry clothes that fit me. I've got so much to do. I need to get a move on."

"Is that the most sensible plan?"

"Yes, because you've got to come up with some spells to save us and the town, and you don't need me there distracting you." I waved my hand when he started to protest. "I'll swing by later, if I don't get killed or slip into an elf-poison coma."

Bryn dragged himself out of the water and shivered. "My house is close. You can shower, borrow some clothes, and Steve can drive you."

My feet did object to the idea of walking farther than absolutely necessary. "I'm tired of floating down the river. My fingertips look like raisins," I complained, shaking from the cold and pulling some twigs from my hair. My stiff body ached in places I didn't know you could ache, but I marched out to the road with Bryn.

As we neared his house, I heard classical music and raised my eyebrows at him.

Bryn cocked his head. "Sounds like *Swan Lake*."

"See, this is the difference between my neighborhood and Shoreside. We never blast Beethoven or Chopin or any of those guys. It's a real fundamental difference between you and me."

"I suppose Sutton has the same taste in music as you?"

"Yep."

"And he likes the same kind of food and has the same politics?"

"Yep and yep," I said, warming to the conversation.

"And he understands you and your family? He'd never do something like force you to see a psychiatrist for disclosing your most guarded secret? Because he understands your background and can completely relate to it more than I ever could?"

A darn trap. Just like Bryn! Him and his mental chess. "What makes you think I saw a psychiatrist?" I asked, choosing to focus on who had blabbed my business instead of on his point. "And that was a long time ago. He's way more open-minded now," I fibbed.

"Sure he is," Bryn said with a patronizing smile.

"Mind your own business."

"I am."

"Uh-oh," I said, spotting the source of the music. A bunch of Bryn's neighbors were sitting in a circle with a woman dancing ballet in the center. She wore a form-hugging blue dress with a flared skirt, but her feet were bare. From the look of her, she was exhausted and one pirouette away from falling flat on her face. Standing behind the circled audience was a big woman in a ball gown, holding a very big gun.

"Come now, really leap!" she snarled. "We know you can do better."

Hellfire and handbags! First the Rodeo Snoopy Parade on my street. Now Shotgun Swan Lake. I sure needed to find a way to re-collect that darn dust.

"Bryn."

He nodded grimly and strolled up to them. "Cecily."

The woman with the gun spun and I jumped. She had thick streaks of gray through her rat's nest of tangled black hair, and her rouge looked like she'd finger-painted it on. When she snarled, her deep wrinkles formed a road map to the fiery hereafter, making me take a step back.

Her expression eased when she realized who it was. "Bryn, it's about time you got here. Join us. Push Charles out of his seat. He's been asleep for half an hour."

Bryn glanced around. The people in the chairs wore mixed expressions. Some looked plumb tuckered out, but some looked attentive and scornful at our interruption of the performance.

Cecily raised the gun barrel at the ballerina. "Miranda, did anyone say you could stop dancing?"

"Holy Cruella Duvall," I mumbled.

I recognized Miranda Castel. She had been a dancer, but she'd retired when I was about ten. Nowadays, she taught dance classes and helped my friend and hairdresser Johnny Nguyen Ho with the town play productions.

At Cecily's sharp voice and the angle of her twelve-gauge, Miranda let out a sob and started to dance again, tearing up her feet as she twirled on the asphalt.

I'd seen more than enough and opened my mouth to say so, but Bryn spoke first with his typical calm, which I felt defied the serious injustice of the situation. I supposed staying calm was smart, but it still made me want to punch him in the arm.

"Why don't we go into your house for some coffee?" Bryn suggested to Cecily.

"Decaf," I added.

"No. I am in charge of this production. For once, the casting will be perfect. Unlike when Mrs. Castel does it."

Good grief. This was revenge for some slight involving the volunteer theater? Some people really do need to get a life. If she wanted something to complain about, she should try getting shot by a poisoned elf arrow or having fireballs hurled at her until she had to park a car on the bottom of the Amanos River. *Then* she'd have something to get mad about.

Cecily swung the gun barrel skyward, so she could step closer to Bryn. "Your father is nearer to my age, but he's rarely around. And you do look so like him." She ran a finger over Bryn's jaw.

I wanted to punch her. In usual Bryn form, he didn't even blink.

"Let's go inside for coffee," he repeated.

"No. Not yet. I want her feet to bleed first." That did it! She started to turn as I charged forward. Bryn caught the gun and yanked it from her hands just before I rammed her. She stumbled back, and several people jumped angrily out of their seats, sending chairs toppling.

I tripped the closest man who rushed us, and Bryn turned and shot the stereo, which exploded to bits. He swiveled the gun back toward his startled neighbors.

"Everyone to his or her own house. Right now," he said.

The protests started low, but rapidly picked up volume.

"I'm calling my lawyer!"

"I won't stand for this!"

"You'll be disbarred!"

Men and women were shouting all at once, and I blinked at their vehemence and their gall. I saw Bryn shiver occasionally from the cold breeze, but the gun never wavered.

"That's enough!" I snapped. "Y'all should be ashamed of yourselves. Shouting like you're on reality TV. This is Shoreside Oaks, not some trailer park." Just as I expected, the insult to their dignity startled them into silence. "Mr. Lyons doesn't want to shoot you, but he will if he has to and a shotgun leaves a mighty big hole." I started pushing people to get them moving. "Go on now."

It was like herding cows, I thought as I circled and prodded them.

"Go on. Go inside your mansion and count your money," I said to the last man.

In the end there was only Mrs. Castel, sitting on the pavement, crying. Bryn and I went and got her up on her poor feet.

"I know just how you feel. Yesterday I skinned my feet something fierce. You know what though? Today they don't even hurt. You just need a good night's sleep. You'll feel better," I said soothingly as we walked her home. "And there's good news. Remember when you used to have to be a ballerina full time? You were one sandwich away from collapsing and couldn't eat it for fear of gaining an ounce? Not anymore. Tonight you can soak your feet and eat chocolate cake if you want. You'll feel a lot better."

She sniffled and rubbed the tears from her face. "Cecily's always been jealous. She lies about it. She says she wouldn't sink to actually performing, but that's sour grapes. She's a witch."

I bit my tongue to stop from saying Cecily shouldn't be lumped in with witches, since most of us are really sweet. "So you have any chocolate cake in the house?"

"No, but I have a gun. A twenty-two somewhere."

Oh boy. "How about ice cream?"

She pursed her lips thoughtfully and nodded. "Häagen-Dazs, strawberry cheesecake flavor."

"Yum."

"I do indulge in a bowl now and then."

"Tonight's a perfect night for it," I said. A thought struck me. My sweet tooth. Honey instead of gravy on biscuits. Powdered sugar on my toast. Chocolate chips in my pancakes from the time I was little. Momma and Aunt Mel never ate them that way. I even drank sugar water for hangovers. It was because I was part fae. Inside, I smiled. It was like I was a jigsaw puzzle that I'd never been able to finish, and Bryn had dumped a bunch of missing pieces on the table, so now I could fill in the empty spots and finally see who I was. It was more exciting than the new season of *Top Chef*.

I slid a glance toward Bryn, fighting the urge to plant a kiss on his brilliant, beautiful lips. Luckily he didn't catch me looking or who knows what Mrs. Castel would've had to witness.

Bryn opened her unlocked door, and I gently pushed her inside. I pulled the door closed behind her and looked at him.

"Should we go in and confiscate her gun?" I asked.

"If we make it our priority to disarm the neighborhoods, it'll take us all night. This is Texas, after all."

Despite the jigsaw puzzle triumph, I rubbed my eyes and shuddered. It was cold out and my clothes were dirty, wet, and stiffening against my body. "We probably should get the guns, but if I don't get a hot shower, I might start shooting people myself."

He nodded, and we walked the rest of the way to his front gate.

He pressed the buzzer and announced us. Steve, who was still working, bless his heart, let us in.

Bryn slowed his pace, looking around. I found I couldn't resist any longer. I caught his arm to stop him and gave him a quick fierce hug and a sound kiss on the cheek.

"What was that for?" he asked.

"None of your business," I said, which made him laugh.

I started toward the house. "You coming?" I asked as nonchalantly as I could manage.

He continued to smile at me. "In a minute. I'm going to check the wards on the property. You go ahead," he said.

I nodded and hustled myself up to the door just as Mr. Jenson opened it.

"Miss Tamara, is he . . ."

"Not cured, but he's okay for the moment. He's down by the gate. Mr. Jenson, as usual when I land on your doorstep, I'm a wreck. I need a hot shower and some more spare clothes. I ruined the heck out of these."

Mr. Jenson ushered me in. "You mustn't concern yourself with trivial matters. A good soak in a hot tub of water will put everything right."

I nodded, shuffling inside, leaving muddy, smeared footprints in my wake on the normally pristine tile. "You have any hot chocolate?"

"Naturally."

"Can I have some?"

"Of course you may."

My shoulders dropped with relief. "Mr. Jenson, will you marry me?"

He chuckled. "That would not be a very good match, considering our relative life expectancies."

"You've got me there. The way I'm going, you're sure to outlive me by a whole bunch of years."

28

AFTER MY SHOWER, I borrowed one of Bryn's white button-down shirts and some black leggings that one of his lady friends had left behind. There were no shoes to fit me, so I just borrowed some socks. I felt like a cross between a pajama ad and a cartoon ninja.

I asked Mr. Jenson where Bryn was and he said Bryn was already down in the library. When I got there, I found that Bryn had showered, too. He was dressed in a black bathrobe and was arguing with someone on the phone. I decided my socks were crooked and spent a few moments just outside the door pulling them up and straightening them.

"No one new to the craft could be expected to be ready for that at the end of a few days' training." He paused. "I don't care. I know what this is about. Let him challenge me outright," he said and paused again. "He's a coward and a prick, hiding behind the position he lied and cheated to get into." He fell silent a moment. "Yes, Andre, I know exactly how that sounds, but absolute tyranny inspires only two things: fear and rebellion. And unlike Barrett, I'm no coward." He put the phone down hard, and I crept into the doorway.

"How'd the eavesdropping go?" he asked.

"I was fixing my socks." I chewed my lip, then added, "I did hear a little."

He folded his arms across his chest.

"Was that about me? About my challenge?"

He nodded and walked around the desk to me. "There's no way you could get through it. It would take Class Three skills at a minimum. You've got the power, but not the control."

"Well, it's good that I didn't waste a lot of time preparing, then. I'll just fix the town's dust problem, then take off for parts unknown. I always wanted to see Graceland. Maybe I'll get a job at a restaurant in Memphis."

"They'd hunt you down."

I twisted my hands, pretending I was rubbing them for warmth instead of wringing them nervously. "What do you say I should do, then?" I said.

"Slip through a loophole in the law."

"I don't even know how to play fair, let alone how to cheat," I said, but I knew well enough that Bryn didn't bring up many problems that he didn't already have a solution for, so I waited.

"There's only one option I can think of. You and I have to bind ourselves in a commitment ceremony."

I felt myself flush as my mind conjured pretty images of candles, long-stemmed bouquets, and Bryn in a tuxedo. I slammed the brakes on my imagination, feeling a stab of guilt for taking it so far. He wasn't for me, and I knew that, but boy did I want him most of the time. "What do you mean a commitment ceremony?"

"It's a partnership where we agree to share magic."

That made it sound very businesslike, but things were never that straightforward between us. "I'm not going to be your apprentice."

He shook his head. "For you, this is a far better deal than that. It means I could legally face the challenge for you."

"And what do you get?"

He pushed a lock of wet hair back from my face and

looked me in the eyes. "I get whatever you decide to give me."

"What if I decide not to give you anything?"

He smiled. "Then it wasn't a good arrangement for me."

I wrinkled my nose, feeling as suspicious as a girl who's offered a diamond for a dollar. "You know what Zach's big brother, the smart businessman, always says? If a deal sounds too good to be true, that's because it is."

"Tamara, John Barrett wants you dead, presumably because he's worried about how powerful we'll be if we join our magic. Even if you don't completely trust what I'm proposing, you have to see that it's better than the alternative." He leaned close, his mouth near my ear, and whispered, "Elfin poison still courses through my veins because I refused to let you die. Doesn't that inspire trust? Tell me," he said, pausing. "What proof beyond risking my own life can I possibly offer?"

I shivered as the words danced along my spine. He was so good at doing that, at making me want him for better or worse, despite all the warnings. I wished I could trust him and have him on my side for always. Who wouldn't when he's all blue-eyed, brilliant, and buff, with years of magical experience? Yet there was the list and Edie's warning. How could I ignore those things?

I took a step back, staring into his glittering eyes. "I'm real grateful for your help, but I just can't. Not right now." I bit my lip. "Probably not ever."

He scowled in frustration. "Then you might as well take all the poison. There's no point in both of us dying. I'll be of better use to the town with my full power restored."

I swallowed hard, trying to pretend that his saying that didn't put a dozen cracks in my heart. I knew it was only fair, but, even so, it shocked me to pieces that he suggested it. Zach never would have. Zach had old-fashioned ideas about men protecting women. But this wasn't Zach. Bryn was more practical than sentimental. And, truth be told, that was exactly what the town needed.

"Okay then," I said with a tremor in my voice. I closed

my eyes and waited for him to kiss me. Nothing happened. And some more nothing happened. Finally I opened one eye. "What are you waiting for?"

"To come to my senses, so I can do this."

Okay, maybe he was a little sentimental after all. "Well, hurry," I said, shoring up my courage as I closed my eyes again and puckered my lips. I wanted to get it over with before I lost what was left of my nerve.

A bunch of seconds passed with my pulse pounding like a drum in my head. I realized I'd been holding my breath. I took a deep one, fighting off the trembling that started in my hands.

C'mon! He needed to get on with poisoning me so I could get back to the things I had to do before I died.

"Get out of here," he whispered.

My eyes popped open. "Can't do it?"

He shook his head, the edge of his mouth turning up in the kind of smile that says you wish you could find something amusing, but don't. I could've kissed him.

Bryn turned and walked to the window. While he looked out, I stared at his back, wondering what he was thinking and wanting to go to him.

Instead, I reminded myself that the town was falling apart so I'd better get my butt moving. Silently, I blew him a kiss and shuffled out of the study and then out of his house. Mercutio was waiting for me on the driveway, and he fell in step with me.

"Just you and me again, Merc."

He meowed.

"Yeah, it's for the best." *Even if it doesn't feel that way.*

29

STEVE DROVE ME to retrieve my car from the road near Macon Woods where it had been parked. I noticed that Earl's TrailBlazer was gone. Maybe the police had impounded it for evidence? They'd no doubt also seen my car. I wondered if they'd found any signs of Incendio.

I drove by Jenna's house, but all the lights were on and I could see shadows moving inside. Not the best time for breaking and entering. I needed those earrings, though, and I might have to go in while they were home, after they went to sleep.

Where the heck was Edie? I needed her help for such a high-risk, likely-to-get-caught proposition. I put my hand over Bryn's shirt and pressed on the locket through the material. Still there. It felt normal to me. So, why hadn't she come back? It looked like I was going to have to seek her out.

I drove across town to my hairdresser, Johnny's. He'd been a big help to me last week, and he was the only one in town besides me and my family who could see Edie.

I knocked on the door and hoped he wasn't out enjoying the pixie dust by disco-dancing or something.

"Be home," I whispered just before the door opened. Johnny Nguyen Ho is about five feet tall, as opposed to his vampire transvestite boyfriend who's about six and a half feet. They make a real unusual couple.

"Hi, Tammy Jo," he said with a smile.

"Hey there. How's your cold from last week?"

"Oh, it better now. Come in. How are you?"

"Great. Well, no, I shouldn't say that. I'm not great. I need a big favor. I'm real sorry to have to ask."

"Come in," he repeated, beckoning me.

He was always so sweet. I hated to take advantage of his generosity. Mercutio raced over to a row of hanging beads in the living room doorway from Johnny's Morocco-meets-the-sixties decor. Mercutio batted the beads, tangling them around his body. "Merc," I hissed.

"He okay. What you need, Tammy Jo?"

"I need to have a séance to get Edie here. She was supposed to get some information and report back, but she didn't. I called her, but I guess she didn't hear me. Since you've got experience with getting her to visit by having séances, I thought maybe . . ."

"I love to see Edie very much. I help you, no problem."

I gave Johnny a big hug.

"I get candles and music and prepare room for her."

"Where's Rollie?"

Johnny rolled his eyes. "He out teasing people. He say the town gone crazy, and it fun to watch."

I grimaced.

"I see what he talking about. My neighbors go naked swimming in the community pool. Mrs. Penelope is eighty-two. Very surprising that she join in."

The dust. Again. "That is surprising," I mumbled, following him as he gathered up the things we'd need.

About fifteen minutes later, Johnny had the spare room ready. Black satin sheets covered the walls and windows, and a midnight blue swath of velvet lay over the table, where five burning tealight candles ringed a grapefruit-sized crystal ball. When he closed the door, the room fell into shadow.

I edged up to the table and sat on a chair that was draped in velvet.

Johnny used a remote to start the stereo, which was hidden from view. The muffled sound of George Gershwin's *Rhapsody in Blue*, one of Edie's favorites, floated into the room.

"Now we put our hands here," Johnny said, placing his on the table so that they formed a *U* shape around the glass globe.

"Hang on," I said, pulling the locket out from under my shirt. I let it dangle over the table as I placed my hands so they mirrored Johnny's. Our fingers touched, closing the circle.

"Miss Edie, please visit us," Johnny said.

I waited, but he didn't say more. I glanced around. "Does she usually come straight off?"

"No, sometimes it take a few minutes. Be calm. Books say better energy."

"Oh. Right," I whispered, and then I tried like heck to relax, but that wasn't happening. My ears perked up at a sound until I realized it was Johnny humming along to Gershwin.

A few more minutes passed, then I felt a distinct rush of cold. The sheets slithered, and I strained my eyes, looking for a telltale orb or a glimpse of her.

The table rattled and uneasiness vibrated through me, frigid fingers of dread twisting my gut.

"What's happening?" I stammered. There was something in the room, but I'd have bet my eye teeth it wasn't Edie.

"I not knowing. Very unusual. It always quite peaceful when she come."

The crystal ball rocked and spun like a top. Smoke twisted into a tiny tornado, and icicles of fear stabbed my heart.

A gaunt face sneered at me. I shrieked and yanked my hands back. The globe careened through the air, slamming into the side of my head and causing an explosion of pain before it skidded off my skull and crashed somewhere behind me.

Too dizzy to keep my seat, I fell sideways off my chair, landing on a pile of pillows.

"Tammy Jo!"

30

A MOMENT LATER, the lights blinked on, and Johnny Nguyen leaned over me. "My goodness. You bleeding! Let Johnny help you."

"Did you see it? What was it?"

Johnny paused for a moment to shrug, then rushed to the door and flung it open. I pressed the heel of my hand to the place at the edge of my hair that was hot and wet. It throbbed, and I eased the pressure, feeling weak and sickly at the thought of blood dripping from my head.

It took about ten minutes of Johnny's ministrations for me to feel well enough to examine the damage. I stood in the guest bathroom with its swirled sable and lavender print walls and tried not to faint. I took the wet washcloth off and peered at myself in the sepia-and-gold-edged antique mirror. My cut was really small, about a quarter-inch long.

"That's not even bad," I chided myself.

"You have a knot there, too. You took hard knock to head. Maybe a concussion."

"That's nothing," I said, straightening my spine. Zach had walked off cuts three times that size before he even hit puberty.

"Why didn't she come?" I yelled at the ceiling. My head throbbed, and I decided I was done shouting.

"It okay," Johnny said, trying to soothe me.

I took a deep breath and rubbed my head. "I should've let you call her alone. It probably would've worked better."

"I try again," he said.

"No! Not with me here and not right away. Whatever was in that room might still be nearby."

"Later, then. Now we have chamomile tea with lavender. That relax us."

We both looked out the bathroom door at the sound of the main door opening.

"Hello!" Rollie called. "You should have seen them," he said, laughing. Then there was an abrupt halt to the sound coming from his general direction. "I smell blood."

He appeared in the doorway, towering into the room. He was dressed in a dark purple shirt and black jeans with a gold-and-mocha-colored scarf. He matched the decor and looked like a seventies rock star—lanky, dark, and tall, with fashionably hollowed cheeks and dark-lined eyes.

"Who's bleeding?" Rollie asked.

I hoped bloodlust wasn't going to turn him all vampy. Usually, he seemed to have pretty good control of himself. Except for that time he'd nearly drained my friend Georgia dry. My heart beat a little faster. Actually, I didn't really know Rollie all that well.

"Tammy Jo bleeding," Johnny said.

"What happened?"

"Magical mishap," I said.

"Ah, so the usual, then." He paused. "You must taste-test a lot of your confectionary creations."

"Why do you say that?"

"Your blood smells chocolaty."

"I've been meaning to cut back. Sometime when the trouble's over, give or take a few years. I mean months."

"May I have a lick?" Rollie asked and ran his tongue over his fangs.

His voice sounded all reasonable, but when a vampire

asks for a taste of your blood, it's like a tiger saying: "Let me see if your head will fit in my mouth."

I didn't like to be rude, but I still said, "No way."

"If I were baking, I'd let you sample the batter," he said. "This is mere professional curiosity. You know you're not my type."

My muscles tightened and twitched as I got more afraid by the second. I knew that for snuggling I wasn't his type, but he'd already proven by biting Georgia last week that he wasn't that discriminating about his human beverages.

"I didn't know vampires had a type when it came to blood."

"We do, but we don't always get to have our favorites," he said with a full-fanged smile. "I'll just have a little sip of you." He moved toward me, and I scampered into the shower, yanking the frosted glass door closed behind me.

"I said no!"

I could see watery images of Johnny and Rollie doing a little two-stepped weave and dodge through the door. Finally Johnny made a squeak of protest as Rollie picked him up and deposited him outside the bathroom. Rollie pulled the door closed and locked it.

Johnny protested, pounding loudly on the door.

I held tight to the shower door handle, knowing what a fat lot of good that would do me. I bit my lip, thinking I really needed to be better armed. I never had a nice, pointy wooden stake on hand for these meetings with Rollie.

"Come on, Strawberry Shortcake, just a little taste. You won't feel a thing."

He pulled gently on the door handle while I clung to it, leaning back with all a hundred and six pounds of me. Most days I was glad I never seemed to put on weight, but this wasn't one of them.

"Get ahold of yourself, Rollie! We're friends," I yelled.

"Exactly, and friends share," he said. "Imagine yourself as a fudge-covered caramel, a mocha-glazed truffle, a hand-dipped chocolate strawberry—"

My stomach growled. "Be quiet!"

"Could *you* really resist? I don't think so."

He yanked the door open, and I stumbled forward right into him, just as the regular door burst open and Johnny slammed into us. We landed in a heap in the tub.

"I think my neck's broken," I grumbled from my breathless, painfully twisted position on the bottom of the pile. I honestly don't know how Zach played football all those years without ending up suffocated.

"That good," Johnny said to Rollie, whose mouth latched on to Johnny's wrist.

"I make a little cut," Johnny explained as a drop of blood welled on his hand. Rollie's tongue darted out and caught it.

"Green tea, sweet almonds, and ginger," Rollie mumbled, then groaned happily.

"Get off me!" I snapped, thinking that blood-drinking ought to be one of those acts that people should be alone for, like making love, watching late-night cable, or getting a spiral perm.

"Come, Rollie," Johnny said, drawing the sinewy vampire away by the mouth.

"What did you hit the door with?" I asked, when I reached the broken door.

"Karate kick," Johnny said.

"Wow." I looked at Johnny as he proceeded down the hall toward his room. He's only about my size. "Next time I come over, can you teach me to kick like that?" I called.

"Oh, sure. Until then, work on getting legs in shape. Practice kicks."

I did a jabbing Tae Bo kick at the air.

"That okay, but for workout I like high kicks, like goddesses in blue and white."

"Huh?"

"Dallas Cowboy cheerleaders. Uniform optional."
Oh boy.

31

THE NEIGHBORHOODS WERE still going full tilt. There was some kind of eighties rock revival on Main Street, and people were drag racing. I grimaced at the sound of squealing tires.

I scanned my block for signs of WAM wizards, who I didn't want to see, and Imposter Abby, who I did. When I got out of my car, Jolene called to me from her front yard.

"Tammy Jo!" she drawled, giving *Jo* about five syllables more than it needs.

I stopped. "Yes?"

"There was a man looking for you. A good-looking, muscular man on a good-looking, muscular motorcycle."

Uh-oh. I looked around sharply for Incendio. "When was he here?"

"When? Hell, I don't know. Couple hours, give or take a couple hours. Anyway, who is he? And is he married or on the market?"

"He's a homicidal maniac, Miss Jolene. Stay away from him."

"So he's single, then?"

I sighed heavily and stomped into my house with Mercutio on my heels. "Well, I didn't want to do it, but we are out of options, Merc. I'm gonna have to call power from the earth and cast a spell. Might not work. Might even cause more trouble. But the universe isn't exactly giving us a lot of choices, is it?"

Merc purred.

"Exactly. None whatsoever."

I contemplated all the things that I needed to make right and wanted to include everything in one big superspell, but including a verse to help me steal the emerald earrings might be considered black magic and I didn't want that tainting the overall spell, so I decided to do my thieving the old-fashioned way.

In preparing for spell-casting, I needed to focus, so I lit lavender- and licorice-scented candles to cleanse my mind. I breathed deeply. I also knew it couldn't hurt to pray. After the werewolves, I hadn't really expected to have to ask for God's help again so soon, but considering how much trouble I was in, it didn't seem the right time to worry about being a pest.

"Hey there, God. It's me again. Tammy Jo. I guess You've probably seen what's going on here in Duvall, but in case You've been too busy with some other part of the world to notice, I have to mention that I've kind of brought on an accidental Armageddon down here." I paused. "Yep. Sorry about that."

I rubbed my scalp until it tingled. "Anyhow, I know You're real busy and all, so I sure don't expect You to clean up my mess, but, as usual, if You could guide me to whatever the right thing to do is, that'd be real helpful. Oh, and if You don't think I'm strong enough to do it all on my own and want to lend a hand, I'd sure grateful. Okay, thank You. Amen."

I went to the kitchen and pulled out a jar of minced garlic. I swallowed a teaspoonful, since it's supposed to be power-enhancing. Then I knelt down and started going through the cupboard. I'd read in my spellbook that black hollyhocks are good for power spells, and I knew that Aunt Mel had some oil she'd infused hollyhock powder into, so I searched until I found it in the back of the pantry. I dabbed it on myself and concentrated on focusing energy.

I needed to call power from the earth, but I didn't want to scald my yard the way I had the week before, so I planned to be real specific. I put on a dark purple bra and panties—yep, a power color—and went barefoot into the yard. Naked probably would've been more powerful, but last week's spell-casting in the nude was one of the things that had landed me in jail.

When I went into the yard, I left the sliding door open and Merc sauntered out. I marked the four corners with a paring knife, then poked my left pinkie and dripped blood onto the symbols.

I took a deep breath. It's possible that I'm not the world's worst poet, but I wouldn't bet money on it. And while I'd like to earn magical energy with a great spell, I wasn't above taking some pity power. I counted on the universe to recognize my sincerity and my desperation.

I took another big breath, blew it out, and cleared my throat. I dug my toes into the dirt, stretched my arms over the ground, and began:

Beautiful Earth, grow my power
Make it tall, like a sunflower
While you do, let prosper your plants
And every living thing, even the ants
Big bold Earth that I admire
Clean your air, make the dust retire
Use your wind and correct this town
For only you can flip my frown
You know that I don't like to meddle,
But that faery dust has got to settle
And while we're at it, the moment's come
To seal those doors so they aren't undone
No one really needs to come or go
Content in their own world, I just know.
Help me heal and protect the innocent,
And bring justice to the guilty, so they repent.
Thank you.

As usual I didn't feel a thing, so I had no clue if anything had happened, but I'd done as much as I knew how to do where magic was concerned. I went inside and washed the dirt off my feet. While I did, Merc came in and ate his tuna fish, which I was glad to see. Now more than ever we needed our protein. I had a quick BLT on toast and explained to Merc about stopping Jenna before she invaded Poland and how we had to have those earrings back if we were going to face flamethrowing Incendio.

Merc licked his paws, which I took as a sign that he was grooming himself for battle. I dug through the closet looking for the stuff I'd need to make myself ready, too.

"YOU KNOW WHAT I bet?" I asked Merc as I smeared some black grease over my face. Normally, it was for football players' cheekbones to stop the glare and stuff, but I decided it could be multipurpose.

Merc meowed.

"I bet that Jenna and her family are under the influence of the dust. I bet their house will be open, and I'll be able to stroll right in. And even if the alarm goes off, I think the police will be too busy or too dusted up to care. How's that for positive thinking?"

Merc looked at me like I was delusional. I waved away his skepticism while spray-painting a shower cap. Since I didn't have a ski mask and red hair's too conspicuous, I had to take steps.

I was glad I had the paint on hand from when I made stenciled signs to announce the bakery specials. After it dried—sort of—I put it on. I looked in the mirror and sighed. My head looked like a mushroom top.

Mercutio swiped the air as if I didn't know that looking like a fungus wasn't my finest fashion moment.

I took a deep breath and gave myself a once-over. Speaking of being blackened . . . between the oily shower cap and the face grease, I had a kind of glossy dark sheen to me. Except for being person-shaped, I looked just like a patent leather shoe. All I needed was a shiny silver buckle strapped to my poofy head. I sighed and looked at Merc. "If we get caught, I don't think I'll let them take me alive."

He yowled.

"Since Edie's got better things to do than to help me save myself and the town, I'll expect you to take her place as my lookout." I squatted down in front of Merc. "I'm counting on you. Like always."

Merc meowed.

"Thanks," I whispered. I pushed the yellow rubber dish-washing gloves into my pocket and stood.

Merc darted to the door, ready. I looked out through the peephole. I was surprised that the neighborhood was quiet. Thankfully, I didn't see Incendio. I wondered again why he'd killed Tom Brick and Earl Stanton. Had the murders been spontaneous acts of violence or planned ahead? And, if planned, were they done with the Conclave's blessing?

I opened my door and looked around. No witnesses in sight, so I crept to my car and we were off, sneaky as thieves in the night.

I had my window down and when I turned onto Jenna Reitgarten's street, the sound of a motorcycle engine made my stomach hit the floorboards. I punched my finger against the knob that works the car's lights. Driving down the dark street with my lights off was eerie. It added to my overall sense that I'm really not meant to be any sort of criminal at all.

I kept my white-knuckled grip on the steering wheel as I parked. Jenna wasn't as dangerous as a murderous warlock or a treacherous faery, but I knew I still shouldn't underestimate her ability to ruin my life if she caught me robbing her house.

The engine's roar faded into the night. I never spotted Incendio, but there weren't that many motorcycles in town. I squeezed my fist shut, trying to get my nerves under control. I sucked in a breath and blew it out. Merc, who never seems to need to compose himself, hopped out his open window and landed silently on the street.

I opened my door slowly, trying to be kitty quiet. After sliding out of my seat, I pushed the door closed with my hip.

I can do this. No problem.

I loped down the street, ducking to stay shorter than the azalea and hibiscus bushes that were conveniently located in rows at the fronts of Jenna's neighbors' lawns.

I studied Jenna's Georgian mansion for a moment. The stucco was the color of sand, with the central pavilion in white. I studied the tree limbs that hung near the right-sided second-story windows.

There were a few lights on downstairs, and the front door was partially open. Their Lexus sedan sat in the drive rather than in the garage, like they might be going out. A girl could hope!

I wondered if I could sneak in the front door and hide in a closet until they went to sleep or left.

I glanced at Mercutio. "If you made a diversion, I might be able to get in there and upstairs without them seeing me. It would be kind of risky for us, especially your part. I don't know if Jenna's husband, Boyd, has a gun, but he probably does."

I crept across the lawn toward the front door and was only a few feet away when it opened farther. I crouched down, pressing myself against the wall and hoping the nearby bush was tall enough to shadow Merc and me completely.

I heard Jenna's voice. "I don't care what his butler said. I'm already dressed, and I'm going over."

"The party's cancelled," Boyd said.

Cancelled! So Bryn must've decided he was too worn-out to play host after all. I didn't blame him, but I hoped calling off the party didn't mean that he was getting sick again.

"We're going!" Jenna flounced out in a billowy pink taffeta dress and crystal tiara that would have been the envy of any princess Halloween costume. Her fine blond hair had been teased into a puff pastry and shellacked with enough hair spray to fill the night air with the smell of it. "Bryn Lyons can't just cancel at the last minute," she said.

I frowned at the thought of Jenna being on Bryn's guest list. If the party hadn't been called off, Jenna would've been eating my desserts. I suddenly felt like part of the hired help. I pictured me and Mr. Jenson banished to the kitchen, making coffee while the likes of Jenna and her moneyed family got served from silver platters in Bryn's dining room. I felt a stab of jealousy that he'd invited her. I didn't want her in his house.

I chewed my lip, knowing it was silly to feel that way. I had no claim on Bryn's place and no right to decide who he entertained. But he was my friend—and sort of more—and she was my antifriend, who, for as long as I could remember, had treated me like something you'd scrape off your shoe. I didn't want them together.

"Boyd, let's go!" she screeched.

I blinked. Jenna was normally a pain, but she wasn't normally crazy. I whispered to Mercutio, "She's under the influence of the dust." *Which might work to our advantage.*

I hoped that they'd forget to lock their front door. I also hoped I could find our family jewelry fast because I knew that if Mr. Jenson had called everyone to cancel the party, Jenna and her husband weren't getting past Bryn's front gate. Security Steve would see to that.

Boyd stepped out, wearing a dark suit and a dark expression. If the dust had influenced him, it sure wasn't to put him in an overly festive mood. He pulled the door shut and locked the dead bolt. I frowned. I'm nowhere near as good a climber as Mercutio, but I was going to have to do my best.

As they drove away in their silver Lexus, I raced over to the tree and shimmied up the trunk. I crawled out on a limb in more ways than one.

I dangled there, using my foot to grab the sill. Sweat beaded on my face and trickled down my back. Luckily, the bark was rough and ridged, because the last thing I needed was to slip and fall, breaking my leg and getting found in the bushes in my Cary Grant *To Catch a Thief* burglar clothes and mushroom headgear.

I rocked my body until I had my lower leg through the

open window, and then I flung myself forward. I ended up in a half split over the sill, and I hadn't done the proper stretching for that tonight—or ever—and felt muscles in at least four places wrench in protest.

I grunted and pulled myself in. I flopped on the floor, trying to let my body get over the insult. I didn't care how risky it was; when I was done, I was leaving through the front door.

Merc did a limber ballet-style leap through the opening and landed next to me.

"Sometimes you really make me mad," I muttered.

He yowled softly.

"I'm just sayin'."

I dragged myself to my feet and put on my thick yellow gloves that could stop not only fingerprints, but any renegade bacon grease or other household contaminant that I came across. I turned on my little flashlight and hurried down the hall, poking my head in rooms. When I stepped out of a doorway, I shined the light and found Merc sitting near the door next to the stairwell.

Knowing what I know about Merc's sixth sense, I rushed to him and opened the door. Sure enough, he'd picked out the master bedroom. I slipped in. "How'd you know?"

He didn't answer. I guessed he was right about it not being the best time to talk. I went through the drawers, but didn't find my stuff. The tops of the dressers had silver-framed pictures, bud vases, and votive candleholders, but no jewelry boxes.

I looked down as Merc brushed my leg. I followed him around the bed and into the walk-in closet. There was a narrow-drawered mahogany stand with spindly legs. I pulled open the top drawer. *Jackpot.*

I found a plastic pouch with my wedding band and Momma's pendant. What I didn't find were Aunt Mel's emerald teardrop earrings that I needed to save my life against Incendio's attacks.

Oh, c'mon! I thought furiously. After all the trouble I'd gone through to rob the place, I deserved to find them.

I went through the drawers again one by one. "They're not here," I hissed, pocketing the pouch with Momma's and my jewelry. I got on the floor and looked around. Maybe they'd fallen on the carpet. I knew that Jenna wasn't wearing them. I'd seen her earrings when she was standing under the porch light. They'd been gaudy crystal chandeliers that matched her tiara.

I searched the closet, the master bedroom, and a couple of guest rooms. Then I saw police flashers. I flicked my flashlight off and crawled on my belly over to the closest window. With my nose touching the underside of the sill, I peeked out.

A deputy's prowler sat in the drive.

"Can you believe my luck?" I whispered. "Every last bit of it bad."

32

THE DOORBELL SOUNDED a doomsday clang, and I rolled onto my back while my heart tried to remember how to beat.

"It's possible we tripped an alarm," I whispered. "Maybe if we're quiet, he'll go away."

Then I heard more car doors and scrambled to the window to look out. Jenna and Boyd were back and talking to the officer. I couldn't see who it was, but I could tell from the roundish shape of the deputy's middle that it wasn't Zach.

I couldn't go out the window with them standing right below it.

"Come on. We'll make a run for it," I said, rushing out of the room. I bumped into plenty of things as I ran and knew I'd be bruised from head to toe later.

When I launched myself down the last few steps, I slipped on the tile floor and ended up sprawled in the entryway as the front door began to open. I scrambled up and dashed into the dark dining room, cowering behind some chairs.

Darn it to hell!

Caught in the middle of my first felony! What I dreaded

even more than jail was facing Jenna. She'd lord it over me, all smug and self-satisfied. To keep from going to prison, I'd probably have to apologize in court and say how sorry and stupid I was.

No! No way.

I heard them in the doorway and knew I should stay quiet and hidden, but my heart was pounding out of my chest, and I couldn't take it. I had to get out. Just as I scrambled around the table, banging into a chair, Mercutio raced out of the dining room.

For one moment there was silence, then shouting and screaming erupted. I should've tried to help him, but instead I went out the room's side door, through the kitchen, and flung open the back door. I shut it and ran, hopping over fences until I was seven yards away.

My thighs were cramping and my lungs burning as I cut back up to the street. When I reached my car, I collapsed against it, gasping. Then I dropped the pack under my car and tried to scrub the black off my face with my sleeve. I'd have to go back for Mercutio. I'd just say that he'd gone up the tree after a squirrel and jumped into their house through the open window. They couldn't prove I'd been inside. They couldn't prove I'd taken anything.

Merc meowed, and I nearly jumped out of my skin.

"You escaped!" I hissed, hugging his neck. I crouched, watching Smitty shine his flashlight around the front bushes of the Reitgarten house. I grabbed the plastic pouch. I opened my door and crawled in, not even minding the feel of Merc's claws as he ran over my back to get to his seat. I pulled the door closed gently and watched out the rear window. Smitty didn't flash the light toward us. I was glad I'd parked so far away.

I waited until he went into the house to start the motor. I slipped out of my spot and drove fast, but not too fast, over to my house. I was inside for about fifteen minutes and had just finished washing my face when my doorbell rang. I pulled on jeans, a T-shirt, and boots before I hurried downstairs.

I looked out and gulped at the sight of Smitty standing on my doorstep. We'd been friends until last week, when he'd arrested me. Bryn got me out of the charges, but I still hadn't forgiven Smitty. Plus, I knew why he was here, and there was no way I was giving our jewelry back to Jenna. My ring and Momma's pendant were safely upstairs in the false-bottomed drawer, and that was where they were staying whether I got locked up or not.

I tucked my cell phone and my wallet in my jeans' pockets. I could go out the back door and climb the fence, but I doubted he'd had time to get a warrant, so running felt premature, especially to my muscles, which were ready to mutiny if they didn't get a break.

"Go hide, Merc," I said.

He cocked his head at the door for a moment and then darted up the stairs.

I pulled the door open and tried to look innocent. "Hey there," I said in my sweetest "welcome to Duvall" voice.

"C'mon," he said, grabbing my arm and hauling me out. He pulled my door closed, before dragging me down the steps.

"What are you doing?" I demanded.

"You're coming with me."

"You have a warrant?"

"Nope," he said.

"Well, we both know how it worked out for you last time you took me in without one."

He yanked open the prowler's back door and shoved me inside.

What the Sam Houston!

"Smitty, you better let me go," I said as he wedged his bulk behind the steering wheel.

"Shut up!" he snapped. "I don't care what friends you got in high places now. *My* friend's sitting in a cell 'cause of you, and you're going to see him. Never thought I'd see the day you'd turn into such a disloyal bitch."

I blanched and pressed my body against the seat, drawing back from him. "What are you talking about?"

"You know, Heather said she saw this coming when you went to work at that hoity-toity restaurant in Dallas. Thought you were too good for all of us. Just biding your time 'til you could move on."

Shock and confusion turned into fury so fast that I hardly had time to be speechless.

"Smitty! What are you talking about?" I couldn't believe his wife, Heather, was saying bad stuff about me behind my back. I'd been a bridesmaid for her. Maybe the dust was working on their minds.

"I'm talking about Zach sitting in a jail cell, covering for you, while you're shacking up with Bryn Lyons."

In a cell? How and why? I opened my mouth to ask questions, but Smitty cut me off.

"Oh, yeah. We been staking out Lyons's house. We've seen you coming and going from there."

Those son-of-a-guns! While the whole town was melting down, the Duvall deputies had been watching Bryn's to figure out if I was having an affair with him?

Smitty went on throwing accusations at me, but I couldn't make heads or tails of what exactly had happened, so I finally yelled at him to shut up.

My cell phone rang, and I pulled it from my pocket. Smitty glared at me in the rearview mirror. I guessed he didn't like his preaching interrupted.

I flipped it open. "Hello?"

"Good evening. Jenson here. We need you to return to the house."

"Is—somebody sick?" I asked, not wanting to say Bryn's name with Smitty listening.

"He's suffering from chills again. We have turned the heat up to eighty degrees, but it doesn't seem to be having the desired effect. More importantly, he's asking for you."

"So he's awake though. That's good," I said. "Well, I'd like to be there, but I'm kind of tied up."

"Miss Tamara, I would like you to know something."
I waited.

"He never asks for anyone." He paused. "Not ever."

I sighed. "I get what you're saying, and I'll be there as soon as I can. Promise."

"How long do you expect that will be?"

"Well, I'm locked in the back of a police car, but I'm hoping I can sort things out at the station pretty quickly."

"I'm sorry about your misfortune and the inopportune timing of it. Well, do hurry, if you can."

I flipped my phone shut.

"Who was that?"

I folded my arms across my chest. "None of your business. Hurry up and get me to the station so I can find out what's going on with Zach. And if you've got him in a cell, you sure better have a good reason because like you said, I've got friends in high places now."

Smitty snorted. "Like Lyons would help Zach. Getting Zach out of the way is just what the guy wants." Smitty shook his head. "You know, I get what Lyons is after. And Zach's easy enough to figure, too. But I don't get you. You've got to know that a fling with Lyons is only ever gonna be that. The guy's way out of your league." Smitty pointed his finger at me in the rearview mirror. "You should use some sense. You're gonna ruin what you and Zach have for nothing. Then when Lyons moves on to some Dallas debutante, you'll be crying in your beer. And don't expect Heather to be there to comfort you. She's disgusted with you, just like all your friends are going to be when they find out."

My cheeks burned, but I clenched my teeth to keep my mouth shut. I didn't have a choice about needing Bryn's help. Not that I could tell anyone that. And not that it was their business.

Plus, I wasn't going to badmouth Zach to his friend, but he'd been hell on wheels when we were married, staying out all night drinking with his brothers. And he'd made me see a shrink. Even if I had been crazy, that jerk Chulley wouldn't have been the right doctor for me. So yeah, I might not be the perfect ex-wife-turned-girlfriend, but Zach hadn't been the perfect husband-turned-ex either.

I folded my arms across my chest rebelliously. Besides,

why would I look to Smitty for advice on good judgment when he was taking me in without a warrant? That was how he'd ruined his case the last time he'd arrested me.

"You got anything to say?" Smitty asked.

"Yeah. My cat would make a better deputy than you."

33

I MARCHED INTO the station and brushed past the desks to get to the holding cells. Sure enough, I found Zach inside the far cell. He was in the middle of it, doing push-ups. On a normal day, watching Zach work out is better than cable, but ogling was strictly a leisure activity, and I didn't have time for it.

"Hey," I said.

He stopped halfway down to the floor and then finished before standing up. Sweat dripped from the dark blond curls closest to his face and neck. He walked to the sink and ran water over a hand towel. He rubbed it over his face and hair before dropping it in the sink.

I waited at the bars for him, aware that several of the deputies had stopped working to watch us. I looked over my shoulder at Smitty.

"Open the cell. I want to go inside to talk to him."

"It ain't locked," Smitty said.

My eyes went wide. With a push, the door swung open. I went in and stood near the bunk.

"So what's going on? How'd you end up in here?"

"I took the Fifth Amendment a lot," Zach said.

"Oh. How come?"

"Somebody claimed they saw you kill Earl Stanton, but I said you weren't there when he died."

"How would you know?"

He smiled grimly. "That's what they asked, which is about the time I exercised my constitutional rights." He cracked his knuckles idly. "Been under arrest ever since."

I frowned. The Fifth Amendment said a person didn't have to answer police questions if the answers could be incriminating. In this case, by saying he knew I didn't kill Earl and then taking the Fifth, Zach was as good as saying that he'd either killed Earl or had been there when it happened.

"We told him that if he's lying, it's a damn fool thing to do, seeing as you're the last person who needs protecting, shacking up as you are with a slick lawyer and all," Smitty said.

I winced and waited for Zach to blow up at me or Smitty or both. Instead, he walked away, pulling his T-shirt off. He rinsed it in the sink and wrung it out.

"I could use some clean clothes. Smitty, why don't you give Tammy Jo my keys, and she can run on by my house for me."

"Hell, Zach, any of us will do that for you," Smitty said.

"Nah. She knows where everything is. Unless you're too busy?" he asked, glancing pointedly at me.

I was way too busy for any errands that didn't involve saving Bryn, the town, or my own behind, but this was Zach asking after he'd laid it on the line to protect me . . . again. I shifted uncomfortably. I wanted to be there for Zach, but there was no way I could desert Bryn either.

"I'll get whatever you need." *Later.* "But first come here, so we can talk," I said quickly. I wanted to move the conversation along.

He studied me for a moment before he joined me again. I leaned close and could smell sweat and him underneath it. It reminded me of kissing him after his football games, and my body tightened. I couldn't believe myself. I guess I couldn't help the effect Zach had on my hormones, but it felt really wrong at the moment.

"I hit Earl in the head with a rock," I whispered in his ear. "It was self-defense. I heard that somebody burned his body. I didn't do that, but I think I know who did."

I leaned back to gauge his expression. It was like we were in the middle of a poker game. He could've been holding aces or nothing at all.

I inched closer and put my mouth by his ear again. "You weren't anywhere near the woods last night. I want you to tell the truth."

He rested his hand on the back of my neck. My skin came to life the way it always did when Zach touched me. "A witness says you lured Earl into the woods, hit him when he was distracted, then poured gasoline on him while he was out cold and burned him alive."

I shuddered. "That's not true! Who said that?" I whispered furiously.

"He messed with you. Lot of people know it. Some of 'em heard you threaten to kill him."

I balled my hands into fists. If I'd killed Earl by accident, well, that was pretty much his own fault. But it sure wasn't fair for somebody to say I premeditated it and killed him on purpose. Who would say something like that? Jenna came to mind. Did she hate me that much? Maybe. But she hadn't been there.

"Well, the sheriff will know that's a lie because there wasn't any gasoline on him," I said.

"Sure there was."

I blinked. "What do you mean?"

"Just what I said."

I leaned back to look at him. He nodded.

I'd assumed since Earl had been burned that Incendio had come back and set him on fire over some argument. I thought about Mr. Brick. No gasoline there. Incendio didn't need it, and I couldn't imagine him slowing down a killing to use it.

I studied Zach's face. What if Zach *had* come to the woods? If he'd gotten there just as I knocked Earl out, would he have killed Earl after I left? No, he would've come after me, to make sure I was okay, and dealt with Earl later.

But what if Zach had somehow found Earl dead and saw some long red hairs on him? Would Zach have burned the body to get rid of evidence that might have tied me to Earl's death? Without a doubt, he would have.

His hand still rested on the back of my neck. Everything about him was calm. Either he hadn't burned Earl up, or, if he had, he didn't have an ounce of remorse over it. I leaned close to him.

"Did you burn the body?"

"I'll have to take the Fifth on that."

"You can tell me. I'd never tell them if you did."

"I know that, darlin'."

But I sure might tell them that he didn't, if he admitted to me he was innocent. Zach probably knew that. Of course, he also might have done it and didn't want me to mentally share the blame over things.

"Who said I killed him?" I demanded. Several heads turned to look at us, and Smitty walked over.

"A little girl. Abigail Farmer," Zach said in a low voice. *The hell you say!* I pounded my fist on my thigh, ready to call her every bad name I knew and then some. But spewing curses at what the deputies thought was a child wouldn't go over too well.

"It's not true," I snapped.

"I know," Zach said.

"She was pretty convincing," Smitty said.

I clenched my fists to keep my fingers from popping a gesture at him that I might regret. Good little witness! More like the wolf in Bo Peep's clothing. For all I knew she was centuries older than all of us!

My head spun from too much fury and frustration, and I slumped back against the wall as I contemplated her. Had she burned Earl's body? She could've. Whether she'd burned the body or not though, she certainly knew that I hadn't done it. So on top of being a child kidnapper and attempted murderess, the Abigail imposter was also a dirty little liar. I began to see why Bryn didn't care much for faeries.

34

SEVERAL DEPUTIES TOOK calls and hurried out of the station, mumbling about how the darn town had lost its mind. I fidgeted, anxious to go myself.

In a low voice, I said, "If you didn't do anything, I want you to tell the truth. Will you?"

"If I told them I wasn't there, guess who they'd arrest next?"

"The person that Abby fingered?" I offered.

He nodded.

"Well, can you tell the truth first thing day after tomorrow? I need a day to put things right." *And if I can't by then, I'll be dead of a wizarding challenge, so it won't matter if the police get a warrant to arrest me.*

He folded his arms over his chest. "Just one day, huh? Guess straightening your life out doesn't include working things out with me."

To explain everything would take hours, and I knew he'd never believe me anyway. Plus, Zach never really was that big on talk. I reached out and squeezed his hand. He didn't intertwine our fingers or lean toward me, so I knew the calm way he was acting was just a cover-up for how mad he was underneath. It made me unhappy, and my heart told me to talk things out with him right then, but my head said there wasn't time. Also, I was starting to doubt that Zach and I even stood a chance if he wasn't going to believe me about the supernatural stuff being real. Funny how I'd just accepted his refusal in the past, but couldn't anymore. I knew on some level that was because of Bryn.

I let go of him and smoothed my jeans. "We can talk tomorrow."

He put his damp T-shirt on. "Smitty, you guys could use some help out there. Ain't no use me sitting in a cell. You know I'm not leavin' town. I'll face the magistrate when the time comes."

"Why don't you change your statement?" Smitty glanced between Zach and me.

"Nope, but we'll get it all sorted out eventually," Zach said.

Smitty scowled at me, and the dispatch phone rang again. He glanced at Zach. "We *could* use the help," Smitty said with a slow nod. When he went to answer the phone, Smitty purposely turned his back.

Zach swung the door wide and stepped out. He grabbed his cowboy hat from a hook near his desk and settled it on his head.

When we got outside, Zach said, "I wondered how long it would take you to come looking for me. Seein' as Smitty dragged you in here, I guess I'll never know if you'd have come at all."

"I would've come. I was tied up."

He looked me up and down. "So I heard."

Guilt washed over me, and the breath caught in my throat, burning there. He yanked the door of his truck open and climbed in.

"I would've come," I repeated. My tone was soft, and I wasn't sure he'd heard me as the motor started. I didn't say it again though. I understood why Zach hadn't called me. He'd been testing me. He believed that people's actions stood for them. Like him taking the Fifth so they couldn't lock me up. And he'd stuck to that story even knowing I'd been with Bryn. Zach didn't have to say the words to tell me he still loved me and would keep his promise to protect me no matter what happened. I was the one who was changing. There had been a time when, if I hadn't known where he was, I would've looked all over town for him. The fact that I hadn't tracked him down in jail meant something, and he and I both knew it.

I swallowed the lump in my throat and squeezed my hands tight as he drove away. It hurt me that I was hurting him. We'd been in love so long that losing him would be like losing a part of me. As the dust settled, I chewed on my lip for a moment. Our relationship needed sorting out. But whatever was going to happen with me and Zach would wait, because it had to.

WITH THE OTHER guys gone, Smitty couldn't leave the station, and he wouldn't have agreed to drive me anywhere anyway, so I started hurrying toward Bryn's on foot.

About half of the businesses along Main Street were closed, and a lot of them had broken windows, like folks had been looting. When I got to Magnolia Park, I spotted some deputies who seemed to have fallen under the dust's spell. They sat at a picnic table playing checkers while people broke plenty of sensible park rules, like the one that said you couldn't have target practice there with real guns.

I got to the edge of the park, keeping my head down and walking in the shadows. Then a bright orange-gold light nearly blinded me. It was like a sliver of sunshine that started on the ground and rose to pierce the night sky.

I cocked my head, peering at it. From out of the light, a spear tip thrust at me. I jumped to avoid it, which made me fall. It missed my skin by a hair. I scuttled backward like a crab and saw a second spear, big as a harpoon, come through and wrench back and forth. The light widened, offering me a glimpse of a monstrous creature with a long pointed face and straggly hair the color of milky charcoal. His mouth formed a snarl, and he snapped his pointed teeth at me.

"Seelie! I'll pick my teeth with your finger bones," he said.

I gasped.

"Open it. Wedge it open!" he cried, and I saw some dirt-smudged hags behind him. They had thin gray hair and hooked noses, and their long warty fingers poked knives and spears through the opening. They levered the blades back and forth, and I realized they were trying to pry the seam between our worlds apart.

Oh my gosh, no!

For a moment, my body went rigid, then I stood up, knowing that I couldn't let them come through the gate. I scrambled over to one of the guys who'd been shooting and snatched his gun.

"Hey, what are you doing?" the guy demanded, but I darted away to the opening and pointed the gun at the faeries.

"Go back," I said.

A blade whizzed out and poked through my jeans, nicking my thigh. I ignored the sharp pinch of pain, stepping back and squeezing off several rounds. The bullets went through the crack, hitting their mark, but none of the fae fell. And none of them bled.

Don't our weapons hurt them?

I dropped the gun and grabbed a spear, yanking it. A hag's hand came through the opening after it, but the seam clamped down on her wrist. She howled and let the weapon slip free of her grip. I flipped the spear around and thrust it through. It banged against the breastplate of the leader and slid off, striking a tall goblin who brandished a serrated iron blade. My spear's tip cut through his muscle into his chest, and he fell hard, levering the spear up, so it lifted me off the ground. My sweaty palms slipped down the metal, and I slid toward the rift—and toward the weapons jabbing through it.

Rather than be skewered, I let go of the spear and fell to

the ground. The leader yanked my spear free from the goblin's body, and it dripped greenish gold blood.

"Tomorrow the doors will open!" the leader announced.

The rest of the creatures cheered, and he glared at me.

"And we'll boil the Seelie witch in oil and feast on her flesh," he shouted.

I shuddered and took a step farther back. "You stay on your side!" I stammered.

The leader laughed and, as they receded from the seam, it contracted into a single beam of light.

"Making friends?"

My heart contracted painfully, and I spun to find Jordan Perth.

Uh-oh. My body went rigid. I wasn't sure whether he was furious with me and would act on that, but I decided to pretend we'd never had a standoff outside town.

"We have to reinforce the doors between worlds or the faeries will get through," I said. "I tried to do it, but my spell obviously didn't work."

"Not surprising. It's an upper-level skill, and your casting talents are, thus far, nonexistent."

I bristled, but knew he was right. "That's exactly why I need magical help."

"We have something to settle first."

He didn't look mad at the moment, so I decided it was probably best not to ask how his wand was after I'd thrown it out the car window.

He glanced around at the dust-crazed people in the park. "Come with me," he said.

"I don't have time for this," I said. I needed to get to Bryn. Not that I could admit that to Jordan.

"Then hurry," he said, cutting into the woods that separated Magnolia Park from the tor.

I needed whatever magical help I could get, so I went a couple feet into the woods after him. "Here's far enough. What do you want to talk about?" I demanded.

"You have to make a decision. Tonight. Right now."

"What?"

"Bryn Lyons has broken the law and will be held accountable. You, however, still have a chance. I can influence the Conclave to postpone the challenge if you prove that you intend to be a law-abiding witch, one who is loyal to the sacred order of magic."

I studied his face. He looked completely sincere.

"Listen, you must believe me," he continued. "Lyons is not your friend. He wants to use you for his own ambition, and the things he intends . . ." He shook his head violently. "He intends to usurp power from the lawfully chosen leaders, and you'll be a pawn in his attempt. He controls a faction, an underground network of terrorists, who are being hunted and eliminated for their crimes. You must disavow any association with him. To do that will save your life and will gain you the World Association of Magic's favor. In exchange, I'll help you rescue your town."

"Is that why you're really here? To keep me from getting involved with Bryn? Was the challenge going to be too hard for me to face alone so he'd be forced to intervene or let me die?"

"I came here to train you. Nothing more. But I can't ignore what I've seen. Lyons has sealed his fate with his own actions. Not that his treachery is a surprise. We've suspected for some time that he's a traitor. We just couldn't prove it until now."

"He helped me when I needed it. *Because* I needed it."

"Only to gain your trust. So that he could use you later."

"You don't know that," I said. There was no way I could know Bryn's motives for things, but I doubted he'd risk his own life for the chance to use my power later. Seemed too risky a gamble.

"You must swear fealty to John Barrett through me," Jordan said.

I blinked. "I don't even know John Barrett."

"He's wizardom's rightful leader. To swear an oath to us is to swear an oath to the magical world order," he whispered fiercely. Bright spots colored his cheeks, and I knew he believed what he was saying. "Anything but absolute loyalty is an endorsement of anarchy. It's high treason. You must not be a party to that."

He grabbed my hand and pulled it toward him. "It's a blood oath," he said breathlessly. "It only takes a few words and a few drops of blood. It'll be over in seconds." He pulled a case from his pocket and withdrew a silver pin.

"No," I said, snatching my hand back in shock.

"You have to pick a side, and you have to pick the right side to survive!"

"That may be, but I don't make promises to guys I've never met. If that makes me a rebel, well, that's what I am."

"You've met *me*. You should trust me. I've been trying to help you from the beginning."

"You have been partnered up with Incendio, who's going around killing people."

"Maldaron is a loose cannon, but don't let that influence you. He was an effective enforcer for several years, but he can't overcome his nature, can't overcome his tendency toward rage. The things he's done here . . . The Conclave will deal with him, once and forever."

"Then I'll wait to see what they do about him."

"There isn't time. You have to choose now."

"I can't," I said. Before he could react, I turned and rushed out of the woods.

I'm not sure if the cracking sound I heard was Jordan throwing spells at me or gunfire from the park, but I didn't look back. I ran as fast as I could and bobbed behind as many big trees as got in my path.

With every step, I knew that I'd made my choice. I just hoped it was the right one.

By the time I reached Bryn's gate, I could barely stand. My muscles cramped and sweat beaded in the hollow of my back as I leaned my whole body against my finger on the buzzer.

"Yes?"

"Steve, it's me," I said, gasping for breath.

The gate opened, and I shuffled to the door. While I waited for it to open, I fought the urge to fall to my knees. I was so darn tired.

The wind whipped my cheeks. I shivered, looking around the yard. It had an eerie cast to it, but I couldn't put my finger on what was wrong. The carefully positioned floodlights were all lit, showing off the sculpted flowering bushes and trees. But leaves blew across the path with the skittering sound of insects, and I broke out in goose bumps. Everything looked right, but felt wrong.

When Mr. Jenson opened the door, I nearly fell inside. "What's happened?" I asked. I braced my weight against the wall, feeling heavy, sluggish, and exhausted.

"Mr. Lyons is—"

My head snapped up, so my eyes could see Mr. Jenson's face. I had heard something tremble in his voice. Sorrow. Heavy enough to squeeze the air from my lungs.

"What?" I said, clutching his arms.

"Please sit," Mr. Jenson said, motioning to the settee in the alcove.

"Where is he?" I demanded, my eyes darting around. "Is he worse?"

Mr. Jenson's gaze slipped to the stairs. "Rest for a moment." The lack of urgency made my blood run cold.

I'm . . . Am I too late?

No!

He reached for my arm, but I rushed past him as Steve hurried toward us. I flew up the stairs.

"Wait!" Steve shouted, pounding up the stairs behind me.

I didn't hear what else he yelled. I ran to Bryn's bedroom door and flung it open. I launched myself inside and would've hit the bed, if I hadn't been yanked back by Steve's arm.

Bryn lay pale, blue, and very dead.

35

"NO!" I LOST my mind, screaming so loud it hurt my ears.

I pounded on the arms that held me, thrashing and kicking my legs, trying to get free. Trying to reach the bed where he lay.

"Let me go," I yelled.

"Don't cross it!" Steve snapped and dragged me out of the room. He slammed the door closed behind us and dropped me. I sank to the floor and sobbed.

"He's not dead," Steve said.

"Don't lie! I saw him."

"It's a spell. He said he'd cross over early, and that you could bring him back."

Tears ran down my face as I leapt up. I tried to get around Steve, but he shoved me back.

"Let me try, then. Get out of my way!"

"Wait!" he shouted.

"What?" I stammered, gulping my sobs down.

"There's a circle. He said you shouldn't cross it until you were ready. He said he won't last long when you pull him back over, that you need to have a cure first or he really will die for good."

"What cure?"

"I don't know." He took a deep breath and steadied himself. "He left you some stuff." Steve started to step away from the door, but then stopped.

"What?"

"You won't go in, will you?"

I felt numb, and my voice sounded hollow when I answered. "Not if he said not to." I leaned against the wall, shaking like tissue paper.

"Miss Tamara, come downstairs. I've made you a cup of tea," Mr. Jenson said.

I walked woodenly down the steps and into the kitchen.

"I didn't know. I didn't know he was so bad," I said, the tears starting to trickle again.

Mr. Jenson didn't answer. I sat at the table and watched him pour two fingers of whiskey into the tea. I took a gulp.

"I should've taken the poison back. I should've done it when we had the chance. I was scared and selfish and stupid." I drained my mug. "It's all my fault—"

"Miss Tamara," he said sharply. "Please calm yourself."

Tears streamed as I set down my cup. "Sorry, Mr. Jenson. I'm just—" I shook my head, and my heart ached like I'd never thought it could for anyone that wasn't Zach.

"Mr. Lyons noticed the difference in the way the poison affected you. He said he cast a spell to deal with the elf poison, but since he didn't recover, he felt there must have been a second poison tainting the first. One that affected him more than it affected you."

I fisted my hands in my hair. If there was a second poison, how was I going to figure out what it was?

Steve walked in and dropped a duffel and a sealed manila envelope on the table. "These are for you."

I unzipped the duffel and stared down at the gun and crossbow. There were about three dozen arrows and two boxes of ammunition. I opened one of the boxes and saw strangely fancy bullets. They were engraved with magical symbols. I lifted one to get a better look. "Iron," I said. "They're made of iron."

I set the bullet into the box and closed it. I lifted the envelope and ripped it open. There was a folder full of papers. Several sheets contained lists of herbs, metals, stones, crystals, and symbols, along with their exact counterparts. Another page was a copy of the spell he'd cast to suspend himself. Lastly, there was a note to me. At the top, in fancy black script, it read, "From the desk of Bryn Lyons."

"His penmanship is generally much better, but he was suffering from chills and lethargy when he wrote it," Mr. Jenson said.

I blinked at Mr. Jenson and gave him a skeptical look that I bet conveyed what I was wondering, namely whether he had lost his mind. As if I'd think less of Bryn because his cursive wasn't pretty while he was dying.

I raised the note and read it with a thumping heart.

Tamara,

I wanted to talk to you in person, but I couldn't hold on long enough. I'm certain there's a second poison that I can't identify. The faery who shot you will know the ingredients, but she won't tell you easily. I leave it to you to convince her to part with her secrets.

You're the only one who'll be able to pull me back from the Valley of Death spell. Unfortunately, the spell will only suspend me until the sun sets again, so time is, as ever, the enemy.

My life is yours to save,
Bryn

Oh my God. I felt sick with fear. I put the tip of my thumb in my mouth and chewed on it, staring at the page. Finally, I rattled it.

"What was he thinking? How could he do this? He knows a lot of smart witches and wizards. How could he put something so important in my hands when I never get anything magical right?" I shook the paper hard like I'd shake some sense into it. "It's crazy," I hissed.

After a few moments, I dropped the note and smoothed it out. I glanced at Mr. Jenson. "He was so desperate he had to leave things to me. God help him," I whispered. "Maybe he thought there wasn't time to call someone in, but he should've tried. I'm sure someone can get here. Lennox or—"

"He didn't want anyone else," Mr. Jenson said.

I stared at him.

"He chose this plan. I asked him if he was sure. I told him that the police had you and that even if you were released, perhaps you would not be capable of accomplishing all of this, given your lack of experience."

"You're right! He was out of his mind with poison when he decided to rely on me. Why didn't you talk him out of it?"

"I assure you he was quite lucid when I expressed my doubts. And do you know what his response was?"

I shook my head.

Mr. Jenson's voice was soft and sincere. "He said, 'I know her, Jenson. She'll find a way. I have faith in her.'"

If it was possible for one sentence to make a heart soar and break at the same time, that one did. I slapped my hands over my eyes and broke down again. I felt too much all at once, overwhelmed that he believed I could save him and scared that I wouldn't be able to. Lots of people had loved me in my life, but nobody ever believed in me more than I deserved, except Bryn. He had always taken me seriously as a witch.

I just plain couldn't stand the thought of him leaving the world because of me . . . because he'd taken poison meant for me and because I wasn't experienced enough to save him. There was a part of me that knew I'd never be the same if he died.

"I need another cup of tea," I said in a wobbly voice. I rubbed my eyes with the heels of my hands. "Okay. Okay," I repeated, nodding. "This is no time for us to fall apart." I slapped my fist in my palm as Mr. Jenson poured more steaming tea in my cup. "Steve, I bet you're tired of working all these doubles, but you have to be sharper than ever. With him gone, there's no protective magic on the house. And there are a couple of wizards in town who, if they figure that out, will waltz right in to take advantage of it. Also, make sure that the sprinkler system's working and that you have fire extinguishers handy. And weapons. Mr. Jenson, you have to guard his body."

They nodded. I sucked my tea down, burning my tongue something fierce. I stood. "I have to pick up my cat. And I'll need a car. Mine's at my house, and there's no time for me to walk home."

"I understand from Mr. Lyons that the Mercedes can't be recovered," Mr. Jenson said.

Since it was at the bottom of the Amanos River, that was true enough.

"Have you ever driven a limousine?" Steve asked.

"Oh, sure, that's my second car. I have the Focus for every day, but a limo for state functions and bakery deliveries."

The three of us looked at one another, and Steve smiled. Then Mr. Jenson did, and finally I managed to. It was that or break down crying again.

A few minutes later, I washed my face and shouldered my duffel full of weapons. I took a deep breath and blew it out as I followed Steve to the side drive where the sleek black limo waited.

He gave me a few tips like "Try not to crash." Then he handed me the keys.

I shook my head as I tossed my duffel in and sat down in the driver's seat. My head was swirling with all the impossible stuff I had to do, so the only thing I could focus on were bits of irrelevant details, which I guess is why I asked, "How much does one of these cost?"

"More than you'll probably make in twenty years."

"Thought so. The insurance is all paid up, right?"

Steve nodded with a half smile.

"I'm not planning on crashing," I added. *But you just never know.*

36

BACK IN MY neighborhood, Imposter Abby's door was wide open, so I went in. The normally tidy house looked like a twister had hit. There were wrappers for Zingers and Oatmeal Creme Pies everywhere, along with empty chocolate milk cartons. Bits of laundry, magazines, and jewelry littered the floor.

I clutched my loaded crossbow and climbed the stairs, stepping over books, papers, dishes, cookie crumbs, and two half-empty honey bear bottles. I did a thorough search of the upstairs, including under the beds, in the closets, and in the bathtubs. Wherever she was, it wasn't home. I tried not to let my frustration overwhelm me.

I thought about exchanging Bryn's limo for my own car when I finished searching my neighborhood, but I didn't want to leave the limo unattended, since the streets were full of people who seemed to think that Mardi Gras had come early.

At my front door, I had to push back some palm fronds that needed a trim in order to get inside. I found Mercutio sitting in the front hall, waiting for me. I explained about Bryn being mostly dead and depending on me to save him.

I ate a couple of Hershey's Nuggets and cocked my head as Merc put his paw on the back door. Could Abby be hiding in my very own yard? Like a supernatural purloined letter? I peered out, but it was too dark to see anything. I grabbed my crossbow and readied myself, then I slid the door open and was knocked back into my living room by a branch. I landed hard on my backside and banged my head on the couch.

"What the Sam Houston?" I gasped as more foliage spilled in, along with half a dozen hobgoblins who were hanging from wandering vines. A six-inch goblin hit me over the head with a cabbage rose, sending blush-colored petals everywhere.

I regained my feet and leaned out to flip on my backyard light. I gaped. It was like a garden that time forgot. Totally overgrown and stuffed full of flowers, bushes, trees, fallen leaves and branches, sprites, goblins, and a few small bats.

Uh-oh.

"When I said to let the plants prosper, I meant protect them! Let them be healthy and grow normally. C'mon, Earth! You know what I meant," I complained, huffing with the effort of trying to push out the branches and vines so I could close the door.

My cell phone rang, causing me to give up on the losing battle. How was I going to save Bryn when I couldn't even handle the plants in my own yard?

I dropped the phone when I realized that more goblins had swarmed over the crossbow and had levered it up against a branch to point it at me.

As I jumped over the end of the couch, I heard the *whump* of the arrow puncturing cushions.

"Hey!" I yelled. "I can't afford a new couch." I marched over and yanked the crossbow up and shook it. They fell off and pulled out their spears.

"No, you don't!" I rushed to the kitchen with the bow tucked under my arm and grabbed my broom. I swept them furiously out the open door.

"And stay out there!" I scrambled to get my phone and

flipped it open while still standing guard with the broom. "Hello?"

"Tammy Jo, it's Johnny. How are you?"

"Kinda busy. How are you?"

The second wave of goblins rushed me, and I had to bobble the phone to sweep them out.

I recovered the phone. "C'mon, Merc, we have to get out of here." I rushed to the front hall. "Sorry, Johnny. I dropped the phone. What's going on?"

"Oh, lotta thing, Tammy Jo. First neighbors get into big fight. They bleeding and Rollie bite one or two."

"Are they alive?"

"Yes."

"Well then, no real harm done," I said. Normally, I have strong feelings against vampire bites, but chaos called for different rules. "Maybe try to lock him in the apartment or better yet, maybe he should leave town until things settle down."

"That the next problem. We try to leave. Can't go."

"Why not?"

"I don't know. Cannot get out of town."

I stopped at my front door. "What do you mean? What happened?"

"Car just stop at county line. Engine running, but it not go. Other cars and trucks stuck, too. Run off road into ditches and onto grass trying to leave. Cars just can't—"

For the love of Hershey.

"Rollie say it some kind of magic. It like someone put a big circle around the town."

I cocked my head. Who would've closed a circle around the town? Bryn was incapacitated, so that left only Jordan and Incendio to cast big spells, but why would they? They might trap me or Bryn inside a circle around the town, but the townspeople and a vampire?

"I say to Rollie that I not understand what he talking about. He say it definitely witch magic, and it like somebody closed an invisible door."

My stomach somersaulted, and I sank to my knees as the

blood drained from my head. "Oh my God." *No one really needs to come or go. Content in their own world, I just know.* My messed-up magic. Again. I clutched the side of my head as my mind reeled.

"So we all trapped. That why I called. Can you come pick us up?"

I shook my head at Mercutio and mouthed, "Big trouble!" To Johnny I asked, "Why don't you just drive home?"

"Well, that the other problem."

I put a hand to my sweating forehead. "What other problem?"

"The plants eat my car."

"What?"

"The bushes and vines wrap around the BMW. All we see now is one tire."

Holy Lord. I slid down the rest of the way to the floor.

"Tammy Jo?" Johnny said.

"Uh-huh."

"You come pick us up?"

I panted and tried to keep from passing out. "Yeah," I said weakly.

"Okay, hurry. It a real jungle out here."

THE POUNDING STARTED immediately after I hung up. I grabbed my crossbow and leveled it at the door before I pulled it open.

Jenna Reitgarten glared at me and shoved my crossbow aside, trying to wedge her twiggy body in between me and the door frame to get into my house. I was in no mood to have my home further invaded, especially while spears were still flying at my back from hobgoblins who needed sweeping.

I gave Jenna a good shove and followed her out.

"Aha!" she yelled, pointing at Mercutio, who joined us on the step as I closed the front door.

"I knew it!" she said. "I knew that cat was yours. He was a distraction while you robbed my house. I want my jewelry back."

"I don't know what you're talking about."

"Yes, you do! You know damn well. The ruby and the ring."

I slapped a hand over my mouth in mock shock. "They were stolen? I'm so sorry to hear that. What about the earrings? Did the thief get my aunt's earrings?"

She raised her chin smugly. "No, as it happens I sold them for three times what they're worth and got a promise that the buyer would never sell them back to you or your family. He was only too happy to agree to those terms."

"What buyer? Who was it?"

"Wouldn't you like to know?"

Yes, I would. I waited a second, thinking she might be overcome with the urge to brag further, but she didn't let anything slip.

Instead, she ignored me and grabbed my door handle, trying to turn it. As it was locked, it refused to open. She turned and glowered at me with wild, beady eyes.

"Earl arranged the sale. Come to think of it, that's probably why you killed him," she said.

I was about to deny that, but a wisp of pale green silk caught my eye as it shimmered under the streetlight. I stepped over the multiplying vines on my steps to get to the sidewalk and narrowed my eyes.

The green silk scarf fluttered behind Imposter Abby as she skipped down the street.

"Merc," I said, to be sure he saw her. I glanced over and found that he had already darted through the tall grass, which now reached midcalf, and was in pursuit. When she saw him, she screamed and bolted.

I pushed past Jenna and ran like a ten-year-old after an ice cream truck. "Catch her!" I yelled.

I saw her run into Charlie Buckland's house and slam the door. Merc went up a tree, probably planning to jump through an open window, but there weren't any. He was back on the ground by the time I got there.

I tried the door, but she'd locked it. I banged on it for a moment and got no answer, so I looked around to see if anyone was watching. Naturally, someone was; Jenna had followed me.

"Merc, go distract Jenna," I whispered.

He glanced at her and then at me.

"Go on!" I whispered in a hiss.

He sauntered over and snarled at her. She yelled at him and at me, but when he leapt forward, she retreated. I took the opportunity to bash in a window with my crossbow. They sure are handy.

I cleared away enough glass to climb through the window into the dark front room. A musty smell had me wrinkling my nose as I peered around. The shadows swallowed everything, and my heart thumped, telling me light would be good since we knew Imposter Abby was deadly despite being small.

"I know you're here. Come out. I just want to talk to you."

She didn't answer, and the hair stood up on the back of my neck, trying to convince me to go back out the broken window.

Life and death. Bryn. The town. You can't lose her.

I kept my crossbow in front of me as I slid along the wall, hoping to bump my back into a light switch. My thigh rubbed against a piece of furniture, and I stepped around it. I was getting close to the front door. I was sure there would be a switch there, and I could open the door for Merc.

Just a little farther.

I heard the cracking sound a moment before I felt the pain in my head.

37

WHEN I WOKE, I was facedown on the carpet with Mercutio licking my cheek. My head throbbed, and I squinted as a face appeared next to mine, owlish eyes blinking.

I tried to draw back, but I seemed to be stuck to the floor, and trying to move made my head and my side hurt. I realized that the face was Charlie Buckland's. He normally wears a suit and tie to his accountancy job, but he seemed to be wearing a rainbow tie-dyed shirt at the moment.

"Dude, what happened to you?" he asked.

"Is that a marijuana cigarette?" I mumbled as he raised it to his lips. He took a puff and offered it to me.

"Want a toke? Go ahead. We'll call it for medicinal purposes, dude."

"Real sweet of you, but no thanks. Why are you talking like that?"

"Trying to get back to my roots. California. The Haight, man, good times."

"What is all this?" I asked, flicking bits of colored flakes off my hands.

"That's potpourri." He ran a hand through spiky, uneven

hair that was clearly a "do it yourself" haircut. Johnny would not have approved one bit.

He said, "Looks like you or your cat knocked over the pewter bowl and spilled it all over the place."

The sudden pounding on the door startled us both. I tried to push up, but couldn't, feeling a sharp pain in my side.

Charlie hurried to the door. "Shit, it's your ex, the cop! Man, I can't deal with this."

"What?" I asked as he fled the room.

I heard Zach's voice outside the broken window. He said, "I am going in. Keep your beads on."

Who's he talking to? Jenna? She wasn't wearing beads, I thought hazily. A few moments later, I saw Zach's boots.

"What in the hell?" he said.

I felt him raise my shirt to look at my back and then I felt something sharp skim my skin.

Suddenly, I could move, and I rolled onto my good side. Zach clutched one of my iron arrows in his hand. My blood stained the tip, and I curled to look at the spot on my side that burned. A bloody groove had scabbed over where the arrow had grazed me on its way to pinning my shirt to the floor.

I picked up the pewter bowl and saw blood on the edge. "She hit me with this," I told Mercutio. "But I guess I'm lucky, all things considered. She could've got me a lot worse with that arrow. Good thing it was dark."

"Who shot you, Tammy Jo?" Zach asked.

I looked around. "And she stole my crossbow! Lousy little thief." My head spun and I swayed. I grabbed my head and tried to steady myself. "Wow, I think one concussion's gonna be my limit from now on." I thought I might throw up so I lay back down.

Zach touched my face. "What happened?"

"I need help. Will you?"

He nodded.

"Abby Farmer. I've got to find her. I know she looks all cute and sweet, but she's a bad seed. I'm telling you. I've got to get my hands on her. Lives depend on it."

"Whose lives?"

"Mine for one." I hedged on mentioning Bryn because I didn't feel that would be properly motivating for Zach. "Or if you don't want to help me find her, I've got other stuff that really needs doing. Like Johnny Nguyen Ho and his friend need to be picked up." I struggled back to a sitting position, rubbing my temples. "I wonder if Charlie's got any aspirin."

I wobbled, and Zach caught my arms to steady me. I said, "You know what? My house is only a few houses away, and I've got aspirin myself." *And my gun with the iron bullets.* "Will you help me up?"

Zach was really quiet. Too quiet given that I'd been hit in the head, shot with an arrow, and now claimed that a child was to blame for it all. Not cross-examining me was very un-deputy-like, but I wasn't going to complain about it.

He stood and picked me up.

"You don't have to carry me. I just need an arm to lean on."

He ignored my advice and walked over to the door, shifting my weight so he could open it, and then walked out. He looked over his shoulder.

"You comin', Spots?" he asked Mercutio.

Merc padded along behind us. I rested my head on Zach's shoulder and closed my eyes, trying to conserve my energy.

"Hey," Zach said, jostling me. "Don't go to sleep."

I heard the worry in his voice and knew I had to reassure him. I was banged up plenty, but I sure wasn't planning to waste time in a coma.

I opened my eyes and offered a weak smile. "I'm okay. I'm just real tired."

"I'm not surprised. It's four thirty on Halloween morning and you haven't been to bed. Seems like you've had a rough night—hey," Zach snapped, looking down at his leg. Merc was swiping it with his paw and then pushed it with the top of his head.

"Mercutio wants us out of the street," I said.

Merc yowled.

"Now!"

Zach jerked forward, and the world twirled like a merry-go-round. I groaned and grabbed my skull as a car two feet from us burst into flames. For a split second, I spotted Incendio behind the blaze.

If it'd been me, I would have been frozen to the spot, but Zach's got reflexes I can only dream about. He flung me over his shoulder and ran across the street. I felt us fly over a row of bushes, and a couple seconds later I was lying on the grass behind a hedge. Zach was next to me on one knee facing the street with a gun in his hand.

"That's the biker? Maldaron?" he asked.

"Yeah. How do you know his name?"

"We can't get to my truck." Zach's gaze darted toward my place a couple houses down. "That's Lyons's limo over there. You have the keys?"

"On the bureau in the foyer." I rolled onto my side and threw up, which made my head feel like an exploding Fourth of July bottle rocket.

I panted and gagged twice more. Then, except for the headache, I felt better. I sat up.

"If you keep him covered, I can make it to the house."

"Hang on," Zach said, rising up to look.

"Look out!" I yelled as a fireball blew through a hibiscus plant. Zach tumbled backward, slamming into a tree. I stumbled to him and smothered the flames that left big, charred holes on his T-shirt and jeans.

He coughed as I pried the gun from his fingers. I spun around and popped to my feet. It was a split-second decision. I could see Incendio's eyes glowing in the darkness. I dropped the barrel slightly and squeezed the trigger.

I saw his leg jerk, and he toppled with a howl. I dropped down and crawled back to Zach. He peeled off his shirt with a hiss of pain.

"Did you hit him?" he asked.

"I fired a warning shot."

"You missed him on purpose?" Zach frowned, regaining his feet and his pistol.

"No. Fired a warning shot into his thigh. Next time it'll

be his head!" I shouted, hoping that Incendio would take the hint and go someplace that wasn't Duvall.

"How far away was he?" Zach asked, pulling me by the arm toward my house.

"About forty feet."

"You always were a helluva shot."

A huge fireball lobbed over us and landed on my front sidewalk. "Hey!" I complained. "Gimme back that gun."

"C'mon," Zach said. We ran across Jolene's lawn to my door. I opened it, and we fell inside. I slammed the door just in time to escape another fiery blast.

A wave of hobgoblin warriors rushed down the hall toward us.

"Oh, no, you're not," I yelled. I grabbed the broom and swung it, sending them sailing through the air.

"What in the hell?" Zach said, just before the front windows exploded.

Fire licked the walls, and I cried, "My house!"

Smoke billowed around us. I grabbed a fire extinguisher and sprayed things down as best I could.

"Get the keys. Let's get out!" Zach yelled.

I snagged them, and Zach pulled open the door. There were flames outside, too.

"Just a second," I said, coughing, and ran to the living room.

I pulled the throw blanket from the couch and tossed it over us. Zach had grabbed the extinguisher and pointed it forward. We rushed out, spraying foam as we went. We reached the limo, and Zach flung the flaming blanket off us as I climbed in. He pushed me to the passenger side. Mercutio hopped in and landed on my seat with me.

Zach started the limo. I spotted Incendio about fifty feet away. He was leaning against a tree. He stretched his hand out and flames ate up the space to the car. Zach swiveled the wheel, and the fire hit only the front bumper.

We careened down the middle of the street, passing Incendio and a lot of burning cars, trees, and bushes. If he didn't stop, my neighborhood would be toast, but I knew that once I was gone, Incendio would probably leave, too.

I hoped people weren't asleep in their houses. I reached over and blasted the horn. I watched some lights flip on at the end of the block. A limo's a pretty expensive fire alarm, but it'll do in a pinch.

My hand slipped off the horn to Zach's chest, and I felt blisters. He'd gotten second-degree burns from Incendio. Fierce anger rocked my body, and I was sorry I'd only shot Incendio in the leg. Next time, I might decide to do things differently.

Zach brushed my hand away from his chest. "Don't touch it."

"Hurts bad?"

"Bad enough. You all right?"

"Right as rain," I mumbled, thinking that there were only about two inches of my body left that didn't hurt, and I didn't have high hopes for them staying pain-free, all things considered.

I rubbed the top of Mercutio's head, and he licked my face. "We have got to find Aunt Mel's emerald earrings. That's the only way I'm going to survive his fire magic," I said to Merc. I was past trying to shelter Zach from the truth. If he thought he was hallucinating everything, that was his problem. But to my surprise, he didn't yell that the town had been poisoned with LSD, and he didn't claim that magic didn't exist.

Instead, he said, "The earrings you pawned?"

"Yep. Jenna Reitgarten bought them, but then she sold them back to Earl. And Earl was going to sell them to someone else or did sell them to someone else." I remembered the night that Earl attacked me in the woods. Incendio had been there. Had he been the buyer? Boy, that would be lousy luck.

"Turn here," I said, pointing. "I want to pick up Johnny and Rollie."

Zach turned south on Hickory like I asked. I found his

silent obedience really weird. Zach had seen Rollie dressed up like a lady, and it had shocked him down to his country-bred bones. Zach might have lived in Austin for two years, but he wasn't what you'd call cosmopolitan.

"What's going on with you?" I asked.

He glanced over at me. "What do you mean?"

"I mean, you're sure taking this 'flamethrowing foreigners, town's come unhinged, and Zach's been in jail' day like it's touch football in Magnolia Park. Why is that?"

"What should I do, darlin'? Have a fit?"

"No, but I just figured you'd be tryin' a little harder to make sense of things and tryin' a lot harder to get control of them."

"Well, it's been a long few days, and it's going to hell despite what we deputies have been doing. Since there's another nineteen hours of Halloween, I decided I'd better pace myself." He gave his head a slight shake. "Especially since whatever's gone wrong with the town is affecting me now, too."

"You're seeing things you can't explain, and this time you don't think you've been drugged?"

He shrugged, frowning. "I honestly don't know anymore," he said.

A thrill roared through me. He was starting to believe! It could change everything for us.

"Listen, we can talk about—" I stopped speaking when the limo's headlights lit up a sight you don't see every day. I cocked my head.

A second later, Zach asked, "What was the name of that man-eating plant in *Little Shop of Horrors*?"

38

"THIS IS *SO* not what I had in mind," I grumbled as we got out of the car.

The bushes, vines, and trees had engulfed the road and the deserted cars. The foliage climbed over itself, roots tangled together in hopeless knots. The enormous green mass looked about the size of a two-story house.

Johnny Nguyen Ho was on top and hanging upside down. His head and arms were trapped in an azalea bush that had grown sideways from the branch of an oak tree, and his legs were entwined in vines of climbing roses. Hundreds of blooms choked every bit of space, making it look like he was sprouting flowers.

"Johnny!" I called.

"Tammy Jo, help," he said as the vine wrapped around his head.

"Do you have a knife?" I asked Zach.

He pulled a huge serrated hunting knife free from his belt. I stared at him.

"Sh—someone told me I might need a big knife. We'll talk about that later."

"Give it to me," I said.

"Tammy Jo, hurry! I not breathe well."

I looked up and saw Johnny struggling against the vines that were winding around his throat.

"How am I going to get through there?" Zach muttered, moving closer to several massive sago palms whose fronds whipped from side to side like the spinning brushes of an automatic car wash. Except the fronds were sharp enough to slice through flesh. "I'll ram the car in closer and then climb out the sunroof with the knife," Zach said and tucked it back in the holder on his belt.

"No. Give me the knife. This is my doing and I'll fix it."

"I don't think so."

As he sat back in the driver's seat, I grabbed the knife and pulled it free. I dove to the ground and crawled under the fronds on my belly. There was an opening behind them. If I could get inside, maybe I could climb to Johnny.

"Tammy Jo," Zach yelled.

I ignored him, trying to think up a spell to help me. It would probably go wrong, but a nuclear holocaust in the middle of the plant explosion could only be an improvement:

> Make this knife aim true
> And help me to cut through.
> Let me save my friend,
> And let this nightmare end.

My heart hammered as a tangle of vines and roots twisted around me. Honeysuckle had my right leg and morning glory, my left.

Zach yelled my name again.

"Yeah, I'm okay," I lied. I hacked at the plants, muttering, "I command you to turn me loose! Right this instant."

They ignored me, but Zach's knife was Texas-sized, and I did my share of damage. I got to an oleander tree and hugged the trunk to pull myself to a standing position.

"Your cat's going right over the top!" Zach called.

"Good for him. This is his territory. Let me know if he gets Johnny loose."

"Come on out of there before you get hurt," Zach said.

I felt something grab my knee and was ready to give it a fast slash, when I noticed the odd white color.

Spindly fingers! Rollie!

"Lemme go, Rollie. I'll free you."

His fingers released me, and I climbed up onto a branch. Vines wrapped around my waist and torso like an organic corset. It was a little hard to breathe, but it anchored me so that I could slice through the thick canopy over Rollie. It was so dense that it was like sawing through a pineapple, but finally I punched open a small square.

Rollie grabbed my branch with both hands and pulled himself up. He tore through the canopy and I saw his head, which was wrapped like a mummy's in green leaves. I heard clumps of dirt raining down as he uprooted himself.

I cut the ivy that had stuck me to the branch, and Rollie ripped the vines away from his mouth and eyes.

"You know," he snapped. "Landscaping is hell. This is exactly why I live in a condo!"

"We have to get to Johnny," I said, pointing upward through the green mass.

"Let's go," Rollie said, dragging his body onto my branch. "Hold your knife over your head," he said.

Suddenly he hissed and retracted his lips so I glimpsed his fangs. He sliced through the vines around us, spitting out strands as he did. He created a small space for us to maneuver and then grabbed me and lifted me above him, propelling me through the din. I hacked and climbed the rest of the way to the top.

The canopy was as thick as a hammock, and I lay across it on my belly to reach Johnny and Mercutio. Merc had clawed the vines around Johnny's neck to help him breathe, but had left bleeding scratches.

"Stop, kitty. Stop now," Johnny garbled.

I carefully sliced the remaining vines from around his

face and chest and was gratified to hear him take in a big gasp of air.

"Rollie trapped below," Johnny said.

"I know, but since he can't suffocate, let's take care of you first." I climbed along Johnny's small body to his legs. The roses smelled sweet as perfume as I hacked them to bits. When I got him unbound, Johnny tumbled free and we both rolled backward end over end. We fell off the canopy and landed hard on the roof of the limo, which Zach was driving straight into the grabby green tangle.

The car's engine revved, but it didn't make any forward progress. "Back up!" I yelled through the windshield. I didn't want the plants to get around the limo and us.

Johnny and I each grabbed the upper edge of the hood where it met the windshield and held on as Zach backed up sharply.

I slid across the slick hood, but managed not to fall off as Zach came to an abrupt stop. I caught my breath and rolled to the ground, spitting out bits of Texas bluebonnet. Rubbing my aching muscles, I watched Merc spring off the canopy and come down a tree trunk, nimble as a . . . well, as a cat. Determined, I stood and squared my shoulders, pointing my knife straight out, ready to charge back in to free Rollie.

I got only two steps before an arm circled my waist, stopping me. Zach had come around that car like a shot.

"Lemme go. Rollie's still in there."

"Girl, you nearly gave me a heart attack." He pried the knife from my hand. "I'll do it."

"But I've got the hang of things now," I said.

He ignored me and strode toward the teeming mass of foliage. Just as he got to the sugar maple tree, a snapping sound alerted us to Rollie's escape. He tore through the lunatic landscape like the Hulk through his T-shirt and britches.

Rollie glanced down and brushed himself off, then he sauntered up to the car.

"Are you all right?" Rollie asked Johnny.

Johnny nodded, and Rollie hugged him. "I told you it was dangerous! If God had wanted us to live in the jungle, He wouldn't have invented concrete."

"I know, but I thought I see Edie's green light circle, and Tammy Jo and I are looking for her. It my duty to check."

"That ghost, missing again," Rollie said with a roll of his eyes, then he glanced at the car. "Nice limo. Or it used to be." There were two dents shaped like Johnny and me on the hood and a bunch of scratches to the paint on the sides where the fronds had done their worst.

"Rollie, is it true that vampires can't be out in the sunlight? 'Cause it's almost dawn," I said.

"I'll be fine behind tinted windows," Rollie said, climbing into the back. "Come on, lover," he said to Johnny.

When Johnny was inside, I closed the back door before turning to Zach.

"Thanks for coming to find me tonight and for bringing a knife," I said. "I couldn't have saved Johnny without it."

Zach nodded. "Yeah, that was something. Seems like if you'd had your own knife, you wouldn't have needed my help at all."

I heard the edge to his voice, but I had way too many monsters left to battle to waste energy fighting with a human being, even one I liked to fight with as much as Zach. I blew the hair out of my eyes. "I need help, but it's maybe not the kind of help I used to need."

"Meaning I'm not the one to give it?"

Exactly. "I didn't say that." My nerves were unraveling like a sweater with a snag. "Don't go putting words in my mouth," I said, opening the passenger door for Merc to hop in.

I couldn't let Zach distract me. Bryn's life still depended on my finding a certain churlish changeling. And my duffel bag full of iron ammunition was at my house. "Can you drive me back home?"

He shoved his hands in his pockets. "There's something I need to talk to you about," he said.

"I bet there's more than one thing." I joined Merc in the

passenger seat. "Can we talk about it while we drive? I'm sure that Incendio will have left my neighborhood by now, but Abby Farmer will probably still be around there. It's real important that I find her."

He sighed. "Are we just gonna talk to her or are you planning to add kidnapping to the list of things they can charge me with?"

A ripple of anticipation went through me. He was going to help me get her? Or maybe he was just kidding? I hoped not. It wasn't fair to tease me when my hours might be numbered.

"Well, I really couldn't say at this point, Zach. These days, I'm kinda flying by the seat of my Levis."

"So I noticed."

"No one said you had to come with me," I pointed out.

"Right, but I'd hate to miss all the fun," he said wryly. He gave me a sideways glance, and his voice softened. "You know how I feel. If you wanna get rid of me, you'll have to tell me to go."

I leaned toward him and planted a kiss on his cheek. "I don't want you to go."

39

I ROLLED DOWN the divider to check on Rollie and Johnny. Rollie was sleeping like a six-and-a-half-foot-tall baby, curled up on the cushioned bench. Johnny sat on the seat that had its back to mine and Zach's. Johnny turned his head to look at us over his shoulder.

"Hi there, Tammy Jo. What you and Deputy Sutton like to drink?"

"What have we got?"

"We have bourbon, whiskey, Coke. Orange juice, fizz water, no-fizz water, and vodka."

"Coke, please. Zach?"

Zach shook his head.

"Hungry? Light to dark, we have: macadamia nut, cracker, cashew, olive, caviar."

"No thanks," I said, taking my Coke.

"The car is stocked with caviar?" Zach said, shaking his head.

"Well, it a limo," Johnny pointed out with a wave of his hand. "But sadly, no milk for kitty."

"Sorry, Merc," I said, taking a swig of Coke. "When we get home, if we've still got a fridge, I'll get you something."

"What is this? A tea party?" Zach mumbled.

"Action heroes gotta eat," I said, unperturbed.

As Zach turned onto my street, the sun rose, letting us take in the full aftermath of Incendio's block party. Five burned-up cars. One partially burned front porch. And several charred trees, which I was sure to hear about from the hobgoblins.

When we got to my house, there was no sign of Incendio. We all climbed out of the car except Rollie. Zach kept his gun handy as we looked around. The front was scorched, the door and windows gone, and the smell of soot was strong enough to choke a smoker.

"I need to see how bad it is," I said, swallowing the lump in my throat. It was just starting to hit me. Incendio had destroyed my home. The place I'd grown up in.

The hall and living room were wrecked, and so was part of the kitchen. I spotted the duffel, but was too shaken to retrieve it. My gaze fixed on the blackened, warped pictures on the walls and the ash that used to be keepsakes and knickknacks.

My eyes swam in tears.

"It okay, Tammy Jo," Johnny said, putting an arm around my shoulders. "I help you redecorate. It going to be okay."

"Thanks, Johnny." I sniffed.

I glanced at Zach, and he held out a hand to me. I moved to him and let him fold his arms around me.

"C'mon, darlin'. Don't cry. Johnny's right. We'll rebuild it, and you can turn it into Marrakech or Bangladesh or whatever strikes your fancy." Zach kissed the top of my head.

"Don't be ridiculous," Edie said.

Edie! Finally!

I whipped my head around to find her standing in the hall, staring at the burned walls. "Some things cannot be replaced. The vintage black-and-whites of the Brooklyn Bridge, of my parents' Park Avenue apartment—those were one of a kind."

"You're here!" I said, wiping my tears away. "I've been so worried. Where have you been?"

"Oh, have you missed me?" she said, her tone light as meringue, but tart, too, like the lemon filling under it. I guessed she was mad at me for letting the house get burned, but maybe if she'd been around to help me, it might not have gotten that way.

I squared my shoulders. "Well, I have been having a lot of trouble. I wish you would've checked on me. You promised to come back with information," I accused. I shot a glance to Zach and froze. He was looking at Edie. *Directly at her.*

"What's . . . What's going on?" I asked.

Edie glided forward and stopped in front of me. "I've been *trying* to see you! About a hundred times a day. I couldn't get through. Someone cast a spell to keep me from reaching you."

I blinked. "Why would they do that?"

"They?" she echoed.

"Jordan and Incendio."

She shook her head. "*They* wouldn't. Incendio's a one-trick pony. Fire. That's his entire repertoire of powerful magic. And Jordan Perth? He couldn't contain a summer breeze, let alone a spirit of my resonance." She glanced at the nails on her curled fingers like she was interested in the state of her manicure. "Let's see?" She buffed her nails against her dress. "Who else in town do we know that can do complex spells? Someone powerful, who always has to get his own way?"

"He wouldn't have done that."

She fixed her beautiful almond eyes on me and raised her thin black brow. "He would and did. The only reason I can be in your presence now is that his spell has failed. I don't know why. I suppose he had to cast something complicated that required all his focus, so he couldn't afford to expend the energy blocking me anymore."

He wouldn't have, I thought helplessly.

Except the spell to keep her away from me had failed just when Bryn's magic ceased to exist because he'd gone into a death coma. A big coincidence. Too big.

The back of my throat burned, and I bit my lip hard to stop myself from tearing up again. How could he have done something like that? She was my family. I took deep breaths, squeezing my hands into tight fists, trying to concentrate on anything except the way my heart hurt.

I felt like I had when he trapped me in that circle. Like a fool. My muscles tightened until they ached. Did he think I wouldn't find out? That it wouldn't ruin our friendship? If so, he'd been wrong. Terribly wrong.

And his life was in my hands. I could decide to help him . . . or not.

Johnny wandered away to straighten the furniture. His tidying up was a lost cause, but I didn't say so. When I finally got my emotions under control, I turned to Zach.

"How long have you been able to see Edie?" I demanded.

He shifted his weight and looked uncomfortable. "I thought I might have seen her on the night I almost died."

"You've known all this time! And you were going to send me to Chulley?"

"No!" Zach put his hands out as if he could use them to ward off my fury. "I thought I imagined her that night. Then she showed up again and kept talking to me . . . It was long after we skipped dinner at TJ's. She didn't appear until after I got out of jail. I thought my guilty conscience was playing tricks on me."

"I suspected that he'd seen me on the night of the werewolf battle," Edie said. "Once a human sees a ghost, the connection between them is forged. When I couldn't break through Lyons's infernal spell, I remembered that. I went to Zach's house and lingered, talking to him rather incessantly. Finally, he told me to go away."

"Which she never did," Zach said grimly.

"A lucky thing for you both," Edie said. "My spirit friends keep me informed. Zach wouldn't have known to look for you in Charlie Buckland's house. You would have stumbled out onto the street, and Incendio would've killed you." She floated over to Zach. "Admit it. I've been helpful."

He nodded, but he was looking at me. "She knew things that I couldn't have known. I finally realized my mind couldn't have been making her up." He looked away, shaking his head.

"I'm sorry as hell that I didn't believe you, darlin'," he whispered. I saw his jaw muscles tighten and, when he looked back, his eyes were bright. The only time I'd ever seen Zach cry was at his momma's funeral, so I was stunned to see him choked up over hurting me.

I swallowed against the tightness in my throat.

"I don't deserve it, but I sure wish you'd forgive me," he said.

I lunged forward to hug him. He held me tight, and relief washed over me. Now I'd be able to talk to him about supernatural things, and maybe we could save our relationship.

It took me a few minutes to remember that there was more going on than my personal life. I pulled back. "We can talk more about everything later," I said with a weak smile.

"That'll be good," Zach said.

"Edie," I said to get her attention. "Abby Farmer is a changeling and to save the town I have to find her."

"A changeling? Here? The gates are closed so tightly that only the tiniest fae can crawl under them. Nymphs, hobgoblins, sprites. Since when can a changeling or anything human-sized get through?"

I shrugged.

"But you're sure?"

"Pretty sure. She's shot me twice with iron arrows and confessed to being one."

Edie wrinkled her nose. "Arrows? It's positively medieval," she said. "They're monsters who call themselves queens and knights and courtiers. They wield javelins and long bows. It's like a Renaissance faire run by Tim Burton."

She called them monsters, I thought, my pride prickling. The ones I'd seen through the rift had looked monstrous, but still. "I have to ask you something, Edie," I said, unable to stop myself. I moved away from Zach and beckoned her, so we could talk alone. I would tell Zach everything, but not all at once.

Edie floated to me.

"Who was my father?" I asked softly.

"You want to talk about this now?"

Yes, I need to know! "I'm half faery, right? So who was he?"

"Who told you that? Lyons?"

"Don't waste time! Just tell me the truth right now!"

Edie sighed. "I wasn't with her," she began. "Marlee visited cousins in Scotland for the summer, while the locket and Melanie stayed here. When Marlee came home, she was pregnant. She told us it was a summer fling with a boy her age. We believed her. There was no reason not to."

"But?"

"But the queen of the Seelie court sent assassins to kill her. Marlee was poisoned, and the magic Melanie had to cast to save her—" Edie shook her head. "Such dangerous magic. Then a faery knight, beautiful and deadly, came to protect her. Settling in Duvall was his idea. A powerful tor that would enhance her powers. And fae territory that belongs to the Unseelie, so that no member of the Seelie court could enter here without starting a war."

"So you moved here to hide?"

"She never admitted that the knight was her lover, but you had his hazel eyes and that golden skin, so unusual for a redhead. When you were six, the boys in the neighborhood were playing cowboys and Indians. You picked up a bow and hit the target ten out of ten times when you'd never been taught. And there was your distorted magic." Edie pursed her phantom lips. "That unnatural union of theirs should never have happened. It ruined your magic."

"What was his name?" I whispered.

"She called him Caedrin, but I don't know if that's his real name. Faeries conceal their true names."

I clenched my fists. "Why didn't you ever tell me? Why didn't they?"

"We didn't want to hurt you."

"Hurt me?"

She nodded. "We always hoped to help you come into your powers. Witchdom would've condemned you for being a half-breed, if they'd known. We kept it a secret to protect you from the shame."

I blinked, taken aback. "You're saying you were ashamed of me. All three of you?"

"No. How can you ask that? Of course *we* weren't."

My head had started to pound. They'd been lying to me my whole life. It was the second time in an hour that I'd felt betrayed. Dizzy and sick, I held my head. All I needed to round out my day was for Zach to say we'd never really been married. That the minister had been an actor, and everyone in town but me had known the truth. I rubbed my temples.

"We only did it to protect you," Edie said. "We adore you and always have."

"Sure," I said hollowly. "Well, you seem to know about them, about faeries, I mean. So tell me. There was a big spill of pixie dust. How can I re-collect it?"

"That I don't know."

I walked to the duffel bag of weapons and iron ammunition. I shouldered the soot-covered bag. "I have to find Abby Farmer."

"I'll help you."

My wounded pride wanted to refuse Edie's help, but I just nodded.

"I'll talk to my friends to see what they know about the changeling, and I'll be back very soon," Edie added, before she disappeared.

When I turned, I guess my face showed how bad I was feeling because Zach rushed across the room to me.

"What? What's wrong, darlin'?"

"Nothing. I have to go."

"Johnny, c'mon. We're going," Zach said.

Johnny's eyes widened. I was surprised, too, but happy that Zach seemed willing to accept my friends along with my secrets.

Zach whistled at Merc and jerked his head toward the door. Johnny fell into step with us.

"Where we going, Deputy Zach?" Johnny asked.

"To find Farmer."

"You want me to come with you?"

"It's your town, too," Zach said.

Johnny smiled. "Yes, it my town, too. Happy to help. Why we need to find a farmer?"

40

THE MAYOR HAD cancelled Du-Fall Days, but people weren't listening to him any more than they were listening to their own good sense. The tailgaters were lined up in parking lots and along Main Street. By seven in the morning people were drunk and disorderly. By midday, we were having to stop every half hour so Zach could break up a fight or lend a hand to the other deputies and volunteer firemen. He helped control the crowds while they put out small fires and rescued people who thought rooftops were good places to dance and dive from. So far, there were eight broken legs, ten broken arms, and three broken jaws that I knew about.

Of course, the thing I cared about most was finding the Abby changeling, and my eyes were always scanning the crowds. To my dismay, I hadn't spotted her once all morning.

Rollie slept through everything. Merc napped on and off, too, and I thought, not for the first time, that vampires and cats have plenty in common. I was so tired that if I'd known a spell for it, I would have turned myself into a tabby and slept on a windowsill. In truth, I suspect that Zach did let me doze a couple of times, because time seemed to bleed away so quickly.

At the moment, I sat in the car waiting for Zach to finish with his keeping-the-peace duty. I looked again at the crayon-colored map Imposter Abby had done at my house. We'd checked out all the parks and wooded areas for her until they'd gotten so overgrown that they weren't safe.

As the territories to check got smaller and smaller, I felt more and more hopeless. Maybe she'd gone underground to hide until the fae army came through when the doors opened at nightfall. Maybe Bryn would be hours-dead by the time I found her.

I checked to be sure the divider was up to protect Rollie from the light before I rolled down the limo's side window.

"Y'all, get off the car, please," I said to the five teenagers who had climbed on the hood. They looked about fourteen, all gangly limbs and shaggy hair.

"No," a pimply-faced boy said.

"In a minute we're going to be driving away from here, and, if you're sitting up there, you might slip off and hurt yourself. So go ahead and get off the car. Please."

"No."

"Listen—"

"There she is!" someone shouted.

I turned my head and saw Jenna Reitgarten rushing toward me with several men and women.

"She's the one who brought this upon us. She's a witch! I saw her."

Uh-oh.

I'd like to have conjured a protection spell, but of course that was beyond my skills, so I did the next-best thing. I rolled up the window.

"Yeah, that'll stop them," I muttered sarcastically. My positive attitude had taken a siesta with Merc.

I locked the doors and started the car. Then I tapped on the windshield to remind the boys that the limo's hood was a no-parking zone. They ignored my warning by lying on their bellies and putting their faces on the windshield to make obscene tongue gestures.

"Stubborn little jerks," I grumbled. "I'll show you." I

turned on my wipers and jammed my finger down on the wiper fluid button. I sprayed them like they were wild dogs I was trying to run off my lawn.

They reacted in much the same way dogs would've. First they were startled by the fluid, then they glowered and snarled at me as the liquid dripped down their faces.

Jenna and her followers banged on the side of the limo. I checked my rearview mirror. A pair of mopeds had parked too close and boxed us in. I looked for Zach, but he was lost somewhere in the crowd.

Jenna slammed her whole weight, about ninety pounds' worth, against the limo. I was tempted to just sit and watch her until she got tired and went away, but her friends were heftier and when one of them brandished a handgun, I apologized to the mopeds and threw the car into reverse.

I crashed into the bikes and rolled over them, swinging the wheel. I shifted into drive and began tapping people with the car at a speed of about half a mile per hour.

"You better get out of the way," I mumbled.

"You hit me!" one of Jenna's crew yelled.

"Just a tap. That's why they named it a bumper."

Despite their profanities and protests, the herding was working. I almost had a clear path onto the street when the man with the gun lost control of his temper. I saw the barrel, my breath caught, and I ducked. I heard the pop, but not what I expected to come next. I opened one eye. No shattered glass. No handgun poking through the window to shoot and kill me where I lay.

I sat up and looked at the mark on the window. Merc yowled.

"Oh, you're up now? It's about time," I said, driving forward slowly. "Look at that, Merc." I tapped the driver's side window. "Bryn's car has bulletproof glass. You've got to admit he's got that planning-ahead thing down pat."

The gunman shouted at me. It was an accident when I ran over his foot, but I wasn't all that sorry about it.

He shot at the window again. The bullet ricocheted, and his buddy in the TO HELL WITH THE DEVIL T-shirt went down.

I slammed on the brake. "Oh, no! He's shot."

Merc jumped onto my lap and pressed his nose to the glass to look out.

The man on the ground was yelling and holding his bloody leg where the bullet had gotten him.

I caught my breath. "He's okay—well, except for being shot. But he's alive, which is what counts on a day like today." I started the car forward again. "C'mon. We gotta get our bulletproof glass away from that guy's bullets! We'll have to leave Zach here."

Someone had parked a half-finished float of Buffy the Vampire Slayer in our way. Most of the floats weren't done. Under the influence of the dust, people just didn't have the proper stick-to-it-ness. Buffy looked like the character in *The Mummy* before he got all the way regenerated, but the half of her face that was finished was real pretty. She also had a big stake in her hand. I was glad that Rollie was asleep. Although, I'm not sure much really scares vampires anyway. Again, they're kind of like jungle cats. I wished I could claim the same.

I put my car in park and gunned the engine, nodding at the boys on the hood. They seemed to sense my determination to get my speed up over five miles per hour because they tumbled off the car.

As soon as the path in front of me was clear of people, I shifted into drive and plowed forward. I slammed into the back of the flatbed trailer carrying the float, making it swing far enough to let me pass.

I heard a thump and looked up. Unfortunately, Buffy hadn't been anchored, so she fell on top of us. Luckily, just like on the show, she was light as a feather. I had to jerk the wheel back and forth to shake her off the roof, then I planted my foot to the floor and roared down Main, swerving to avoid people and finally mowing down some shopping carts to get onto Elm, which thankfully was deserted.

I slowed down to the speed limit out of habit and looked at Merc. "What should we do? Try to track Imposter Abby on foot?"

He cocked his head.

"Or should we assume she went back to the fae and try to sneak into their world?" I shivered at the thought. How would I even do that? And if I got inside, how would I keep them from killing me while I looked for her? I shook my head. Overwhelmingly bad odds.

Merc swiped the air with his paw.

"I know it's not a great idea, but what do you suggest? The sun's going down in a couple hours, and I've got to save Bryn's life. It's the right thing to do even if he is a backstabbing, ghost-blocking traitor." I took a deep breath. "Besides, if he dies, I won't get to give him a piece of my mind. And I mean to."

As if she knew I was talking about avenging her, Edie appeared in the passenger seat.

"Did you find her?" I demanded.

"Better," she said with a smile.

I frowned. She stroked Merc's fur with a phantom finger.

"Well?"

"Say you forgive me." Her rosebud lips fashioned the perfect pout.

"Do we have time for this?" I said, exasperated. "No, we don't!" I added, in case she didn't realize that was one of those rhetorical questions.

"Say it."

If she'd been alive, I would have killed her. Merc hissed at me to hurry up. I sighed.

"Yep, okay. I forgive you."

"That didn't sound especially sincere."

"Edie!"

"All right!" She smiled. "I got her name. Her *real* name."

I blinked and looked at Merc, who stared back blankly at me. I turned my head toward Edie again. "What good does that do?"

"Oh, not much," she said, glancing at her nails casually. Then she raised her eyes, and they met mine. "It just allows you to call her to you and to command her to do your will."

I slammed on the brake, causing me and Merc to lurch forward, and from the sound of the thump for either Johnny or Rollie to fall on the floor in the back. Edie, of course, sat serenely in her seat, polishing her fingernails against her wine-colored satin gown.

"Is that true?"

"Absolutely. I got her name from a ghost who owes me a favor. The door at the base of Macon Hill was partially ajar, and the Unseelie Queen's First Ambassador called the changeling to him to give her orders. My friend overheard it all."

I slapped my palm against the steering wheel. "Finally, a break! What's her name and what do I do to use it?"

"All's forgiven?"

I huffed a sigh. "Yes."

"Nixella Pipken Rose."

"Okay," I said, flinging the door open.

"Just one thing. You have to remember that she'll do exactly what you say, so choose your words carefully."

My muscles tightened. Why did everything have to be tricky? I got out of the car and stood looking around, not totally believing it would work.

"Nixella Pipken Rose, I command you to come to me now."

With the soft pop of a quarter dropping into a glass of water, she appeared.

"How dare you!"

"Be quiet," I said.

"How did you find out my name? How? How? How?" she shouted in a whisper.

"Be silent."

Her voice disappeared like a light flipping off.

Wow. "Hang on," I said, and she grabbed my arm and held it. "Um, no. Let go. I meant wait there."

She rolled her small eyes at me, and I made a face before reaching in the car to get the duffel. "I have a list. I want you to mark every ingredient that was on the poison arrow you shot me with."

I dug the list out of the bag and gave her a pen. Nixella looked at me sullenly.

"Do it now," I added.

She took the papers and started checking things.

"Poison?" Edie asked me, concerned.

"I'm okay. I just need to make an antidote." *For the family's archenemy.*

Nixella finished and thrust the papers at me. I didn't put my hand out.

"On the back of the first page, write down anything else that was in the poison or on the arrow or inside the arrow that's not on the list."

She made a face at me and started writing. After about five minutes I took the list from her and looked at what she'd written.

Iron, you stoopid witch.
Water, you retch-ed cow.
Mud from the Camaron bog, you rotton bitch.

Then there was a bunch more misspelled profanity. Guess there are no spelling bees in faerie land.

"Iron, water, and mud? Nothing else? Nod for yes, if that's true."

She nodded.

"The bog mud. Is it poisonous? I command you to answer my questions without cursing or shouting."

She clenched her fists and jumped up and down until her face was as red as a stop sign. "Not to you. Not to witches."

"But it can be poison?"

"Yes, to selkies."

"Selkies?"

"Magical creatures. Shifters. They live most of their time as seals, but they can turn into human form. Unlike your terrible race, they're very pure of heart."

Well, that ruled Bryn out.

"What's the antidote for it?"

"Why do you care?" Nixella spat.

"I command you to answer."

"It's shark oil."

"Are all the herbs and metals listed as antidotes for the poison ingredients correct?"

She snatched the list and tore it down the middle.

"Stop!"

She froze.

"I command you to look at the list and tell me if those ingredients are right for making an antidote. And I command you to stay still except for looking at it and talking to me."

"They are! They are correct. Now let me go!"

"Give me the list."

She shoved it at me.

"You told me that the dust will keep circulating around Duvall because of the wind here. How can the pixie dust be re-collected?"

"Smear honey or syrup or warm molasses on the tree trunks in the four corners and center of the town. The dust will be drawn to the sweetness and get trapped in the stickiness."

"If the doors of the land of faery are closed until All Hallow's Eve, how do you get in and out?"

"Any fae can return to the Never anytime he wants, but getting a greater fae out through a sealed door is harder than shoving a big fat human through a keyhole. In my case, it's easy peasy because I have a special talent for it. It's one of my many gifts," she said smugly. "Unlike some untalented half faeries who most of the time can't even see the creatures of the Never or the doors to come and go."

Since I'd only just figured out that I was a faery, saying I wasn't a very good one didn't really hurt my feelings. On the other hand, my side ached where she'd shot me, and I felt like dropping her on her smug little head. Maybe when we were a little less busy.

"Nixella Pipken Rose, I command you to apply the honey and syrup to the trees in a way that will re-collect the pixie dust as fast as possible. And then I command you to sneak into the land of faery to get Abigail Farmer. You will return her to her parents without letting them know she's been gone, and, while you're doing the stuff I command, you won't tell anyone what you're doing or why. You won't cause any trouble or endanger any human beings. And when you're finished, you'll find someplace to hide until I call you to me again. Go now."

She disappeared. I turned to Edie and found her smiling at me.

"Aren't you just the bee's knees?" she said.

"Can you do me a favor?"

"Of course, biscuit. What?"

"I need Aunt Mel's earrings so I can face Incendio. Last I know of, Earl had them, but he was going to sell them to someone. I'm not sure who. Can you find out what happened to them?"

"Absolutely. Leave it to me."

41

WHILE I'D BEEN dealing with Nixella, Mercutio had gotten out of the car. I called to him several times and searched the surrounding area, but didn't find him. I glanced at the sun, hanging low in the sky. I was almost out of time; I needed to go. Luckily, Merc could take care of himself.

"Merc, I have to try to save Bryn. Meet me there!" I yelled.

The drive to Bryn's was interesting. People were milling about like cars had never been invented. They wandered into the streets for a stroll or a game of touch football or to play hockey on Rollerblades. If there was a rule of the road, they ignored it, which meant I had to do the same. I drove around them, riding curbs, crossing sidewalks, and going over grass, rocks, and between trees. I doubted the limousine people ever thought of it much as an off-road vehicle, but it did really well.

Steve let me through the gate, and Mr. Jenson waited for me at the open front door.

I hurried in, clutching the pages in my hand. "I need to make a potion."

"This way," he said, leading me down the hall to a locked door. He opened it with a key and turned on the light. The windowless room smelled spicy. There were floor-to-ceiling shelves full of bottles and jars. On a granite-topped work-bench were half-used candles, a mortar and pestle, a thin silver ice-pick-looking thing, and half a dozen bottles and jars. I glanced through the labels on the bottles and matched them to the things on the pages. Eleven ingredients matched the antidotes checked on the list. I removed the bottle of cloves from the others and set it aside. Then I looked at the shelves.

"Are they in some order?" I asked Mr. Jenson, stepping to the shelves. There were thousands of bottles. "I still need dandelion root and shark oil."

My eyes darted over the labels. *Lemon Extract. Lemon-weed. Marstone.*

"I'm not sure, but if I know Mr. Lyons, it will be—"

"Alphabetical," I finished, hurrying over to the "D" sec-tion and pulling bottles off the shelves until I found the jar I needed. I set it on the counter and rushed to the "S" section. I couldn't believe anyone would have shark oil, but there it was, between something called "shade silt" and "ground silkworm."

I grabbed the mortar and added two pinches of the dry ingredients and four drops of the liquid ones. I ground it together and stirred. It had a good consistency.

"I need a spoon," I said.

"Won't you need this, Miss Tamara?" Mr. Jenson asked, holding up the silver spike.

"What for?"

"Mr. Lyons used it to—well, it was rather like tattooing himself, I suppose. He has a great connection to the stars and introduced the previous antidote under his skin in a very particular pattern, that of the constellations Pisces and Tau-rus, he said. He intended for you to do the same."

Connected to the stars? Was Bryn's magic mainly celes-tial? And would my spell-casting work on him since mine wasn't? I took a deep breath. It would work. Because it had to. He might be connected to the stars, but he was magically connected to me, too. I'd felt the proof of that every time we touched.

I thought of the word in Bryn's instructions for the counterspell that I hadn't been familiar with. *Subcutaneous.* I'd looked it up and found out it meant "below the skin," which hadn't made sense to me, and I'd figured I'd misread the word because the handwriting had been so shaky. But now I realized I'd read it right after all. Subcutaneous . . . yuck.

"He expects me to poke him with that?" I asked, grimacing.

Mr. Jenson nodded. "If need be," he said, then hesitated with his brows drawn together. "I can assist you with that portion." From the look on his face, it seemed like he'd rather have had a hammer to the head.

"No, I can do it. Where's the pattern he used?"

"He did it from memory."

"Of course he did. He's probably got a thousand star charts tucked away in that brain of his, but since I don't usually have to pilot the space shuttle, I need a book."

"Yes, I'm sure he'd have anticipated that and left you one, but he was weak and pressed for time. Let me see what I can find."

I caught his arm. "I'm real sorry. I shouldn't have snapped at you. I'm just nervous."

"Understood. No need to apologize. Give me a moment to find you an adequate volume."

Ten minutes later, he gave me a book with nice big pictures of the constellations. I took it with me when I crossed into the circle in Bryn's room. Mr. Jenson and Steve waited downstairs, saying they didn't want to intrude. Apparently raising the dead calls for privacy.

I figured Bryn's back would be the best canvas, so I rolled him on his side and lifted his shirt. Lucky for him I'm an expert cake decorator, so copying patterns is a skill I actually do have. It was real creepy, though, to dip the needle-tipped spike in the potion and then poke it through his waxy, bluish skin. It was even creepier when he didn't bleed.

If I didn't get my pastry chef job back, two jobs I knew I wouldn't apply for were mortician and tattoo artist. I shuddered and pressed on.

I consulted my book and made sure I had all my stars just so. Then I rolled him on his back and put a couple dabs of the potion on the back of his tongue with my fingertip, hoping it might drip down into him.

He hadn't left me any verse or counterspell to say. I guessed he didn't have time. I decided to keep it simple:

With you gone, your soul I miss
Return to me now, with this kiss.

I pressed my lips against his, not feeling a thing.
Please!

I crawled on top of him and kissed harder, holding his face in my hands as I mumbled the words again, blowing my breath into him.

Like a flame on the head of a match that's just been struck, the power flared to life and blossomed.

His body was still cold and stiff, but I went on kissing him and mumbling the verse until I felt his heart start to beat in his chest. He took a deep breath and swallowed.

I sat back, holding one of his hands, and watched his skin. The blue faded to pale white, almost glowing, and then returned to normal. It was nothing short of a miracle.

I smiled my triumph.
Not such a magical menace now, am I?

His palm warmed against mine, and he opened his eyes. They were lighter than usual, and it seemed to take time for them to focus.

Aren't I just the cat's pajamas? I thought, wishing Merc had been there to see me do something right.

"Hey there," I whispered, giving Bryn's hand a squeeze. "We may be antifaery at the moment, but the *Sleeping Beauty* fairy-tale thing sure worked. I used a kiss to wake you up."

Bryn's lids drifted shut, but he spoke, his voice raspy and soft.

"Saved my life, huh? Knew you could do it."

42

AT FIRST, I was so relieved he was alive that I was content just to watch him breathe, but, as time ticked by, I started to get anxious. I jostled him, giving his arm a pinch when he didn't wake right away.

He stirred, and when he opened his eyes, they were their usual bright blue.

"How come you didn't kiss me awake this time?"

"Because you weren't dead."

A faint smile lifted the corners of his mouth. "For future reference, I still prefer it."

"Can you get up?"

"Possibly, but I'll need help undressing."

Huh?

Oh! My cheeks burned, and I slapped his arm. "No flirting. We've got work to do." I opened my mouth to accuse him of blocking Edie, but closed it again. I wouldn't bring up the Edie spell when there was still so much to do.

"I need a little more time to recover. Get me some black tea. Tell Jenson to put ginger and a moonstone in it."

"I'll be right back."

I hopped up and rushed downstairs. By the time I came

back with the cup, he was sitting up with some pillows behind his back. He looked normal, his eyes clear and alert.

I gave him the tea, and he drank it down, then he stretched, grimacing when he twisted his torso.

"If your back hurts, it's because I poked you once or twice." *Or twenty-eight times.* "Mr. Jenson said I should."

He climbed off the bed and walked to me. "I feel fine, sweetheart. You did a great job." He brushed his lips over mine, making them tingle. My traitorous body reacted like he hadn't betrayed me. *Cut it out*, I told myself and took a step back.

"Okay, let me give you a list of all the stuff that you have to help me fix," I said. "First, we've got to reinforce the doors before the fae come through to murder half the town. Second, we've got to blow the wind toward the four corners so the dust can get stuck to the traps. Third, we've got to unspell the trees and plants to keep them from growing five years' worth in an hour. Fourth, we've got to unbind the town so that people can get in and out of Duvall again. Did I forget anything? Nope, I think that's everything."

The left edge of his mouth curved up, all sexy and amused. "You've been busy."

I frowned. He wasn't moving as quickly or taking the trouble as seriously as I wanted him to. "Think we've got a chance of putting everything right?" I asked.

"Anything's possible." He paused at the doorway to the bathroom to steady himself.

"You feel weak?"

"I feel half dead," he said. Then he smiled. "Which is decidedly better than feeling all dead." He winked at me and stepped into the bathroom. He didn't bother to shut the door, and I was about to turn away when I saw him open the medicine cabinet. I wondered what magical thing he had stashed in there. An amulet or a packet of strength-boosting elixir that he kept nearby in case of emergencies?

I waited and then gaped when he took out shaving cream. I stalked over to the doorway as he squirted some white foam into his palm.

"Please tell me this is from some special ritual."

"It's a daily ritual," he conceded, rubbing the foam on his face.

"You're taking time out of our busy schedule to shave? Now?"

"The whiskers itch. It's distracting."

I yanked my shirt up and turned so he could see the wound on my side. "This is from the second time I was shot by an iron-tipped arrow. You think it doesn't hurt? You think the throbbing isn't distracting? But you don't see me saying I'll pop a pain pill and sleep until I feel better, do you?"

Bryn looked me over and then turned to his own reflection. He pulled the razor down his jaw, relaxed as you please, totally oblivious to my objection.

Anger ran through my veins like a runaway locomotive. "Well? What do you have to say?"

"You've got a great belly button."

Surprisingly, my head didn't explode. "Are you kidding me!" I shouted.

He paused from shaving to brace himself, holding the sink tightly. "Tamara, you want me to spell-cast. I can barely stand upright. I'll need every ounce of concentration I can muster. That means eliminating any distraction I can, even the minor ones."

Oh. The fury drained out of me, leaving me a little less rattled. "Okay." I stepped into the bathroom with him and touched his arm. "Sit. I'll help you."

He handed me the razor and sat down, tipping his face up. He closed his eyes and his breathing turned even. I slid the razor over his skin, stopping a couple times to rinse it under the trickling water from the sink's tap.

It was weirdly intimate. I stood back as far as possible, but I could still smell the spicy-scented foam, could still feel the curve of his perfect jaw as I pulled the razor along it. I tried to concentrate on the trouble we needed to fix, but all I could think about was his gorgeous face . . . and the fact that usually being in the bathroom while a man shaved meant that you'd spent the night with him.

Pull yourself together!

"Easy," he said.

I winced as a drop of blood formed where I'd nicked him. "Sorry." I finished as quickly and carefully as I could.

"Done!" I announced, tossing the razor in the sink and wetting a towel.

He opened his eyes and studied me. I backed away, tossing the towel to him. It landed on his thigh, but he never looked down. His blue eyes glittered at me in that way they do, like God gave him priceless sapphires instead of eyes.

He lifted the rag and wiped his face while watching me.

"Um, I'll wait for you out here," I said, hurrying back into his bedroom where I was sorry to see that taking up the better part of one wall was still his king-sized bed.

I clenched and unclenched my fists. *Physical attraction doesn't mean anything. Don't forget you can't trust him. He blocked you from seeing Edie, which is probably why he's on the family list. And from what Jordan Perth says, Bryn's the leader of some anarchist terror group. Plus, he's a lawyer!*

"Tamara—"

I spun around and pointed a finger at him. "I'm mad at you."

He glanced over his shoulder at the bathroom and then to me again. He raised his eyebrows. "You know, your mood swings could give a man whiplash."

"I wasn't going to bring this up until after we saved the town, but I decided it can't wait."

He walked over to the plush chair in the corner and dropped into it, putting his feet up on the matching footrest. "Talk to me."

"You cast a spell to keep Edie from getting to see me, and—" I waited for him to deny it. The jerk didn't even bother to lie to me. "And I'll never forgive you for it."

He leaned his head back and looked up at the skylight. "You know, never's a very long time. Longer than say . . . a week or two."

Freaking smart-ass. I was glad I'd brought him back to life. It's too darn hard to get even with someone who's dead.

"I know how long it is!" I snapped. I dragged a few breaths into my lungs and lowered my voice. "I was just starting to trust you. How could you do that to me?" I whispered.

He raised his head and looked at me. "She was a threat to us."

"You had no right! She helps and protects me."

"By keeping you away from me? Her primary purpose in death?"

"What if it is? You and I are not supposed to be together. I mean, look what you did. Blocking a member of my family from seeing me—it doesn't get any more wrong than that."

"Disenfranchised spirits are dangerous. They are not to be trusted."

"You don't know her. For your information, I couldn't have saved your life without her help."

"Well, that's ironic," he said. "But she still doesn't belong in our world. Maybe if you let her go, she could move on."

"Or maybe she'd still be trapped and, on top of it, she'd be all alone. By doing things like that spell, you just reinforce what she believes, that I need to stay away from you."

He smiled wryly. "Undoubtedly. A man who risks his life, who turns himself into a wizard marked for assassination, for a woman's sake—yes, that's a man she needs to be warned about."

I threw my arms wide. "I appreciate all that stuff, but I'm not sure why you did it. You could have—probably do have—an ulterior motive. Everyone says you're out to trick me. I don't know what to believe."

"That must be difficult for you."

I heard the hard edge to his voice. He was angry and frustrated that I didn't just let him convince me, but Edie had been blocked. I folded my arms across my chest and squared my shoulders. My posture made him clench his jaw.

"There's one thing you can believe, Tamara," he said, the

dark-edged tone going darker. "If you want to save this town, you need my help." He held out a hand to me.

I couldn't go share a chair with him when we were in the middle of a fight. Seconds ticked by, and his hand stayed stretched out where it was.

"We're in here and it's quiet, but I think you know it's not quiet out there," he said. "If the fae army comes through en masse, people will die. Are we letting that happen, or are we trying to stop it?"

Just once I wanted saving Duvall to be someone else's problem. "My powers work best when I have bare feet touching the ground. I think we should go outside," I said.

He dropped his hand. "That's good thinking." He stood and motioned for me to precede him out the door. We walked silently down the stairs.

Mr. Jenson saw us and smiled. He was relieved to see Bryn up and it showed.

"Well-done, Miss Tamara."

I forced myself to smile. It wasn't a real smile, but I hoped he wouldn't be able to tell.

43

BRYN AND I went out the back door that led to the court-yard with the pool. I glanced at the fountain. "I wish Mercutio was here. He helps boost my power, too."

"Where is he?"

"Don't know. But whatever he's doing, I'm sure it's important or he'd be here. Him I can always count on."

Bryn didn't argue with me, but his silence was icy.

I stopped as soon as I hit the grass, but Bryn kept walking. He studied the sky and stopped about thirty feet from me.

"Here's better." His voice was calm and smooth again, which made it easier to approach him, but I took a step back when he pulled his shirt off.

"Skin to skin works best. You know that," he said, glancing at the horizon.

I did know that, but I wished I didn't. "It's freezing out here," I complained.

"I don't think that'll be a problem for very long."

I took my boots and socks off first, then curled my toes into the grass until I felt the cold dirt. My fingers shook as I pulled my T-shirt over my head. Goose bumps rippled over my skin.

"This is as far as I strip," I said, glancing down at my purple lace bra.

He hooked his fingertips in the waist of my jeans and pulled me to him. The power sizzled to life. I put my hands on his chest, trying to keep some distance between us. He let go of me so fast that I had to take a step back to stop myself from falling.

"What?"

"She's still in the way," he said.

I looked around. "She's not here."

"I don't mean that she's in the way physically. I meant she's making you resist me."

"It's not Edie's fault. It's yours! You did something terrible, and that's why I don't want to get too close to you. You make me mad and . . . you scare me."

He opened his mouth to protest, but I cut him off.

"In my heart, I don't believe you'd hurt me directly, no matter what anyone says. But you can do things, spells that are so beyond what I can comprehend. And people like you get where you are by being ruthless. Edie was in your way. So you did a spell to get her out of it. That makes me scared. If I could do things to you that you couldn't control, wouldn't that scare you?"

"You do things to me that I can't control, Tamara. The difference is that when you're ruthless, I never ask for an apology."

My eyebrows shot up. "I'm not ruthless."

"Are you here for my company? Or are you here to use me?"

I stamped my foot. "That is not fair! I saved your life."

"You would have done that for anyone," he countered.

"Stop twisting things around. You're such a—such a lawyer!"

He smiled. "Is that the worst you can do?"

"Admit you were wrong to block Edie!" I snapped.

His smile faded and he nodded. "Yeah, it was a mistake. An ironic one." He paused and tapped his thumb against his thigh, as if he were picking out his next words carefully.

"Your safety and your happiness are important to me. That's why I take risks for you. Risks I wouldn't take for anyone else. So the fact that I hurt you wasn't just unintentional, it was the exact opposite of what I was trying to do." He shook his head, adding softly, "You throw my world off its axis."

My breath escaped in a rush as I stared at him. His eyes were like open windows into his soul, and I could feel the truth reflected there. Right then, if he'd reached for me, I would've been his for the taking. He was that irresistible.

I licked my lips. "Um, okay," I said, fidgeting. "I—yep, you're forgiven." I shoved my hands through my hair. "Ready to get back to saving Duvall?"

The corner of his mouth curved into a smirk, and he nodded. "I think we've established that when you want something from me, all you have to do is ask."

I walked close to him and dug my toes into the dirt. "What next?"

He leaned his mouth close to mine. "You know."

The minute I kissed him, he slid a hand behind my head and one around my back. We bruised each other's lips with the force of the kiss. Parts of me thought that wasn't good, but other parts thought that was better than perfect. My feet were rooted in the earth as he crushed me to him.

The wind blew and the earth rocked, and everywhere we touched, power burned like a white-hot flame. The darkness broke apart, and bright light blazed through my closed lids.

Every thought dissolved into sensation. His skin, warm and smooth. His muscles, hard and tight. His breath, ragged and lost to me every time I inhaled. I let it curl down into my lungs like the smoke of a sandalwood candle. My tongue touched his, caressed it, and tried to swallow the power. We fought for it, my nails digging into his back, my hips pressing against him like I'd walk right through his body and soul.

I leaned back, not knowing why, until the arch was so deep that we lost our balance and slammed to the ground. I felt the power of the world slice through me to touch the heavens.

I could have a piece of that raw power if I wanted it badly

enough, and I surely did. Bryn's body slid along mine, making me ache to the core. That place inside me without a name knew he was mine and wanted the proof of it. I slid a hand between us and fiddled with his clothes. He seemed to be of the mind that we could make love with our clothes on because he didn't help me. It turned out I didn't need his help.

We clung to each other, and I swallowed the words he said against my mouth. I opened my eyes and the stars pulsed overhead, their light like needles tattooing his back and my hands.

He drew the power to him, and I didn't care. I just wanted to feel good, to tip over into that body-clenching, skin-tingling place. And then I did, tumbling into an ecstasy more intense than any I'd ever known.

He followed me over, and it was glorious . . . until he gave me more than what his body had to offer.

The power screamed through me like it would tear my skin off to get out. I shrieked and tried to grab him as he slipped away.

"Take it back," I wailed.

I barely felt his fingers on my face. I couldn't see him through the white light that blazed in front of my eyes. It was like staring at an overexposed picture.

"Concentrate, Tamara." His voice was a distant echo in my head.

I thrashed, begging him to get it out of me.

"See the doors. See them in your mind? Burn them closed."

I felt one of his hands squeezing my arm. It was painfully reassuring. "See them for me." He kept talking. He whispered against my skin, spell after spell, until the words closed around me like a fist. I saw an army of monsters pouring into the world. I drew Bryn's spells to me and cast them out. I saw the beasts scatter, and the golden doors slam shut. The heat made the doors warp, melting along the edges. They were too soft, too malleable. The monsters would push through them, like gilded warriors.

I wanted to cool the doors, and Bryn's new spell chilled

my skin. I made the wind mine. It whipped icy water. Some hands and faces froze into the doors as they hardened.

There was still power left. I tried to concentrate, but couldn't remember what else needed to be done.

"Want to fix the rest," I mumbled. It was hard to untangle my thoughts.

He spoke in my ear, in my head. I saw the flowers and trees. I saw the dust floating on the air. I saw the edges of Duvall as I flew over it. I was a tempest. I twirled like a ballerina in an endless pirouette, and at the last moment before I lost my balance, I flung my arms out and cast the power.

When I was human again, I turned my face away from rain that pounded down on me. I wiped my eyes and opened them. Bryn was lying next to me, one side of his face under mine. He'd been saying the spells against my neck, near my earlobe.

"We closed the doors," I said breathlessly. "Yay us." I paused. "I didn't expect it to hurt like that." I put my hand out to block the rain from hitting our heads. "You alive?"

"Hard to tell," he mumbled.

"I'm surprised you gave me the power."

"Didn't have a choice. It was too soon for me to draw that much in. I couldn't have contained it and cast at the same time."

"It was too soon after waking up from being half dead and poisoned?" I asked. He didn't answer. "Bryn?"

"Hmm?"

"Some of the fae came through. Somebody's gonna have to deal with that."

"Somebody besides us." His breathing grew even as he fell asleep.

I sat up and righted my clothes, then his. When all our bits were safely tucked away, I kissed his temple and stood.

Blood ran down from the reopened wound in my side as I strode to the house. It hurt, but I did my best to ignore it. Soon I would get to rest, too. But not yet. *Not yet.*

"Steve!" I called.

Steve appeared a moment later.

"Go collect your boss. He's sleeping on the back lawn."

Steve raised his eyebrows, his lips curving into a smirk.

I gave him a stern look. "You know, it'd be a real good thing if you didn't start with me right now." I cleared my throat and tried to look dignified. "Now, where the heck's my gun with the iron bullets?"

44

AS I REACHED Magnolia Park, Rollie woke up and did a full-body stretch in the backseat of the limo.

"How was your beauty sleep?" I asked.

He moved so that he could better check himself out in the rearview. "Apparently very well, since, as usual, I look fabulous."

I parked and grimaced at the pandemonium. More fae had gotten through than I'd thought.

"There are a bunch of bad faeries loose. Want to help me deal with them?"

"It'll put my nails at risk, but that's why God invented acrylic. Let's go," he said. He bent and gave Johnny a peck on the cheek. "You stay here."

Johnny protested, but I agreed with Rollie and asked him to stay behind. Johnny's hell with a blow-dryer and brush, but he's no Calamity John.

I tucked the gun in the front of my jeans and shouldered my duffel, which contained another bow that I'd gotten from Bryn's. While loading up on ammunition, I'd asked Steve how big Bryn's arsenal was. Steve had smiled and said,

"Unless the U.S. Army invades, big enough." I hoped I'd borrowed all I would need.

When I flung the car door open, I had to sidestep Rollie. He was leaning against the limo, surveying the field of faeries gone feral.

"How many?" I asked.

"You expect me to count them, too?" he said, waving a dismissive hand. "They're running around too much. It'll be easier to count them when they've stopped moving. What have you got for me in iron that's stylish?"

"You want a gun or a long bow?"

"Neither. Don't you have any pretty daggers? Or a short spear?"

"I wasn't planning to get that close. How about these arrows?" I asked, giving him a handful.

He admired the tiny magical symbols engraved on them.

"Very elegant. I'll take them," he said. With that, he pulled his lips back, exposing his sharp white fangs, and then he sauntered right into the middle of things.

Being quite a bit less indestructible, I kept my head low and took cover. The police and a number of concerned—or at least annoyed—citizens were shooting, but the faeries weren't falling.

There were some people on the ground, but not as many as I expected. Some women and children were cowering under picnic tables. The monstrous human-sized faeries danced around, jeering at the people and making scary, malicious faces. That's right. Before they slaughtered people, they were taunting them.

On behalf of Duvall, I was officially madder than a hornet. It already wasn't a fair fight. I counted nineteen practically immortal faeries, fully armed. I spotted Zach on the far side of the bonfire. He was bleeding from his leg and reloading.

I crawled across the grass, keeping out of sight by staying below the level of the disposable coolers. Rollie provided a nice distraction. Five big fae had surrounded him and were poking at him with their spears. Two of them pulled off the tips so the wood underneath was exposed. Stake size: extra large.

If lightning moves faster than faeries and vampires, I'd be real surprised because the action was a blur. I pushed up onto my knees, took aim, and squeezed off two shots. *Pop. Pop.* I dropped back onto my belly and peered around a cooler, resting my chin on an empty can of Miller beer.

I'd hit the two faeries who were by the farthest picnic table, and they were down. I crawled commando-style to Zach.

"What are you doing here?" Zach whispered fiercely.

Saving your cute butt. "This gun's got bullets that will kill them," I said, handing it to him. I looked at the gash in his thigh. It wasn't bleeding much because the flesh around the wound was burned.

"The thing had his spear in the fire before he stuck me with it," Zach explained.

"Well, here's your chance to get even. That gun's not on fire, but the bullets will burn plenty when they go in."

I arranged my arrows so I could reload the bow quickly. Rollie was doing well in the center. Two faeries were down with arrows sticking out of their chests, but Rollie also had a spear in his belly. Too low to kill him, but it had to smart.

I raised up and shot a charcoal-skinned faery with spiked black teeth, who was dancing near us. I dropped down and reloaded. When I rose again, there was a feral face with oily eyes right in front of me.

I gasped and stumbled back. He was on me in an instant. I'd like to say killing him was planned, but the arrow just slid into him when my elbow hit the ground and jarred my arm. He rolled off of me, bleeding shimmering green blood that disappeared when it hit the earth.

I reloaded, sweating and breathless. They moved very fast, but I could still sense the hum of Bryn's power under my skin. It made me feel fast enough to fight them.

Zach was on one knee next to me when I rose up. I sent my arrow flying, reloaded, and sent another into the air as Zach squeezed off two shots.

The faeries spotted us, their long haggard faces glowering.

Uh-oh. A rush of fear coursed through me.

I sent three more arrows up in quick succession, then grabbed the gun from Zach. I squeezed off rounds, then yanked the bullets from my pockets and reloaded.

They were on us, so I jumped up and ran, drawing them away from Zach. I shot over my shoulder. As you might imagine, that was less accurate, but I still managed to hit about half of the things I aimed at.

When there were only two left, I just turned and shot them point-blank as they rushed me.

Rollie yanked the spear from his belly with a grimace. "That blood's going to ruin my pants," he said.

He looked down at the five dead fae at his feet, before glancing around the area at the ones I'd shot. "Well, look who's the little showboat," he said, clapping for me by tapping his palm with the fingers of his other hand.

I drew my brows together. "Yeah, I used some magic I conjured earlier actually, and I couldn't have done it without your help either."

He laughed. "Haven't I taught you anything? If you're a fabulous little killing machine, you don't apologize or explain. You just say, 'Rollie, what color cape would look good on a redheaded superwitch?'"

I turned and saw Zach, kneeling not far from us. He stared at me like I'd just won the Olympic gold medal in a sport I'd never told him I played.

"Hey, honey," I said, walking to him. "How's your leg?"

"Not too bad," he said and stood with a grimace.

"You want me to bandage it up? We can go—"

"No," he said. "Is this it? Or are there more . . . creatures loose?"

"I think we got 'em all," I said, not counting Rollie since he was on our side.

Zach nodded. "I need to ride over to the station to check on things. We've got a lot of guys wounded." He looked me up and down.

"I'm wounded, too," I said quickly and raised my shirt to show him my injury, remembering too late that he'd already seen it.

He looked at me. "I thought it was deeper than that."

I glanced down, startled to find it was almost healed. Just like my shoulder, where the flesh had closed and the bruising had faded much quicker than expected.

"It's a lot better. That Neosporin is a miracle drug."

"Uh-huh," he said skeptically. "Why don't you go to Georgia's to rest? I'll see you later."

"I could help you," I offered.

"Nah, you've done enough," he said.

Chewing on my lip, I squeezed my fists tight to keep from reaching for him when he turned away. I watched him limp toward his truck.

"He didn't even ask me for a kiss," I murmured, realizing sadly that Zach and I were not okay. He might have accepted the fact that there were monsters in the world, but he hadn't come to terms with it or with my needing to fight them.

Rollie slung an arm around my shoulder. "Oh, doll face, it's better this way. You can't have all the men in town, and frankly, I think Bryn Lyons is the kind of guy you'll need both hands to handle. But I suppose you know that, since I smell his magic all over you."

I stood rooted to the spot, watching Zach drive off. "Bryn's great." *When he's not casting spells to block my family members from seeing me.* "But Zach and I, we've loved each other our whole lives."

"Oh, please. Your whole life? You've been alive for about five minutes. Besides, he might just need a few days to get used to the new you." Rollie gave me an encouraging nudge, and I walked back to the limo with him. Instead of getting in though, Rollie held the door open for Johnny to get out.

"Johnny and I are going to take a stroll," he said. "You go home and get pretty, and we'll meet up later to have a nice glass of champagne to celebrate your killing spree."

45

I WASN'T GOING home. I was going to help collect the wounded people, too, but first I needed to check on Neutered Nixella's progress. I called her and, when she first appeared, I didn't recognize her. She had skin the shade of a ripe avocado; I guess she was showing her true colors—literally. Her fingers and toes and ears were twice as long as a human's, and I studied her warily.

"Did you do what I asked? I mean, commanded?"

"Yes," she said glumly.

"Are there any more fae loose in Duvall who wouldn't have been if the doors hadn't opened?"

"No."

"All right, I command you to go home and not to come to Duvall ever again unless I call you."

"Wait," she said.

I waited.

"I want to make a deal. If you promise never to use my name to call me and you promise never to tell anyone else my name, I'll tell you something you don't know, but would want to."

"Nixella Pipken Rose, I command you to tell me what I don't know, but would want to."

"Your friend Georgia Sue bought you a black cocktail dress for Christmas. She thinks your other one is too worn. She doesn't know why you still wear it when the color's faded."

I gasped, slapping a hand over my mouth. Faeries are so mean. And so are best friends apparently. "That was the information you wanted to trade for?"

"No."

"Well, then what was the secret?"

"There is none."

I knew she was a trickster, but I also had this weird feeling that there was something that I needed to know and didn't.

"Tell me the information that's worthy of my promise not to call you again."

"Do you promise not to call? And to keep my name secret?"

"Nixella Pipken Rose, I command you to tell me the worthy information right now."

"Incendio Maldaron has your cat. If you don't get to the inn immediately, he'll be dead."

I felt the blood drain from my face. "Go home," I shouted. She disappeared instantly, and I started the car. I jammed the gas pedal to the floor and paid no mind to the cars or bikes I ran over.

I careened down the road as fast as I could. I can't say how long it took me to get to Old Town, but since I couldn't travel in an instant, it took too long.

I threw the car in park and scrambled into the Yellow Rose, but the second I crossed the threshold into the parlor, I heard a pop that sounded suspiciously like when Bryn had closed me in a circle.

"What's going on? Mercutio!" I ran to the doorway, trying to step into the dining room, but bounced back. Sure enough. Trapped! I looked down at the symbols in the doorway and then into the next room.

Mercutio was locked in a cat carrier. Incendio was lying on the rug, unconscious with blood pumping from a wound on his head. Jordan Perth was reading from a spellbook.

"What are you doing?" I asked, nausea roiling in my belly.

Jordan's gaze flicked up for a second and he smiled. Then he continued reading, tapping his wand in time as he did. "This transfer I seal with heart's blood," he said as he closed the book and dropped it to the floor. I cringed as he pulled a huge knife from his crimson robe's pocket.

"From the ten fires of Hell, I draw his power," he said. Walking around Incendio, he repeated the same line over and over. "From the ten fires of Hell, I draw his power."

Mercutio hissed, but Incendio never moved.

"Incendio, wake up!" I yelled. "Incendio!" I sure wasn't a big fan of Incendio's work, but everyone knows it's wrong to kick someone when he's down, let alone to stab him in the heart and steal his powers.

Finally, Jordan knelt next to Incendio. I slapped my hands over my eyes. There was a blast of heat, and I staggered away from the doorway. I could hear Mercutio yowling.

"Give me my cat!" I yelled.

The air cooled rapidly, and I peeked back in, immediately wishing I hadn't. Jordan licked some blood off his knife, and I gagged, slapping a hand over my mouth.

He came to the doorway, grinning like a dirty, rotten psycho.

"Thank you for sparing me the trouble of finding you. Saves time, which I value. And thanks for shooting Incendio. That made him more vulnerable to my attack, since he needed help getting inside."

"Why did you kill him?" I stammered. For a small town, we sure had more than our share of homicidal maniacs these days.

"Someone has to take the blame for Tom Brick. It might as well be the thug who killed him. And while he's at it, Incendio can take the blame for Earl Stanton's murder, which was mine. And yours and Bryn Lyons's. Mine and mine."

My murder! And Bryn's? My heart banged in my chest. I needed to get out. I turned and ran, trying to break the circle by going out the front door, which didn't work.

"Trapped," he said with a smile.

"Uh-huh. So I see." *Plan B: Stall!* He looked so pleased with himself, I bet he wanted to brag. "What the heck did you kill Earl for?"

"Stanton double-crossed me. He had some powerful jewelry. Incendio wanted it to help him control the tor—something to do with your family's claim on it."

What? The tor? The only jewelry Incendio would've been after that Earl had were the earrings, but maybe Incendio had lied to Jordan about why he wanted them. He might not have wanted a wizard to know he had a weakness.

". . . I paid Stanton twice the money, but he gave them to Incendio anyway. Incendio, who didn't need more power," Jordan hissed. "I couldn't let him have it. I'm the one who was born with too little. But not anymore. Now I have Incendio's magic to eliminate you and Lyons. With you both dead, I'll stake my claim on the tor here and be as powerful as anyone in the Conclave." He grinned. "No one will ever dismiss me as insignificant again."

"Why did Incendio kill Tom Brick?"

"Brick wouldn't cooperate, and Incendio flew into a rage. We needed Brick to lower the wards on his property to give us access to the Amanos. The river was the only way to get to Lyons's property to spy on him. His wards on the land side were too powerful."

"You *were* here to spy on Bryn!"

"We were here to find an excuse to kill him. I was surprised to see him so preoccupied and reckless because of you. Not like Lyons to get distracted. And now I hear he's been weakened. Poisoned by elf magic." He smiled and licked the bloody knife again. "I do hope I'll get most of his magic intact when I cut out his heart."

He turned and walked away from the parlor doorway.

"Wait!" I yelled.

He ignored me and kept walking. He opened a French door on the opposite side of the dining room and stepped out.

Seconds later, there was a blast that shook the house and flames swept in. Mercutio went wild in his cage.

"No!" I screamed. "Help! Help us!" I kept screaming as the fire spread up the curtains and walls. Black smoke billowed through the rooms, choking me, and the heat smothered me.

"Nixella Pipken Rose, come to me now!" She appeared in Mercutio's room.

"Come here," I said.

She skipped toward the doorway, but stopped short with a laugh. "You're stuck, you stupid witch," she said.

"I command you to cross the circle and break it."

She grinned. "You can't command me from inside that circle. I wasn't compelled to come when you called this time. I came because I wanted to see you burn." My heart sank, and from the other room, Merc yowled. My eyes darted to the doorway.

"Nixella, take Mercutio outside."

"No."

"If you do, I promise I'll never call you again, and I'll never tell your name to anyone."

She laughed. "You'll never do that anyway." She looked around at the smoke and flames.

"Please! Please take him. It's not his fault he's here."

She walked over to the cage and looked at him. "I do like cats," she said. "He's got beautiful eyes. Almost as nice as a faery's."

I prayed my hardest, clenching my hands together.

"All right, but he stays in his cage until this house burns down with you in it." She picked up the carrier and skipped out.

I lay down on the floor, coughing as I rummaged through my pockets and pulled out my cell phone. No signal. Too much magic around. I moved to a corner of the room and curled up.

Sweat drenched my shirt and I concentrated, calling for rain, sleet, snow, a bucketful of water. Nothing happened. Trapped and helpless! I felt sick and scared, my head throbbing, my stomach churning.

I still had Bryn's and my magic, but I couldn't seem to

use it in the circle. I felt a pang of worry over Bryn. Would Jordan get to him? Bryn was weak. Steve and Mr. Jenson would try protect him from Jordan, but with Incendio's firepower . . .

I pulled my shirt over my face and tried to breathe through it. My lungs burned like the fire itself. The ceiling blazed over my head, and I squeezed my eyes closed because they hurt from the heat. It would all be over soon, I thought as I choked on the smoke.

46

"TAMMY JO!" EDIE'S voice called.

I squinted my watering eyes, trying to find her among the thick smoke. "Here!" I rasped, my heart leaping at not being alone.

"Where are you?"

"I'm trapped in a circle."

I held the locket in my hands and finally saw her, glowing despite the darkness.

"This way, darling. Come this way."

I crawled along until I got to the doorway leading to the stairs.

"Come with me."

"I can't," I said, tears sliding down my gritty face.

"Of course you can. Be brave."

"No, it's the circle," I said, shoving my hand against the barrier to show her, only it went through.

"I broke the circle when I came in."

Really? Was it true? Hope surged through me as I inched forward. "How?"

"My soul is tied to your witch magic, to that of the family

line. When I crossed the circle, so did a sliver of your own magic."

I turned. I couldn't see the way out, and all four walls were on fire. It was still too late.

"This way!" Edie said. I had no choice but to climb the stairs on hands and knees with the walls of the stairway burning around me. The heat was so terrible, my skin felt like it would melt off my bones.

"Hurry!" she cried.

I followed the halo of light that surrounded her.

I can't breathe. I pressed my hand over my mouth. Every breath I took seared my throat. The heat burned my eyes, too, and it was hard to see through the blur of tears. I felt dizzy.

"In here!" she said.

I stumbled forward. We were in a bedroom. Her phantom hand rested on the top drawer of a side table.

I pulled the handle, but it didn't open. I didn't hesitate. I threw it on its side and slammed it up and down until it cracked open like a walnut.

"What?"

"The earrings!"

I sifted through the rubble until I came to a small white box. I flipped it open, and there they were. Aunt Mel's emeralds.

"Hurry."

I choked down mouthfuls of smoke.

Can't—can't breathe!

I pushed the first one into my ear and snapped it shut. I stabbed the second one through the hole and flipped the back closed.

A blast of cold fresh air smashed through the ceiling and funneled around me.

Oh my God! I held my head, overwhelmed to be able to breathe again. "I can't believe it," I rasped, shaking with relief.

Edie laughed and clapped her hands. "Yes, wonderful!

This way. You have to get out. You could still fall or get crushed."

I followed her to a second-story window and smashed it with a lamp. I shimmied down the drainpipe, engulfed in flames that didn't burn me. I landed hard on the ground, then struggled to my feet, still coughing and sputtering. I ran around the house and found Mercutio.

I wanted to shout for joy, but my throat hurt too badly.

"You're okay," I croaked, yanking the carrier open. He leapt out, and I grabbed him, hugging his neck.

He yowled.

"Yeah, I'm okay, too." We ran to the car and got in. Edie appeared in the passenger seat with Merc.

"Thank you, Edie."

She smiled and blew me a kiss. "Incendio forgot about me. He shouldn't have done that. A ghost saw where he hid the earrings. One of us always sees," she said with a self-satisfied smile.

"You're awesome!"

"I can't disagree," she said, tilting her head as she began to fade. "Must rest though. Creating light in such darkness is tiring. Stay out of trouble," she said and shimmered into a faint orb that disappeared immediately.

"Incendio underestimated more than ghosts, huh, Merc? You believe Jordan Perth murdered him?" I shook my head. "Surprised the heck out of me." My voice sounded like I had a bad case of the croup, and every time I talked or swallowed it felt like someone was rubbing sandpaper up and down my throat.

"I guess you realize it's up to us to stop Jordan."

Merc purred that he did.

AT BRYN'S, THE security intercom had been fried, literally, and the front gate had been firebombed open.

I parked the limo and rushed into the house. I called out, but no one answered. I went through the door to the courtyard and found Mr. Jenson treading water in the pool.

"Mr. Lyons insisted!" he said.

"Where is he?"

"He and Steve went to the river."

"Stay here."

I ran through the courtyard to the lawn.

"Oh my gosh," I said, staring at the ring of fire. It was at least fifteen feet tall, and Jordan was walking around it, marking symbols in the ground. I couldn't see through the flames, but three guesses who was inside.

I rushed toward Jordan, but he spotted me before I was close enough to knock him down. He sidestepped my attempt to dive at him. I rolled away as flames shot from his wand.

I lunged through the fire wall to get inside the circle. God bless Aunt Mel's earrings.

Bryn was on his hands and knees, sweating, and mumbling what seemed to be a pretty ineffective spell. Too bad someone had borrowed all his magic, or he might have been able to do a better one.

"Hey," I said, dropping down next to him. "Wanna go for a swim?"

He didn't answer me.

"Bryn, honey, can you hear me?" I pulled on him, and he collapsed facedown on the grass, totally unconscious. "No way," I said. I kissed him and did my best to transfer some power to him.

His eyes opened, and he blinked at me.

The fire wall came down suddenly. I looked around and saw that Merc had distracted Jordan, who was blasting balls of fire out of his wand. Merc zigged and zagged all over the lawn.

"I need you on your feet, Bryn," I said.

He squeezed my arm. "He said you were dead."

"And doesn't that make him look silly now? Shouldn't count his chicks before they're barbequed. I want you on your feet," I said, only it came out as a rasp so soft I could barely hear it myself.

"You!" Jordan screamed.

He threw flames from his wand, and I threw myself in front of Bryn.

"You will burn!" Jordan snarled.

But I didn't burn. Yay for me and my family's magical earrings.

I jerked on Bryn's arm and felt him move. I stood up as he did, and his fingers entwined with mine as we backed up toward the river. Jordan tried getting around us, but I kept Bryn behind me and moved toward the water. Finally, Jordan tried throwing other spells. He shouted random words and I saw bright white energy come from the end of his wand, but Bryn's arm shot out and deflected it. Even as weak as he was, Bryn's defensive powers were better than Jordan's regular abilities.

Jordan turned and put up a wall of fire in front of the water's edge.

"Turn back, right now!" Jordan said. "You're not leaving this property."

He tilted his wand and the fire wall started to wrap around us. It herded Mercutio toward us, and I yelled for him to get back. I talked to Bryn over my shoulder. "We're going into the water. Stay as close to me as you can until we get past the fire and then you get under the dock."

He didn't say anything. I didn't even know if he could hear me with my froggy voice. But when I pulled on his hand and started moving forward, he came with me. I closed my eyes and barreled toward the sound of rushing water. We crashed into something, and then fell into the water, going under. Cold water shocked my system.

When Bryn and I surfaced, I let go of his hand. Jordan was in the river, too. He was what we'd rammed.

Jordan sputtered and cursed as his robes took on water. I saw my chance and dove under, swimming toward him. When I felt his robes against my face, I surfaced suddenly and yanked his wand from his hand.

He howled in fury. I tried to swim away, but the current was strong, and he grabbed my hair. I snapped his wand in half. I guess he felt it because he screamed like he'd turned banshee. I threw the wand pieces. A part landed on the dock. The other hung up in some tall grass.

Jordan tried in earnest to drown me. It was working pretty well. I twisted, which wrenched a clump of hair out of my head, but when I came up, he and I were face-to-face, and I punched him right in his perfect nose.

Blood splattered, and he looked stunned. I socked him again, and he let go of me and grabbed his face.

I turned and tried to swim upstream toward where Bryn was calling for me. He and Steve were making a human chain. Steve held the dock with one hand and Bryn's right arm with the other. Bryn stretched his left hand out to me.

I swam my hardest, but the current pulled me farther away. My legs burned from kicking, and my arms felt heavy. It was like I'd used up all my adrenaline fighting Jordan, and my body just didn't want to fight to survive anymore. I bit my lip.

C'mon! He's not that far!

Bryn yelled at me, and I tried to reach him, but I couldn't. I heard a splash and Merc was with me, swimming and pulling me by the shirt.

The river wanted me though. It sucked me farther from the dock. Even treading was getting hard. I sank under the water and bobbed up sputtering. If I drowned, I wasn't taking Merc with me.

I pulled him off. "You can't save me. You get onshore. Get onshore, Merc, right now," I said, shoving him away.

He yowled.

"Let go," Bryn said to Steve.

"No, Steve. Don't let him go!" I yelled in a voice full of gravel.

"Let go," Bryn snapped, and I felt a pulse of magic. Steve dropped Bryn's hand like he'd been stung.

Bryn swam, taking only a few moments to reach me.

"Put your arms around my neck."

"We're not going to make it," I sobbed. "Why did you let go?"

"Put your arms around my neck," Bryn repeated, yanking them into position. My weight dragged us both under for a moment. I came up, sucking air. Bryn licked his lips.

"It's all right," he said.

"Let me go! You save yourself."

He shook his head, holding on. The river widened and its fast grip propelled us downstream, sucking us under and splashing us with icy water when we bobbed up for breath. The roar of Cider Falls filled my ears.

"When I kiss you, hold on. Don't let go of me for any reason."

"Are you strong enough to cast a spell to stop us falling and getting smashed on the rocks below?"

I saw the answer in his eyes, but I'd known it anyway. I could feel there wasn't any magic left. We'd burned through the power we had.

"Promise me you won't let go," he said.

"No one goes over the falls and lives," I said, coughing out water.

"Then I'll damn well die with you kissing me. Swear you won't let go."

My body burned in response, and I knew a part of me was already in love with him. "I—Yes, I swear."

In the last few feet, I couldn't hear anything over the sound of the water, but I did feel his mouth. I held on as tight as I could just like I promised, even when the falls flipped us over, pounded us with fists, and dropped us over the edge.

47

I WAS DEFINITELY drowning. We were flipping and flipping and flipping. And then I was being dragged down and down and down. The world started to fade. Then the river spit us out. Moments passed with us just holding tight to each other and gasping for breath.

Everything hurt, especially my ankle, but my head was above water, and we were floating downstream, easy as you please.

"How come we're not dead?" I asked dazedly.

"There's a deep hole at a certain spot under the falls. I used a little magic to put us in it. Unfortunately, there's an incredibly powerful eddy. It felt like a tornado underwater, didn't it?"

"How come we're not drowned?"

Bryn laughed softly. "The water doesn't want me."

"Huh?"

"Just a silly old story that Jenson tells. I don't even remember. Something about a pond." He paused. "Your hair tastes like smoke. So did your mouth."

"Yeah, before I almost drowned, I almost burned to

death. Tomorrow I'm going to let someone shoot me out of a cannon. Then I'm retiring."

STEVE COLLECTED US about a mile downstream from the falls. When we got back to the house, I had to hobble in with Steve half carrying me. But there was tea and cookies, and we got to lie down on a soft bed.

Mercutio sat in the corner eating raw chicken, and my first order of business should have been to sleep, but it wasn't. I'm as curious as that Pandora girl, so first things first; while Bryn took a shower, I had to ask Mr. Jenson about the pond.

Mr. Jenson sat in a chair next to the bed and poured himself a cup of tea, putting in a generous splash of whiskey.

"We were in the old house then. In Ireland. I heard my wife calling for him and wondered where he'd gotten to. Under furniture, I expected. Then she rushed in, demanding to know where the bairn was. At the same time, Rory Cameron came through the kitchen shouting that he was going to kill the dogs for the racket they were making, barking at the duck pond like fiends. Her face went as white as that pillowcase," he said, nodding to it. "And we all rushed out, running as fast as we could.

"I spotted his body. So did she, and she let out a cry of grief such as would turn the angels stone deaf. The dogs went deadly silent, and we kept running until we were knee-deep in water, which is when I realized he wasn't facedown. He was faceup to the sun, floating on his back.

"Then he flipped onto his belly and paddled toward us like a puppy dog would. But no one had taught him that. He was only thirteen months old. Too young for swimming, or so we thought. Well, she snatched him out of that water and ran straight to the house.

"Later, we guessed he'd learned to swim by watching the dogs. But the floating confounded us. The lads, unbeknownst to us, decided to try him out again in a big tub of water. They dunked him, but he floated right up and never cried. When she found out about the dunking, the wife was more furious than I'd ever seen her. And the next time someone mentioned the pond, she cut him right off and announced to the room that there would be no more talking about that day. The water didn't want him, and that's all there was to it, she said.

"We never spoke of it again. And she never liked him in the water, though he was a superb swimmer. She was superstitious, you see, and thought that the water might change its mind and take him from us in the end. It didn't. Something keeps the water from claiming him. A magical spell of some sort, I think."

"Well, I'm sure glad the water didn't claim him today. Or me. It definitely felt like it wanted to when we went over those falls."

"That must have been quite frightening."

"Yeah, after the past two weeks, my adrenaline gland's running on empty."

WHEN BRYN CAME back, I took a shower, too. This time Mr. Jenson gave me blue silk pajamas, and they weren't too tall for me. They fit perfectly.

"Where did these come from?" I asked.

Bryn lay on the left side of the bed in black pajamas that looked like maybe Ralph Lauren had designed them, except where the logo should have been there was a small white Celtic cross. He shrugged. "I guess Jenson found them in a drawer."

Uh-huh. Like once when Georgia Sue told me a few junior leaguers were going to drop by my house, and I made two pitchers of iced tea and a whole tray of finger sandwiches and then pretended like that was normal for me to have on hand. I thought about Mr. Jenson telling me Bryn's baby stories. And the way he and Steve had started to treat me like I belonged in Bryn's house. I was beginning to suspect that there was a plot to make me so comfortable that I'd never want to leave.

"There's a new toothbrush in the medicine cabinet," Bryn offered.

"Mr. Jenson told me. It was real convenient. Thanks."

"Something wrong?" Bryn asked. I guess he heard the suspicion in my tone.

"Nope." I pretended to yawn. "Well, you should probably go up to your room now. I'll just sleep here for a couple hours if that's okay."

"Sleep here as long as you want." He gestured for me to lie down. When I didn't move, he added, "I'll go up in a minute."

I sat cross-legged on the bed, facing him.

"Your throat sounds sore. Jenson left you some cough drops on the nightstand," he said, nodding toward them.

It's a conspiracy. I turned and glanced at the bag. Part of me wanted to resist, but it was the part of me that wasn't my throat. I test-swallowed. Yep, still scratchy. I grabbed a honey-lemon one, unwrapped it, and popped it in my mouth. "I don't know the etiquette of this, but I'd like to ask for your butler's hand in marriage."

Bryn chuckled. "I think Jenson's got someone else in mind for you."

I sure wasn't letting the conversation go there! Plus, there was something that I wanted to bring up, something that I'd been thinking about the whole time I'd taken a shower.

I tucked my hair behind my ears. "Speaking of what Mr. Jenson thinks about things, he believes there's a spell that protects you from drowning."

"There's no spell. If there was a spell on me, even a protective one, I'd know it."

"Most babies who fall in ponds drown," I pointed out.

He shrugged. "I must have learned to float before that. Maybe in the bathtub."

"You know how you thought there was—" I stopped myself and took a deep breath. "Wait. Let me ask you something first."

He nodded.

"Let's say someone had to tell you something that you

might not like. Something that might make you embarrassed or even ashamed. Would you want to know?"

"Yes."

"Hold on. Really think about it. Maybe you wouldn't."

"I would want the truth. Tell me whatever it is that you think you know."

I hesitated. "Well, I don't know anything for sure." I tapped my fingers together. "You've probably already thought of it and decided it wasn't true." I sat silently, thinking things over. I didn't want to sound silly. What were the chances that I'd thought of something that Bryn hadn't?

"Tamara, for pity's sake, spit it out."

I looked up then. "Okay, number one," I said, holding up my index finger. "You didn't drown either today or as a baby. Number two," I said, popping up my middle finger. "You could feel my magic when I was a faery even though you shouldn't have been able to, even though you cast spells to block most of that kind of non-witchfolk magic." I lifted my ring finger with the others. "And number three, there was a second poison on that arrow tip they shot me with. It was mud from some special bog, but it shouldn't have worked on you. It shouldn't have worked on a human or a wizard. It should only have worked on a selkie. There were only two ingredients missing from the antidote you mixed for yourself. Dandelion and shark oil. The shark oil being the antidote for the bog mud."

He ran a hand through his glossy black hair.

"The selkies in the legends all have dark hair and light skin. They're all gorgeous as new shoes and just as hard to resist." I paused. "You never talk about your mother. What do you know about her?"

"Enough to know she wasn't a selkie." He glanced at the ceiling for a time, and I was proud of myself because if his brain was working that hard, it was because I'd given him something interesting to think about.

He finally glanced at me as he got up.

"Where are you going?" I asked.

"To bed. Aren't you tired?" He pulled back the covers.

I maneuvered myself into bed and let him tuck me in.

"Should I have held my tongue about my theory?"

"No." He rubbed his thumb across my bottom lip in a way that made my toes curl. "I always like to hear what you're thinking."

"So is it a crazy idea?" I asked because I couldn't resist.

He hesitated a moment. "Lennox's mother swam incredible distances in water so cold you'd never want to put your toe in it. So it was a great irony that, after a terrible fight with my grandfather, she went into the water and never came out. There was a storm that night. It sank boats. Of course, even a great swimmer would've drowned."

"Maybe," I murmured and looked at him. "Or maybe she couldn't drown . . . You were born a great swimmer, huh? No one had to teach you?"

"So it seems." He paused. "Also there's a story Jenson and Lennox haven't heard. Once in college, while I was playing hockey with my friends, I fell through the ice. They claim I was in the water for twenty-five minutes, but I was sure they must have exaggerated because when they pulled me out, my heart was still beating."

I digested that information, getting more excited by the moment. I clasped my hands tightly under the covers. "So maybe you're like me. Part wizard. Part something else— part magical creature."

He nodded.

I didn't realize until then how keen I was on not being the only magical mix-up in town. Being unusual's great if you're, like, the world's best basketball player or something else that pays millions of dollars and makes everyone admire you, but it's not so great if it makes your family live in exile and hide what you are. "So it could be true. How will you find out for sure?"

He bent forward and brushed his lips over mine. Then he walked away. When he was at the door, he glanced back over his shoulder and said, "I'm already sure."

48

MERCUTIO WOKE ME by tapping his paw on my cheek.

"I'm asleep," I said.

"Give her cheek a little scratch with those claws. That should wake her," Edie said.

I opened one eye. "*He* wouldn't do that. Mercutio loves me."

"Wonderful, you're awake. Get up and dress, then. You're meeting the cowboy in the park in fifteen minutes."

Cowboy? Who, Zach? "What? I'm—what time is it?"

"Or I could go there and tell him he can find you here at Lyons's house."

I glared at her, but sat up.

"Be in Magnolia Park in fifteen minutes," she said before disappearing.

I wrinkled my nose in annoyance, then looked at Mercutio as I stumbled from the bed. "Are my car keys here?"

He yowled softly.

"What about my car?" I mumbled, yawning. *No, it isn't. I'll borrow Bryn's limo one last time.* I glanced down at my bare feet and silk pajamas. I didn't have any daytime clothes to wear. I shuffled out of the guest room and through the dark house. A clock said it was fifteen minutes to seven in the morning.

"You know, Merc, losing my job sure isn't how I thought it would be. Getting shot, saving the town, getting up before dawn . . . Being unemployed is a lot of work."

FOR THE FIRST time in days, the town was quiet. I saw some of the places where Nixella had scraped the dust off the trees, leaving behind just the sticky concoction she'd used to trap it. *Our own collection of Honey Bunches of Oaks,* I thought with a smile.

Merc stayed in the limo as I got out and walked to Zach's truck. He wasn't inside, so I looked around. I spotted him sitting at a picnic table.

Flower petals covered the ground, and the air was thick with their perfume. I ducked under a canopy of vines, thinking overgrown gardens weren't all bad.

"Good morning," I said.

"Is it?"

"We're not dead," I pointed out.

"I love that about you, darlin'. When it comes to looking on the bright side, you're the world's expert."

I smiled and sat down. He tipped his tan cowboy hat back.

"So you were right," he said.

"I usually am," I teased. "About what?"

"About witches and monsters and all that."

"Yeah, too bad I am right about all that."

He paused, and I waited for him to ask me questions, but he didn't. Instead, he said, "Abby Farmer claims she can't remember anything about the night Earl died. I swore out a statement that says I didn't kill Earl. They'll probably want one from you, too. Just a formality. With so many people claiming hallucinations and all the chaos and confusion of the past few days, I wouldn't worry about it. They'll have to chalk her original statement up to the town's mass hysteria."

"That's good."

"So," Zach said and paused. "I'm leaving town for a little while."

My head snapped up. "Where are you going?"

"I figured while your house is being fixed, you could housesit for me." He slid a key over to me.

I stared at it, my chest squeezing tight. "You can't go. Your job's here and your family."

He reached over and ran a thumb along my jaw. "Darlin', you and the town needed me, and I couldn't help you, not like I wanted to."

"You helped—"

He held up a hand to silence me. "Your aunt tells me that there are places where human beings train and learn about the secret part of the world. Kind of a SWAT team to fight monsters."

My mouth dropped open. I didn't know anything about that. "My aunt? You mean Edie?"

He nodded and stood. I got to my feet, too, as he walked around the table. "So I'm going to see about it."

"You don't have to do that."

"The hell I don't." He smiled. "You think when trouble comes calling, I'm going to hide behind my girl?" He bent his head and kissed my lips, stealing my breath. "I plan for us to sort out our relationship when I get back. Is that all right with you?"

I nodded.

"Lyons won't give up trying to steal you from me," he said.

It's not really stealing. "What I do isn't up to Bryn." I paused. "But I can't promise that I'll never talk to him or see him again. He's—he helped me a lot this past couple weeks."

"You want to be with him instead of me?"

"I—" I rubbed my thumb over my palm and stared at his face. I took a deep breath before saying what had to be said. "If I'm being honest, I'd have to say that I don't know for sure what I want. You and I, we haven't been able to make things work, but that doesn't mean that I don't hope that one day we could. But I've also needed Bryn's friendship, and he's given it to me. I can't slam my door in his face."

"Do you still love me?"

"Yeah. Of course," I said softly.

He nodded. "Well, can I ask you for one thing, then?"

I held my breath.

"Don't decide anything while I'm gone." He squeezed my arm. "Wait until I come back, when he and I will both have the same chance."

I exhaled slowly as I stared into his denim-colored eyes. "Yeah, that I can do."

He gave me a heartbreaker smile. "Give me a kiss good-bye?"

I nodded and he kissed me. I melted against him, and his strong arms held me tight. I still cared about him so very much.

When we came up for air a few moments later, he tugged my arms from around his neck. "All right, that's enough, or I won't be able to leave." He smiled once more before turning to go.

Silently, I watched him walk to his truck, get inside, and drive away.

Everything is changing.

I sat back down at the picnic table to think. I was half witch and half faery. I'd saved my town, but helped cause the death of a member of the World Association of Magic. What would all that mean in terms of my life? What did I want it to mean?

I wasn't sure, but I was pretty certain that I'd never go back to just being a pastry chef again. With magic being in my blood from both parents, maybe I'd always been destined to become more. That was definitely what Edie believed. And now Bryn, who was so often right about things.

I smiled softly, watching the horizon. The sun rose, golden and warm as it ushered in a new day.

TURN THE PAGE FOR A PREVIEW OF
KIMBERLY FROST'S NEXT
SOUTHERN WITCH NOVEL

HALFWAY HEXED

*COMING TO BERKLEY SENSATION IN
MASS MARKET IN MARCH 2014!*

THE REASON I don't normally bother to plan my schedule is that something unexpected always seems to come up and throw it off. That Friday when I got kidnapped was a prime example.

It was only four days after I'd almost been incinerated and drowned, but I was hopeful that I could balance my new life as a witch with my old life as a pastry chef. I'd accepted a commission—my first ever—from an accountant who donates her time to the Texas Friends of Fish and Fowl. As a celebration of their third anniversary, they were holding a regional fund-raiser in Duvall, and the centerpiece was to be a chocolate sculpture designed by yours truly. They wanted it to involve birds and fish, which was a bit of a challenge to my creativity because although fish are tasty—as anything but dessert—I just don't see them as art.

I was hard at work on a woodland scene with fish popping out of a brook when the bells chimed, announcing that someone had opened the front door to Cookie's Bakery. I glanced at the clock. It was twelve twenty, so Cookie hadn't returned from her lunch break yet. In the bargain we'd struck, Cookie would let me use the bakery, if I covered her lunch hour and one Saturday.

I wiped my hands on a rag and walked out to the glass counter to find my mailman, George. Technically he's not mine. He belongs to the town, but he's delivered the mail to our house since I was five, and his route always seems to be expanding. Truth be told, George would like to be the only mailman in town. He considers postal work a calling.

"Hey, George. Are you in the mood for a cinnamon roll or a caramel pecan one?" I asked with a smile.

His bushy silver eyebrows rose. If a hedgehog ever mated with a hobbit, George could've had a twin. "I'm not on a break, Tammy Jo. I'm here on official postal business."

I smiled a little wider. "Okay, then. I'll take the bakery mail," I said, holding out my hand.

"No need," he said, rounding the counter to set the mail into Cookie's straw mail basket. That was George. Mail delivery with military precision.

"All right, have a good day on your route," I said, moving toward the back.

"Just a moment, young lady."

"Yes?" I said, turning to face him again.

"We've got to discuss the situation at your house."

I frowned, thinking about our family home, which had sustained fire damage and was under repair. I was staying at my ex-husband Zach Sutton's house while he was out of town. I'd had my mail forwarded there. "Well, the situation at my house is being handled. Between TJ's construction crew and Stucky's brother-in-law, Chuy Vargas, who's the best carpenter in a hundred miles, they'll put it to rights. Chuy did the built-in bookshelves at Bryn Lyons's house, and I can tell you firsthand, he does the most beautiful work you've ever seen."

"That may be the case, but that still doesn't address the situation *I'm* talking about."

"I had my mail forwarded, George. Filled out all the paperwork two days ago, and the mail already came yesterday. You guys are a top-notch operation."

George rattled off Zach's address with a frown.

"Right, that's where I'm staying."

"It's not on my route."

My jaw dropped a little. "Right, but I'm not moving off your route permanently. It's just until my house is fixed."

"Shoreside is on my route. Highest tax bracket in Duvall, and I'm on that route *by request*. I believe you could stay there if you wanted to."

"I can't move in with Bryn Lyons just so you can deliver my mail!"

"You've got a package all the way from London, England. Airmail. Express with insurance attached. You going to trust something of that nature to the likes of Jeffrey Fritz?"

"I've got a package from England?" I asked, half amused that George couldn't stand for a high-priority package to be delivered by his rival. "I haven't ordered anything. And I don't know anyone there."

"International mail," George said with a solemn nod.

"Sounds important. Do you happen to have it on your truck?"

"In my bag," George said in a grave whisper, as if the package contained state secrets that spies in foreign countries had lost their lives to bring us.

"Well, that sure is convenient. Do I need to sign for it?"

"No. I've got my computer. I'll take care of everything," he said. He took out the small package and scanned its label, then handed it over. "Zach Sutton's mailbox isn't large enough to hold that."

"George, how did you know I'd be here today? I didn't arrange with Miss Cookie to use the bakery until last night. I can't imagine who even knew I'd be here."

"You're part of my route," George said crisply.

I laughed and couldn't help wondering whether George might have one of the town ghosts as some sort of spirit guide. No one was better informed than the Duvall ghost network.

With his sworn duty fulfilled, George marched out of the bakery, head held high.

I took a pair of scissors and carefully opened the box. There was a double layer of bubble plastic, which I unfolded to find a disc-shaped object, heavily wrapped in white foam packing sheets, making it about three inches in diameter. I raised it. Concealed underneath was a folded piece of thick stationery. I lifted the corner to read the note.

Never let it be taken from you. Keep it secret. Keep it safe.

A chill ran down my spine. I turned the paper over. No signature. Nothing written on it besides the three sentences in fancy black script.

I flipped up the box flap to look at the label. No return address. I set the note down carefully and returned to the mystery object. I pulled off the tape and slowly unrolled it. Peeling away layer after layer, I finally uncovered a beautiful antique cameo brooch. It was about two inches tall. The carved white image of a young woman's profile stood out from the pinkish-red background. There were flowers tucked into her upswept hair, and she had delicate features, angelic and pretty. The oval rim of the brooch was laced in gold and dotted with the tiniest pearls I'd ever seen. So many precious details. It made me feel like factory-manufactured jewelry ought to be outlawed.

Could Momma or Aunt Melanie have sent it? If so, why hadn't they written a longer message? And why would they be in England? Or, if it wasn't from them, who else in the world would have sent it to me?

I reached down to touch it, and a jolt of electricity shot up my arm. My brain seemed to rattle in my skull for a moment and then my vision blurred, the bakery receding.

I staggered, blindly catching myself on the counter just as she appeared. A woman with thick chestnut hair and high cheekbones. Her disheveled clothes, a blouse and skirt, flared out as she ran. I heard her panting breath, the clicking of her heels, and I smelled damp, rain-soaked streets. The haunted look in her wide eyes made my heart contract, and her fear consumed me. I reached out to her, to rescue her, but she went past me and disappeared.

I stood, staring at the spot where she'd been, but there was only black. Trying to catch my breath, I sank shakily to the floor.

Who is she?

The darkness faded, and the bakery reappeared around me. The smell of melted chocolate and baking bread. The ticking of the wall clock that was shaped like a country apron. I shook myself. I was safe at home in Duvall. The girl had been part of a premonition—my first ever. Were they always like that? Yikes. I hoped not.

And who or what had been chasing her? She'd been terrified, running as if her life depended on it. I'd felt what she was feeling. I wasn't sure if that was normal with psychic visions or not, but it didn't really matter. Only one thing was important; I had to find out who she was so I could save her from whoever or whatever was chasing her.

From national bestselling author
KIMBERLY FROST

Halfway Hexed

· *A Southern Witch Novel* ·

Pastry-chef-turned-unexpected-witch Tammy Jo Trask is finally ready to embrace her mixed-up and often malfunctioning magic. Too bad not everyone wants her to become all the witch she can be. One thing's certain: this would-be witch is ready to rumble, Texas style . . .

Praise for the Southern Witch series

"An utter delight."

Annette Blair, national bestselling author

"Full of action, suspense, romance, and humor."

—*Huntress Reviews*

penguin.com
facebook.com/ProjectParanormalBooks

Exploring the spirit world has never
been this much fun—or this much trouble . . .

FROM NATIONAL BESTSELLING AUTHOR
Madelyn Alt

A Witch in Time

Maggie O'Neill—Stony Mill, Indiana's newest
witch—is dealing with both her burgeoning love
life and her sister's giving birth to twins when she
learns that a local teenager has been found dead.
Later, at the hospital, she hears a whispered conversation that sends chills down her spine. Could the
conversation be related to the teen's death? Or to a
murder that hasn't happened yet? It may take all her
witchy intuition to find out.

facebook.com/TheCrimeSceneBooks
penguin.com

M999T1011

NEW FROM NATIONAL BESTSELLING AUTHOR

Madelyn Alt

Home for a Spell

Indiana's newest witch, Maggie O'Neill, needs a new apartment. But when she finally discovers a chic abode, Maggie's dream of new digs turns into a nightmare: The apartment manager is found dead before she can even sign the lease. And Maggie finds herself not only searching for a new home—but for a frightfully clever killer.

penguin.com

M761T0810